I0582518

THE ROSETTA MIND

BOOK TWO OF THE ROSETTA SERIES

CLAIRE MCCAGUE

EDGE SCIENCE FICTION AND FANTASY PUBLISHING
An Imprint of HADES PUBLICATIONS, INC.
CALGARY

The Rosetta Mind
Book Two of the Rosetta Series

Copyright © 2022 by Clair McCague

EDGE SCIENCE FICTION AND FANTASY PUBLISHING
An Imprint of HADES PUBLICATIONS, INC.
P.O. Box 1414, Calgary, Alberta, T2P 2L6, Canada

The EDGE Team:
Producer: Brian Hades
Edited by: Brian Hades
Cover Design: Brian Hades
Book Design: Mark Steele

ISBN: 9781770532137

EDGE Science Fiction and Fantasy Publishing and Hades Publications, Inc. acknowledges the ongoing support of the Alberta Foundation for the Arts and the Canada Council for the Arts for our publishing programme.

Title: The Rosetta mind / by Clair McCague.

Names: McCague, Clair, author.

Description: Series statement: Rosetta series ; book two

Identifiers: Canadiana (print) 20220270694 | Canadiana (ebook) 20220270759 | ISBN 9781770532137 (softcover) | ISBN 9781770532120 (HTML)

Classification: LCC PS8625.C355 R67 2022 | DDC C813/.6—dc23

FIRST EDITION
(20220729)
Printed in USA
www.edgewebsite.com

Publisher's Note:

Thank you for purchasing this book. It began as an idea, was shaped by the creativity of its talented author, and was subsequently molded into the book you have before you by a team of editors and designers.

Like all EDGE books, this book is the result of the creative talents of a dedicated team of individuals who all believe that books (whether in print or pixels) have the magical ability to take you on an adventure to new and wondrous places powered by the author's imagination.

As EDGE's publisher, I hope that you enjoy this book. It is a part of our ongoing quest to discover talented authors and to make their creative writing available to you.

We also hope that you will share your discovery and enjoyment of this novel on social media through Facebook, Twitter, Goodreads, Pinterest, etc., and by posting your opinions and/or reviews on Amazon and other review sites and blogs. By doing so, others will be able to share your discovery and passion for this book.

Brian Hades, publisher

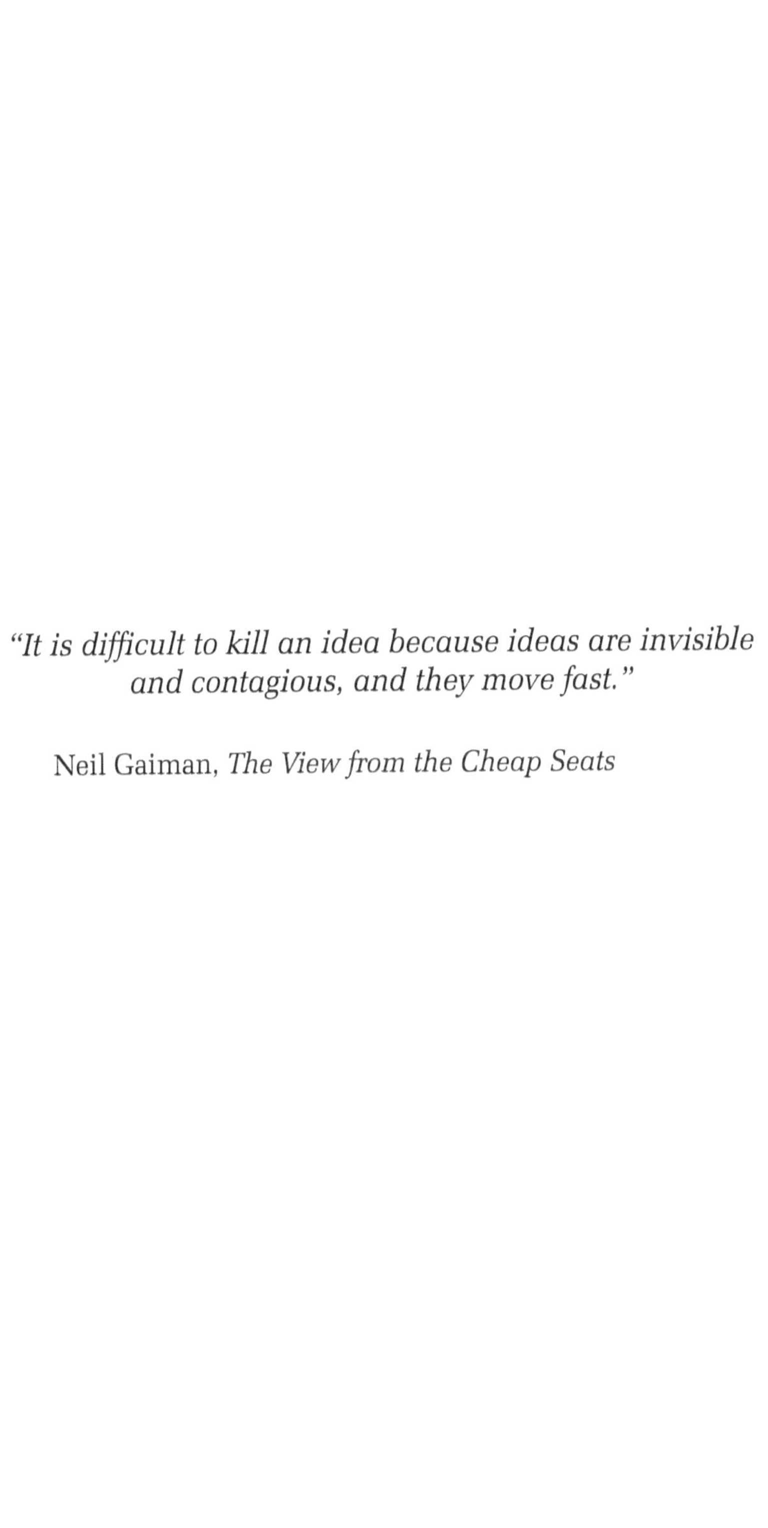

"It is difficult to kill an idea because ideas are invisible
and contagious, and they move fast."

Neil Gaiman, The View from the Cheap Seats

Prologue

Twin Butte, Alberta

The banging on the front door progressed from hesitant to insistent to resolute.

In the attic room, Estlin stared at the rumpled blankets on his bed. His life had taken a ludicrously sharp turn, and it was disconcerting to be home again where everything was exactly how he'd left it. He wanted to lie down. He wanted a few minutes of quiet, not to sleep but to wake again. The banging from below demanded an answer. It meant that the world had noticed the improbable object hovering over his old farmhouse and had sent someone to his door.

"Are you getting up?" Estlin asked the pair of Waes resting in the shadows of his open closet.

There was no response.

He left the bedroom, following the short hallway to the top of the stairs.

"I'm coming," he hollered as he descended to the kitchen. Soft, blue-tinged light was spilling through the windows as though the calendar had stepped forward from summer to winter's first snow fall. He opened the door and found a fireman on his porch, wearing the full kit, heavy yellow overalls, bulky jacket, helmet, breathing mask and air tank.

It took Estlin a moment to recognize Bill, who owned the closest hardware store and volunteered with the local fire station.

Bill pulled down his mask, sweat dripping from his face. "Mr. Hume, are you alright? Is *this*," he gestured skyward, "is this some kind of emergency?"

"It's not an emergency," Estlin answered. "Not exactly. It's...aliens."

It wasn't necessary to point at the vessel obscuring the sky, so he didn't.

"Aliens," Bill said. "It does look like an alien sort of thing. I thought I'd check on you before the military marches in."

"I'm sure they're coming." Estlin considered how much of the convoluted story he should tell. "My friend, Harry, is a biologist. He had the first encounter in Wellington, and he flew me down to see if I could translate for the visitors. Things got complicated. That's not a ship. It's a tank full of ocean and cuttlefish. A lot of cuttlefish. Swimming up there."

"Aliens and cuttlefish. That does sound complicated." Bill looked at the structure supporting the water above them. "Your UFO is weird. It doesn't quite touch the ground. It goes right out to the edge of the road, like a wall, with a notch at your old postbox. When I walked toward the notch, a tunnel opened along your driveway." He wiped the sweat from his forehead. "What do the aliens look like?"

"They're kind of small and spiky." Estlin dropped a hand to just above knee height. "And they like to climb, except for the ones that like to swim. Two of them are taking a nap on a shelf in my bedroom closet."

"Your closet?"

"Do you want to come in?" Estlin stepped back from the door. Three squirrels took the opportunity to dash around their feet and into the kitchen. Estlin ignored them. "Can I get you a glass of water?"

"No, thanks." Bill looked again at the structure that enclosed the house, particularly where it rose from above the roof to arc over the nearby tree. "I'm going to get quarantined, aren't I?"

"Probably."

"I should report back." Bill took a step backwards, and a second step.

"Wait," Estlin said. "When the cavalry arrives, tell them I want to see Harry when he gets here."

"Sure." Bill pulled the mask over his face as he descended the steps, picking up speed as he went. He jogged across the yard, visible until he passed the tree, and then the ice-and-ocean structure closed behind him.

Chapter 1

Three Days Later

The arched tunnel forming before Harry, and collapsing behind him, was concealed by a roiling fog that suggested the air was being rapidly cooled. The rutted, weedy driveway was long, and he wondered how the first person to check on Estlin had kept his nerve through the journey, unable to see where he was going and not knowing if the farmhouse was still standing. The tunnel peeled open a gateway that swept the mist into an open space. Currents of air and light flowed around his feet as the sides of the gateway reached down, and then curled back up without bending a single blade of grass. Harry stepped through into the pale vaulting structure that created a cathedral around a copper beech tree, surrounding it with diffuse light.

Two corporals were standing at ease just off the driveway before it curved around the tree to the house. Their pixilated green uniforms were tucked into tan boots, and they were without rifles or other visible weapons. Princess Patricia's light infantry secured both ends of the tunnel, and Harry wondered how these two would react to his unscheduled arrival. One glanced at her watch, the other inspected the security pass dangling from Harry's neck and waved him by without comment.

At the edge of the tree canopy, Harry took the compact camera that had been forced on him and lobbed it towards the base of the tree. It skidded across the dirt and stopped against one of the thick pale roots. Continuing around the tree, he found Estlin standing on the porch, staring out at the featureless wall.

A horde of squirrels had gathered close around him, and three rabbits were hanging out under the porch swing.

"Lyndie?"

"I need a minute," Estlin said, raising one hand.

Harry shrugged, dropped the cooler he was carrying at the foot of the stairs and unstrapped the oxygen tank from his back. Sitting on the steps, he looked at the reservoir of ocean suspended above, covering a few acres of Canadian prairie grass. It mirrored Estlin's property line almost exactly, in a way that seemed both ridiculous and considerate.

A flock of sparrows burst through the white-blue wall. Harry grabbed at the step, threatened by the erratic movement and chatter of the birds. The knot of sparrows skimmed up the path, circled the house and settled in the beech tree. Estlin descended from the porch to sit next to Harry.

"Were you flying?" Harry asked.

"They were lost," Estlin answered. "Whatever the Waes do to make the water behave like a cauldron of ice messes with avian navigation. The birds fly in a spiral. The cuttlefish like watching the air swimmers, but birds need branches." Estlin stretched and grinned. "It's good to see you. How was your trip?"

"Long. Interesting. Boring," Harry answered. "The Russians will land an Antonov anywhere. Your police rolled out to the plane, lights flashing, and handed them a ticket for parking an unlicensed vehicle on a dirt road. The Russians had to stay and deal with the Canadian border guards, but the RCMP gave me a very fast ride over here in their truck, which was helpful. How was your trip?"

"I don't remember."

This concerned Harry, but digging into a memory gap that spanned two days and half the Pacific was not his first priority. He pointed at the house. "So, this is your inheritance. Bit of a fixer-upper."

"There's usually more of a view," Estlin said.

"I like the tree bubble. That's unexpected."

"You brought an air tank."

"Pointless, I know," Harry answered. "If this comes down, we'll be crushed before we drown. I'm glad I refused the wet suit."

"What else did you bring me?"

"Sandwiches." Harry opened the cooler. "And Russian beer. I'm loving the small talk, by the way. Have you been short on company?"

"Not exactly." Estlin pointed to a pile of diving tanks stacked next to the stairs. "What kind of sandwiches?"

"The kind you like," Harry said. "The waewae tapu and a thousand cuttlefish are hanging out in a puddle over your house. You've got everyone's attention."

"One thousand three hundred and sixty-one cuttlefish."

"Right." Harry handed Estlin a sandwich. "So, you've been directing bird traffic and talking to cuttlefish. How's that going?"

"Cuttlefish are weird." Estlin took the sandwich. He unwrapped it and ate silently.

Harry used the step edge to slap the metal cap off a bottle of Ohota. "I hear you kicked everyone out this afternoon."

"Yeah, I needed a nap."

Harry swallowed the urge to argue, washing it down with a mouthful of beer. He'd been too trusting in Wellington. He'd guessed that his friend's unusual skills might crack the communication barrier, but the instant interdependence that formed between Estlin and the yellow-eyed visitor, Wae, had been a shock. He'd failed to recognize how risky it was to be the world's only effective translator. Within hours, Estlin was snagged and dragged across the South Pacific by global powers trying to control first contact.

"If you're trying to handle this alone...." Harry paused. He couldn't ask Estlin to let everyone in when the inclusive approach taken in New Zealand had collapsed into a breathtaking fiasco.

"Yidge is here," Estlin said.

The flat statement jolted Harry. "Yidge is dead."

"I know." Estlin looked at the tree next to the house. "The Waes' recording of who she was is here, and it talks to me. *She* talks to me."

"That does not sound good."

"Do you want to see her?"

"No."

Estlin's shoulders sagged. He looked at the half-eaten sandwich in his hands. "The blood is gone. I mean, they cleaned up the image."

"Fucking hell." Harry had glimpsed the Wae's projection of his young, impulsive assistant in Samoa and had no desire to see it again. Yidge had been shot in the chest on a Chinese cargo ship. Whatever actions she'd taken to put herself in the middle of that situation didn't shift the fucking tragedy of it.

"They took it all while she was dying." Estlin closed his eyes. "It was like the Waes ripped who she was past me. Everything. A life in seconds. She had just enough time to know she was dying. And now some fraction of her is here, in a little disk upstairs."

"I'm sorry."

"So am I," Estlin said. "She seems okay with it—which is awful—that *acceptance* isn't her. It must be some effect of the process."

"Is that why we're out here?" Harry asked. "There's a ghost in the house?"

Estlin considered this and did not answer.

"I hear the Waes are living in your closet." The care and feeding of the visitors had been Harry's responsibility in New Zealand, in part because he was a biologist, but mostly because they arranged their *discovery* by breaking into his truck.

"They're out in the tree now," Estlin said. "They like it more than the closet."

"Welcome to first contact." Harry raised his bottle.

"Yeah, thanks for the translator job," Estlin answered. "Am I still getting paid?"

"I have no idea," Harry replied. "Apparently, the United Nations has an Office of Outer Space Affairs. They've flown in an official, Ulz Lichtwardt. He thinks it's his job to represent humanity."

"Good."

"Good?" Harry's brief encounter with the UN man had not filled him with confidence.

"Do you think I want that job?" Estlin asked. "I've been evicted from every place I have ever lived!"

"But that's just your squirrel problem, not your sunny personality." Harry looked at the squirrels surrounding them, attracted by Estlin's inexplicable gift. The gift connected Estlin to all kinds of living things and separated him from humans. The squirrels looked harmless, but he knew they'd ruined every job, degree and relationship Lyndie had attempted.

"Why are the cuttlefish here?" Harry asked.

"They want to have a conversation with me." Estlin stood and walked out on the grass, leaning back to look at the structure above them. "Apparently, I agreed to this without knowing it. The images they projected of their ocean home were an invitation. I responded with images of my home, and they accepted."

"And suddenly talking to cuttlefish is more important than talking to the Waes," Harry said. "Do I want to know why?"

"The cuttlefish are very concerned."

"Concerned?"

"They think we might blow up the planet."

"And you've used this opportunity to assure them that we won't blow up the planet," Harry suggested bluntly. He received a shrugged response from Estlin, which he did not appreciate. "Lyndie?"

"It's more complicated than you think."

"Aliens have arrived. It's knocked the wind out of everyone. But we aren't going to nuke ourselves."

"Harry—"

"It's a mess out there, and it will get worse, just like Wellington."

"That's not—"

"Lyndie, you trust rabbits more than humans—fair enough. But if you let the cuttlefish think we're going to do something stupid, they may ask the waetapu to *fix us*. And then things really will get stupid."

In Wellington, Wae and Waewae had proven they could move through secure facilities with ease by deceiving the eyes and minds of those close to them. Harry knew what he'd witnessed was no where near the limits of their capabilities.

"Are the cuttlefish asking the Waes to help?" he asked. "Maybe unplug our mutual mass destruction toys? Can you imagine how that might inflame the situation?"

"The cuttlefish have survived multiple ice ages," Estlin said. "They aren't worried about nuclear winter."

"Bugger." Harry hated threats that hit the scale above atomic incineration.

"They're worried about Sanford and Bomani's equations—their understanding of the Rosetta Burst."

The intense electromagnetic pulse that marked the *arrival* had a complex frequency spectrum that physicists had peered at and picked apart. The physicists viewed the Rosetta Burst as though the signal offered the keys to a dangerously powerful interstellar transportation system.

Estlin glanced again at the water above him. "The cuttles think we might try to eat the dross spilled by the Waes arrival. They think that, a thousand years from now, we'll make a mistake that could boil the oceans and the bedrock." He looked to Harry. "How do you disarm that kind of threat?"

Harry had no answers and stayed seated as Estlin took a beer from the cooler, walked up the steps and across the slanted porch into the house.

—— «» ——

Dr. Ulz Lichtwardt was surprised by the full-length mirror in the staging tent. He checked the polish of his shoes, and the bright UNOOSA pin on the lapel of his suit. Technically, his boss should have come to speak on behalf of the Secretary-General of the United Nations, but the aliens' mind-bending technology had knocked the job one notch further down the food chain.

He was ready for an alien encounter. He'd landed in Wellington the day the aliens and their translator had vanished, and he'd raced to Pago Pago to find they had disappeared overnight. During his flight to Alberta, any anxiety about meeting the aliens was supplanted by his fear of missing them again.

He used the mirror to watch Serese Saie as she inspected one of the orange hazmat suits hanging on a rack next to a metal bench stacked with wide rolls of tape. She was wearing a flowing silk shirt of muted pinks and grey. The medal of the Order of Canada, a red maple leaf on a stylized snowflake, hung from an ornate collar and stood out against her shirt. Her natural black hair had a short, tapered cut, and her shoes were practical. He'd read her profile after meeting her and found she had no scientific background, having been anointed as Governor General of Canada based on her fame as a retired dancer.

Accompanying the governor general was Lichtwardt's fastest way to access the aliens. His boss thought he needlessly conceded to the Canadian prime minister, but Ulz felt that wrangling for greater recognition of UN authority could wait. His political skills were limited as he was primarily a science advisor with a background in astrophysics applied to the orbital trajectories of space debris.

A middle-aged scientist bustled into the room, carrying a coffee, notebook, and binder. "I'm Bernie Springer. I was part of the team in New Zealand."

Bernie saw Serese, tripped over his own feet, and spilled coffee on his shirt. "Oh, nuts." He didn't have a hand free to swipe at the spill. "It's fine. The coffee's cold. Good morning. I'm here to tell you about the aliens."

"Good afternoon." Serese offered her hand.

"Right. I haven't slept enough since…" Bernie was visibly unable to correctly count the number of days. "Since this whole thing dropped on us. Miss—your excellency—what do I call you?" Bernie realized that he had to put the coffee, notebook, and binder down on the bench to shake hands.

"Serese."

"I'm Dr. Lichtwardt from the United Nations." Ulz extended his hand, which prompted Bernie to release Serese's hand.

"Good to meet you," Bernie said. "You've both seen footage of the waetapu?"

"Yes," Serese answered. "They're intriguing."

"Intriguing, unnerving, sure," Bernie said. "*Waetapu* is from waewae tapu, which is how the Māori refer to travelers from far away. Harry named them and it stuck because, when you are with them, *alien* feels like an insufficient word. We named the two from Wellington Wae and Waewae. Wae has yellow eyes, and Waewae has orange eyes. By *eyes*, I mean the pair of finely facetted structures on their heads that we think are broadband multi-channel receivers. But they really do look like eyes.

"The way they camouflage is really alien. They trick your brain. A camera sees them as they are, which means your eyes see them. But the signal gets wobbled in your brain, so you think you're seeing an animal—something exotic, something about their size. I haven't proven this, but I bet that when they camouflage, they can control whether each of you see the same image or different images."

"Very sophisticated." Ulz suddenly recognized the name of the scientist. "Dr. Springer, you wrote the report on the particles they release."

"Yes. It's a kind of dust that sticks to your eyeballs, likely to gather and relay signals." Bernie picked up the binder and flipped to a page filled with magnified black and white images. "Ovoids. Named for their shape. They are ridiculously small and very structured. We've got a few guesses at how they work, and we know how to burn them out."

He closed the binder. "Bigger picture. While the climbing pair of waetapu were visiting us in New Zealand, a pair of swimming waetapu were visiting the cuttlefish. The cuttlefish are here because our translator, Estlin, lives here. I hope you read a briefing about his background because it sounds ridiculous when I try to explain it. The Waes really like him. I mean, their eyes literally light up when he enters the room."

Bernie flipped to the back of his binder, to a full-page image extracted from the Wellington sessions showing Wae fixated on the translator.

"The Waes have created a big tank of ocean above Estlin's house. The walls of the tank are made of ice that's not ice. It's too strong and too warm to be ice, but if you point a spectrometer at it, all you see is water. We assume they are using a field to manipulate the molecules. Water has an extremely complex phase diagram. I think the blue walls are a dense, glassy water structure. Crystal structure fails by fracture, but glass can flow. I'm trying to collect some evidence on this but…. You don't care."

"There must be a spaceship in the middle of it," Ulz said.

"We don't know," Bernie answered. "That's a good guess, but we haven't seen it on the satellite images. We don't want to ping it with active sonar or knock a chip off the tank with a chisel because we don't want to risk disrupting the water structure. We don't want to dump the bucket here."

"That would be bad," Ulz said.

"Very bad," Bernie agreed.

"Do you think that's a possibility?" Serese asked.

"Yes. If the ovoids have any role in relaying signals that control or maintain the ice tank, there is an obvious vulnerability. In Samoa, after I shared my theories, the Americans zapped everyone with jamming signals from their aircraft in the stupidest experiment I have ever seen."

For Ulz, this dropped into the puzzle like a missing piece—a reason for the aliens to suddenly leave the island. "They understood that the particles are linked to the aliens, like an expansive, extra-sensory system?"

"Yeah, it was like tazering them, and not expecting a negative reaction. It was ugly. The Waes vanished into the night, and they took Estlin, probably to protect him from us. His eyes were bleeding." Bernie pulled down one of his lower eyelids. "I ended up with eighteen little red burn marks on my eyeballs, and it could have been worse.

"The Canadians have forbidden overflights by manned and unmanned aircraft," Bernie continued. "If you see any plane—Prowler, Growler, drone—anything that looks like it's going to fly over the ice tank, you should run away."

"Run away?" Ulz couldn't win a footrace against a flood.

"The tank is about 30 meters deep," Bernie continued. "It covers twelve acres. An acre is a chain by a furlong— which is awesome, I had to look it up for the calculation. We have roughly 1.4 million tonnes of water overhead. The Canadians are risk averse. They're tracing signals and removing hardware. They asked everyone not to play with jammers or electromagnetic pulses. They asked really nicely, and with great technical detail, but the border is an inch away, every airstrip is full, and we are relying on everyone having good manners."

"Which way would we run?" Serese asked.

"Away," Bernie answered. "From here, don't bother, you'll never see anything coming in time. If you're out in one of the big campsites, and you see a problem flying at us. Run away or jump in a vehicle and hope it floats." Bernie checked his watch. "You are due in there now. Do you have any questions?"

"Should we be suiting up?" Serese asked.

"Only if you want to," Bernie answered. "I've been directly exposed to the waetapu, and you've been exposed to me. Also, the ovoids are microscopic, move actively, and defeat all the filters and barriers we've thrown at them. In New Zealand, we had paperwork about it. No one here has forced me to sign a waiver yet, but it's understood that you visit with aliens at your own risk."

Bernie waved at the other corner of the tent. "You can bring an air tank if you like. It was mandatory until this morning. Now, it's your choice. The lightest cylinder we have is four kilograms. The oxygen concentration under the bucket has been steady so far, but I only have a day of data. No one thought to tape a sensor to the house when the thing arrived."

Bernie crouched to open an aluminum case next to the bench. "I'm also supposed to offer you these." He lifted out a pair of goggles with thick glass, metal rims and thick rubber seals. "They just arrived. Custom built, but I think they could have ordered a crate from the steampunk emporium."

"Are they effective?" Ulz asked.

"Pure placebo," Bernie answered. "They might be effective for a minute and a half. Not long enough to matter. Also, you'd have to put them on and walk through one of the decontamination zappers otherwise you're just adding a layer of containment to the ovoids you are already carrying."

"I appreciate your honesty," Serese said.

Ulz wondered if Serese's continuous air of sincerity was genuine or a performance. Bernie dropped the goggles back in the box before he could express his interest in trying them.

A man with the cool demeanor of a security escort entered the tent. He was wearing a black suit, a red tie, and sunglasses. Serese beckoned, and he approached, removing the sunglasses and sliding them into his pocket.

"This is RCMP Constable Mike Hirakawa," she said. "He leads my protective team. He'll be joining us. If a security issue arises, please follow his instructions."

"Today, we're keeping the number of visitors low," Bernie said. "So, it's you three and that's it. Try to resist the urge to push the situation. Abrupt changes are scary."

"Personal recording devices are not permitted. Possession is enough to get you tossed and use will get you tossed with prejudice." Bernie handed them each a compact video camera with a stereo microphone mounted on it. "I'd appreciate it if you could keep these recording at all times and return them after your visit."

He walked through the open door of the tent with them. "Follow the driveway. The arch will open in whatever direction you choose. One guy tried to cut across the grass. He missed the house and popped out on the other side. If that happens, you'll have to walk back here to try again. We don't know how. We don't know why. That's just the way it works. Have a good trip."

Ulz glanced at Serese and caught her shift from a nervous smile to a confident one. Her Constable Mike led the way.

Chapter 2

Estlin gave the squirrel on his table a crunchy piece of lettuce. He was breaking his own rules, but he wanted to be in the moment with the squirrel folding the morsel in its hands into one cheek. The squirrel tilted its head, considering the rest of the sandwich.

"Mine," Estlin said.

The Russian beer had a distinctive sour tang. Estlin decided it was acceptable. He drank and picked through the words he needed to discuss the current significant problem with Harry. He'd spent each encounter with the cuttlefish drowning in the shallows. He believed that humans actually were dumb enough to pick up an explosive idea from the Waes, try to develop it, and accidentally burn the planet. How was he supposed to represent humankind if his instinct was to concede the key point and start negotiations from the wrong side?

Harry entered the kitchen. He placed his empty beer bottle on the counter, borrowed a glass from the dish rack by the sink and filled it with water. "When all this is over, I'll hang around and help paint the porch."

"Crap." Estlin let his head drop to the table. "My yard will be a tourist destination."

"Are you going to pack a sad over being home?" Harry responded. "It could be worse. Hell, it was worse four days ago."

"Oh, fuck you," Estlin said. "It took you long enough to get here. I thought you had a Royal Air Force lift."

"The Americans refused to refuel the Harrier, and there was no room for me on any of their flights."

"So, you hitched a ride with the Russians?"

"I knew I was being parked. And then an Antonov Cheburashka planted itself on a runway with a honking crater in it. The spook it was there to pick up offered me a ride and I took it. The Cheburashka stopped hard, backed itself up, popped a door for us and took off with a swearing F-18 escort, but it didn't have the fuel to get here. We flew to Kiribati and waited for a cargo lifter from Vladivostok."

During the longer flight aboard the massive Antonov 124, Harry had lost at cards, shared the vodka, and slept on one of the narrow bunks. "You really don't remember how you got here?"

"I woke on the floor in the bedroom upstairs, slightly damp. You phoned a minute later."

"Bernie spotted the puddle over your house," Harry said. "How often do you talk to the cuttlefish?"

"They drop by when they feel like it." Estlin finished his sandwich. "Short visits and long visits. They ask weird questions. They haven't asked about the *concern*. I know about that from Yidge—from the Waes—and I'm not bringing it up. The first cuttlefish meeting was at night. That was a mistake. I couldn't see clearly. The micro-whatzits the Waes spread around for communication sensed that I wanted to see and plugged me into a cuttlefish perspective. Imagine a pair of independent, spectrally shifted wide-angle views that pick up which way the light is rotating, and then add pattern sensing skin. I nearly puked over the side of the porch."

"How far did you make it?" Harry asked.

"Kitchen sink." Estlin had fled from the dark porch, stumbling into the kitchen to grip the counter by the sink until the heaving in his guts subsided.

Harry blinked at him. "I meant in the conversation. What did you learn in the first conversation with the cuttlefish?"

"Nothing. It didn't have a beginning, middle and end. It was just confusion, followed by complete disorientation, followed by puking. It lasted about twelve seconds."

"But you've made progress since then."

"Oh, yeah." While he'd rinsed his mouth and the sink, a crowd in orange hazmat suits had lumbered into his house to ask absurd questions and complicate every other conversation he'd attempted. "I can manage the confusion for minutes at a time now, but I can't figure out why it's necessary, given the translating power of the waetapu. The ones swimming with the cuttlefish seem to be fully engaged, but my pair...? They're up a tree, being useless."

"What is Wae telling you?"

"That this is my conversation, not theirs." The whole thing made Estlin angry. "But that's a cheat because the cuttles know the waetapu can predict our probable future from our reaction to first contact stress. I think that's what they care about, and it's completely beyond me. Would you like to guess what kind of trouble we'll be in ten or a hundred generations from now?"

"Difficult."

"Impossible," Estlin answered. "Even for the Waes. As far as I can tell, they collect data for the prediction. They don't make it. This isn't something you work out on the back of an envelope!"

"Is that what's expected from you?" Harry asked.

"I've been told that I am speaking for myself." Estlin forced his fingers through his hair. "Whatever that means."

"That sounds simpler."

"Yes, very simple," Estlin said. "I couldn't possibly get it wrong and ruin everything for everybody."

"I am glad I dropped Bernie's camera out by the tree," Harry said. "Has your kitchen been bugged?"

"Fuck if I know. Why bother with spy tactics when there are cameras everywhere?" Estlin waved at the red light shining by a lens propped atop a monopod leaning against the nearest corner.

"You're swearing a lot," Harry said. "You probably should have taken that nap you wanted."

Shake your tail, Estlin told the squirrel on the table, pushing for the squinine territorial *fuck off* gesture. The squirrel ignored him, sniffing around for sandwich crumbs. Estlin finished his beer and watched with suspicion as Harry returned his glass to the dish rack. Harry rinsed their beer bottles, stashed them under the sink, and grabbed a broom that was leaning against the wall in the corner.

"So, when is company coming?" Estlin asked.

"Did I say that company was coming?"

"You are sweeping."

Harry looked at the broom in his hands in surprise. "I'd mop if I could."

"You were sent here ahead of someone else," Estlin said.

"Is that you or are the Waes stealing information?"

"Me." Estlin's connection to the Waes made it easy to borrow perspectives, so he asked one of the squirrels to clamber to the edge of the tree canopy and look for him. "They're on the driveway."

"It's the guy from the UN," Harry said.

"And you left the front door open?" Estlin wiped the sandwich crumbs from his shirt and dismissed the squirrel on the table with a flick of his fingers.

——— ⟨⟩ ———

The weathered farmhouse was illuminated by bright yet soft light, as though a storm had passed, lifting the clouds but not releasing the sun. The alien structure swept over the immense tree that sheltered the house. Serese found the bright surface difficult to look at—there was nothing to lock one's eyes on as each smooth curve met other smooth curves without creating any edges.

"The door is open," she said. "Do we go in?"

Serese followed Ulz up the steps, pausing to knock on the doorframe. The wallpaper in the hall and kitchen had a faded yellow and brown flower pattern, and the vintage fridge was avocado green. Estlin was slouched at the kitchen table, thin, weary and surrounded by squirrels.

"I'm Dr. Lichtwardt of UNOOSA," Ulz said. "The United Nations outer space office."

"Hello, Mr. Hume." Serese entered the kitchen, leaving Mike to occupy a corner in the entrance of the house. Estlin rose, rubbing his palms on his jeans before taking her hand with a firm grip, meeting her eyes. From the colours, she judged the bruise on his face to be a week old.

"I'm Serese Saie."

"Yes, you are," Estlin answered.

"You've been in a challenging position these last few weeks," she said. "Are you well?"

"Well enough. This is my friend, Harry Hatarei. He was the first person to meet the Waes in Wellington."

Serese shook Harry's hand and gained some confidence in a snap decision she made earlier in the day. When the contact site was placed under her authority, she reviewed the roster of people with access to the house and decided to fix the most obvious gap first.

"Are the aliens upstairs?" Ulz asked.

The most accessible, comfortable alien photo Serese had seen was of the Waes curled next to each other on the shelf in Estlin's bedroom closet.

"They are outside in the tree," Harry answered.

"I didn't see any sign—" Mike spoke from the entry way.

"You wouldn't," Harry said. "You don't see them unless they want you to."

"They saw you," Estlin said. "You're not the first to come wanting to speak to them. But they are watchers, not speakers, and they are resting in the leaves."

"Is that your opinion or a translation?" Ulz asked.

"You can go out and yell at the tree if you want," Estlin said

"Why would I do that?"

"Because Wae and Waewae are sixty feet up."

"Do they respond if you shout at them?" Ulz asked.

"No. They've abandoned me to deal with the cuttlefish on my own," Estlin said. "That's been the depth of the conversation since we got here—except for the morning they wanted me to try to help them talk to the tree."

Serese could read Ulz's disappointment. "Will progress with the cuttlefish lead to progress with the aliens?"

"That's possible," Estlin said. "Do you want to talk to the cuttlefish?"

"It's their first visit to Canada." Serese wanted to limit expectations and invest in each step of the learning process. "I can welcome them. Dr. Lichtwardt, would you like to introduce yourself to the cuttlefish?"

Ulz cleared his throat. "How?"

"Lyndie will help," Harry said. "Do you want to be introduced as representing the UN or just the spacey wing of the UN?"

"Keep it simple," Ulz suggested.

"Is the UN everyone?" Estlin asked.

"Almost everyone," Ulz replied. "I don't think you should list the exceptions."

"Governor general…" Estlin absorbed the strength of Serese's presence. "I think that will translate as one who represents both the selected leader of the northern half-continent and the hereditary leader of many places."

Serese nodded her approval.

"It may be less specific," Estlin said. "I'd like to do this before sunset. Night visits are harder."

"How do we proceed?" Serese asked.

The squirrels in the room shuffled, responding to a change Serese could not sense. They collectively scampered from the kitchen. Mike's expression barely shifted, but Serese caught his double-take assessment, flashing from the squirrels, to Estlin, and back to the squirrels as their fluffy tails brushed by his feet.

"I've extended the invitation," Estlin said.

Serese watched Ulz pace around the kitchen, stopping to look out the window above the sink.

"Why did you bring the aliens here?" he asked.

"They brought themselves here," Harry was quick to answer.

"The cuttlefish suggested that I meet them at the bottom of the ocean," Estlin said. "I guess it would have been simpler, but I didn't understand the invitation at the time."

"I'm glad they didn't park over a city," Harry said. "Does the UN have an Office of Ocean Affairs?"

"Ma'm," Mike spoke from the entranceway, flicking his eyes towards the door.

"They're getting ready." Estlin left the kitchen, and Serese followed.

The light outside changed as a bright box of smooth, glassy ice flowed down the side of the larger structure, descending on asymmetrical arms that formed and folded back into the expanse of thicker ice.

"This chamber is separated from the main one," Estlin said. "It's a shallower tank, so the walls are thinner and clearer."

"It's amazing." Serese reached out as the tank settled in front of the porch, but did not touch the translucent wall. "Do you know how it works?"

"That's a frighteningly precise manipulation," Ulz said. "If they can force water to solidify, they can freeze the blood in our veins."

Six cuttlefish glided into view. A pair remained high in the tank, within reach of each other, but their arms were still. Serese realized their W-shaped eyes were tracking together. A smaller cuttlefish led a threesome. The final, solo cuttlefish remained close to the back wall of the world's strangest aquarium. Its skin was textured and carried colours that were darker and more continuous than the light cloud formations rolling over the backs and bellies of its companions. Serese reached out and the nearest cuttlefish turned with the barest shift of its undulating fins and extended an arm towards her. Their flickering skin tones had both autonomic and thoughtful qualities. What did anger or laughter look like?

Serese settled her shoulders and straightened, ready to introduce herself.

———— «» ————

Estlin stayed on the porch, behind Serese and Ulz. He didn't need a direct view of the tank, but wished he could connect with the cuttlefish without getting wet. The shifting sensation of being both gravity-bound and afloat with the balanced buoyant *rightness* of the cuttlefish made him seasick.

He couldn't tell if he'd met the individual cuttlefish who were considering Serese. The cuttles didn't fix their identities to names or roles. After contemplating the qualities of stones with *one-who-likes-smooth-stones*, he realized that if they met again, and the conversation jabbed a sharper topic, *one-who-likes-smooth-stones* might identify as *one-who-swam-too-close-to-the-pointy-end*.

As Serese stepped forward, the flow of movement in her arms and clothes was inviting, and the light reflected from her metal medallion was distinctly different than the light from her shirt and black skin.

"I am Serese Saie, Governor General of Canada."

The translation of Serese's role was unexpected, but it was grounded in how she perceived her job. He translated it back to her. "One selected to convey recognition to individuals who make exceptional contributions to the group, one who promotes unity, one who swims with those who defend the group."

"Thank you," Serese said. "I welcome you, explorers, to Canada. A country spanning mountains and plains, forests of dark pine and fields of grain. Land of lakes and rivers, glaciers and oceans."

"Place of standing water," Estlin echoed, "flowing water and frozen water. Place against which the northern, rolling water breaks."

"The first people have lived here for thousands of years," Serese said. "Hundreds of years ago other people came from distant lands to explore, to take objects and stories home. They returned to take this land as a new home. People from around the world have built homes here, including this house in this field. I welcome you to Canada."

The time frame for the formation of Canada translated as both countless cuttlefish generations, and the fleeting edge of a single day. The response from the cuttlefish flowed back as a smooth, drifting pattern of light that Estlin had trouble translating. "The cuttlefish.... Our courtesy is foreign to them, but open patterns accept the tide."

Ulz stepped forward. "I am Dr. Lichtwardt. I am here to speak on behalf of the United Nations Office of Outer Space Affairs."

The representation of Ulz's job suggested he was a piece of space debris, who lived in a box, and studied the sky-above-the-sky. He spoke for those who observed the Earth from a fixed orbit, able to see the world's perpetually changing half-face and the thinnest edge of where light ceded to dark.

Estlin decided that translating this would not be helpful, but it was clear Ulz was waiting for a pronouncement.

"How strange for you," he said. "Their reply not mine."

"Please tell them the cuttlefish fishery has been shut down," Ulz said.

"Is that where you want to start?"

"Yes. It's important," Ulz said. "We need to start off on the right foot."

"Or tentacle." Harry rocked back on the creaking porch swing. His exaggerated, relaxed posture masked intense focus.

In contrast, RCMP Constable Mike Hirakawa stood nearby, his sunglasses in place, his back against the clapboard siding of the house.

"Please translate," Ulz insisted.

Estlin obliged, assisted by the waetapu in the water.

"It's an odd choice," Harry said. "Asking him to visualize cuttlefish being pulled from the ocean, cooked and eaten."

"I didn't," Ulz protested.

"This type of translation relies on visual concepts and physical sensations," Harry said. "How can he communicate that we've stopped doing something without showing us doing it?"

Estlin waved Harry off and tried to ignore the extra colours the side conversation created. He didn't think ignoring the reality of the cuttlefish-human relationship was healthier than acknowledging it. His graphic presentation wasn't too graphic, and he tried to be open to the layers of their reply.

"The cuttles will continue to eat," he said, because it was true, and it was the simplest part of the reply.

"Eat what?"

"Cuttlefish eat until they become food." Estlin saw Ulz's confusion. "They aren't considering veganism. Also, they find it interesting that you begin with deception."

"You told them I was lying?"

"I didn't believe you, but that doesn't matter," Estlin said. "You know the UN called for the cuttlefish fishery to be closed, but hasn't accomplished it yet. You knew it wasn't true, so they know it's not true. The understanding the waetapu gather to share with the cuttlefish is direct. I'm not as necessary as you might think."

"He is necessary," Harry said. "The last time they tried to send a message to a group of us, it was like a spike in the eye."

"Don't worry. The cuttlefish associate deceptive behavior from smaller males with intelligence." The words were out of Estlin's mouth before he realized a less accurate translation would have been better.

"Do they have a leader?" Ulz asked.

"I don't know," Estlin said. "Are you asking them?"

Ulz stepped forward, looking at each occupant of the tank. "How do you make decisions? Who is your leader?"

The response from the cuttlefish was like a swift undertow with sand in the current.

"The water chooses," Estlin said. "The water chooses who is here to see and learn, and who returns to the place where they emerged small and hungry. Of all who give their young to the water, it is those whose young the water chooses to hold safe and nourish that are...*leaders* is the wrong word. Their primacy is passed forward."

"Is that a Darwinian answer?" Ulz asked. "The ones that reproduce win?"

"That's a fraction of it."

"Do they make collective decisions?" Ulz asked. "How are the questions formulated and communicated? How are the answers collected and tallied?"

Estlin approached the question using the symbol pair he'd worked out, the on/off sensory association of the cuttlefish. For squirrels, the active/inactive idea-pair was hungry/satiated, and for lizards it was hot/cold. The yes/no of the cuttlefish was translucent/opaque, although choices seemed more trinary than binary because opaque objects could be inert or living, and living opaque objects required translucent water. He found that his approach was wrong. The cuttlefish corrected him, representing the collective choice as accepting/rejecting an object passed from cuttlefish to cuttlefish. The trinary essence was still embedded because an object could be accepted (held) without being accepted (used for creation of life/death seeds).

"It's their children that decide," Estlin said. "No, sorry, it's their children that know."

"Know what?" Ulz asked.

"Know what has been decided."

"The children know." Serese seemed to float forward, drawing attention. "Their inherited knowledge is that specific?"

Estlin had his own immediate question and followed it to a realization. "This group is all one generation. No elders. No children here."

"These answers are taking us away from the key question," Ulz interjected. "What do the cuttlefish want from the aliens?"

Ulz's key question was safer than other sharper keys, so Estlin took it. His impression for *want* started with hunger, which always required clarification. The response was clear, but he flowed it back and forth with the cuttlefish, testing Ulz's patience and confirming the answer before relaying it.

"The cuttlefish did not want for the far swimmers," he said. "The far swimmers wanted for the cuttlefish. Why else would they swim so far?"

"That doesn't make sense." Ulz turned away from the tank to face Estlin, while Serese reached out for the transparent wall.

"Ma'm," Mike called to her. "Please don't touch it."

"New question," Ulz said. "What do they want from us?"

"From Estlin, you mean," Harry responded. "They are here to visit him not us."

Estlin didn't want to talk about the primary concern of the cuttlefish.

"The cuttlefish must want something," Ulz said.

"They crossed the Pacific," Serese said. "They crossed the mountains. Imagine the journey, Estlin. Why did they ask for this?"

"Imagine." Estlin stepped forward. "A future image. A tomorrow dream today." His skin prickled, fine hairs rising, as colours rippled behind his eyes. "They don't dream forward. The cuttlefish dream of yesterdays and years ago and the deep long gone. The far swimmers say they swam with the cuttles in the distant deep. In a space—a time—so long ago that the cuttlefish can't reach it in their dreams."

"Explain, please," Serese said.

"I think it's a literal answer," Estlin said. "In sleep, their minds travel back, they dream about the past, not the future."

"I asked about plans, not dreams," Ulz said. "We can't negotiate if the cuttlefish don't have a desire or plan. This must be a translation issue. You need to be more specific. Start with the immediate future, the next year or two years or five, and you need to focus on their waking thoughts about the future, not dreams."

Estlin visualized the concept and received a clear and cloudy answer. "They will be memories. Drifting in the depths."

Ulz huffed in frustration. "I have to report to the Secretary-General. He won't accept philosophical poetry about water. Are they evading the question?"

"No. That's their answer." Estlin pressed his fingertips against his eyes. "In a year, they will be dead. Cuttlefish have short lifespans."

Estlin realized that Ulz was looking at the cuttlefish before him, their skin pulsing with bright patterns, and imagining them drifting on the ocean floor. The images were an echo-overlay from a documentary, a vision of cuttlefish dead and gone, their pale skin sloughing off—food for the fish.

"Oh, don't." Estlin knew it was too late.

The cuttlefish jetted to the top of the tank. The base of the tank thickened, and it began to ascend, pressed upwards by a curling tongue of ice.

"What happened?" Ulz searched the water for further signs of movement.

"They're going," Estlin said. "The image of dead cuttlefish rolling on the bottom, you probably didn't mean to share it, but that was a real conversation killer."

"I didn't—" Ulz stopped short. "I did. I flashed on it for a second, but only because I knew what you said was true."

Estlin stepped forward to watch the bright tank merge into the larger structure over his house. "It's over for now."

"What about the other cuttlefish?" Ulz asked.

"Not tonight. I'm sorry," Estlin said, though he was actually grateful.

"It was not what I expected," Ulz said. "An awkward, brief conversation with six cuttlefish."

"Four cuttlefish," Estlin corrected him.

"There were six."

"Two waetapu were with them," Estlin said.

"The swimmers," Serese said.

"Yes," he answered. "The two that swim came to see you and to translate for the cuttlefish. The two that like climbing—the ones that talk to us—they've taken the night off."

"Four cuttlefish and two aliens." Serese watched the rising tank. "Two of them moved differently. It was subtle. I saw them, but I didn't see them."

"They are good at concealing themselves behind images from your mind," Estlin said. "They translated for the cuttlefish. I translated for you. If I repeated your words, it was to help you understand how they were being received. The waetapu read humans fairly well. I mean, they get inside your head." Estlin turned to Ulz. "That's how your death image was transmitted so strongly."

Ulz turned in place, looking from Harry to Serese to Estlin. "The aliens were here, and I didn't ask them any questions!"

"You weren't meant to," Estlin said.

"I've been trying to catch up to them for weeks!"

"Your cameras saw them," Harry said. "You'll be able to see them on the playback."

This answer clearly did not satisfy Ulz. "You should have said something."

"Why would I? They didn't," Estlin responded. "They aren't here to talk to us."

"How do you know?" Ulz asked. "In some cultures, offers have to be repeated many times before they are accepted. Maybe if we persist. If we wait out here, and you call them back—"

"I won't," Estlin said. "They'll be back in the morning."

"Did they say so?" Serese asked.

"No, I'm making an assumption," Estlin said. "I assume that if I tell you they'll be back in the morning, there is a chance you will leave me alone until morning."

Ulz took a step towards Estlin. "Your attitude is—"

Harry was on his feet. "I think you should come back in the morning."

"Mike?" Serese looked to her RCMP escort, who answered wordlessly.

"We'll go," she said.

"See you tomorrow," Estlin responded. "Please let the birds follow you out."

Chapter 3

Ulz's mouth filled with saliva as his base-level biology suggested imminent vomiting would be a good idea. He swallowed and trudged after Serese and her security man, the birds circling overhead, tittering at him. The tunnel was wider and higher than earlier, and the only landmarks were tufts of grass breaking up the gravel driveway. He was relieved when the end of the tunnel opened, the birds diving ahead to fly out.

Bernie was waiting next to the roadside postbox, holding an open umbrella. Several members of Serese's security team were with him, along with the soldiers posted on watch. The birds let loose, spattering the group as they rose skyward. Bernie was the only one protected.

"The crows were worse," he said to no one in particular and closed his umbrella. "We heard you coming. The ice tunnel makes a low noise as it moves. Is everything okay? That was a short visit. The night shift isn't ready yet."

"We met the cuttlefish," Serese said. "But we stumbled after introducing ourselves. Please schedule us for the first visit in the morning. We'll have to give the cuttlefish time to introduce themselves." Serese handed Bernie her small camera. "Do you need anything further?"

"Paik will ask you to make a written or video summary," Bernie said. "And there's a doctor—I've forgotten his name— he's tall and English, and he really likes blood samples."

"Thank you," Serese said. "I'll see you in the morning."

Ulz unclipped his camera, reluctantly handed it to Bernie, and tried not to guess how many people would see the footage.

"I think I need to watch this right away," Ulz said. "That was... There is so much I didn't see."

"It's a real kick to the head, isn't it?" Bernie said.

"Es ist demütigend." Ulz realized his brain had skipped. He softened the words as he switched to English. "Yes. It's humbling."

"Everyone blinks through their first session," Bernie assured him. "Estlin is the only exception. Actually, I'm wrong. He blacked out, but he accomplished way more than anyone else before that happened."

"I thought I had prepared," Ulz said. The words sounded foolish as soon as he spoke them.

"Drink some juice," Bernie said. "You'll feel better."

Ulz looked at Bernie.

"Trust me," Bernie said. "After you come out, there's a drop, like your brain runs out of processing power. Sugar helps. Give yourself a day or two. You'll build up some stamina. There's juice in the tent."

"Juice and debriefing," Ulz said. "I want to watch the footage. And I need to talk to an expert on ancestral memory."

"About the information the Waes archive in their spikes?" Bernie asked.

"No." Ulz stopped. "They keep information in their spikes?"

"I think so," Bernie said. "I don't know if anyone's confirmed it."

"The way Estlin spoke about the cuttlefish." Ulz paused. "He suggested the information passed to the next generation was not simply subconscious or instinctive, it was more complicated."

"Instincts are complicated," Bernie said. "Being born able to hunt and hide, identify prey and predators, know where on the globe your life should begin and end…it's all very complicated."

"It's not about complexity," Ulz said. "Complex is the wrong word. Deliberate? Deliberate genetic memory. Is that possible? I can have my office find someone, but—"

"The expert you want is me." Bernie pointed at himself. "I've studied biochemistry, neurophysics, and behavioural science. I mean, we'll still need an *expert* expert. I haven't focused on epigenetic molecular memory, but I know who to call."

"Of course," Ulz said. "Wellington had so many experts. Is that group coming here? I met the military commander when I arrived, but who is leading the science team?"

"The Canadians," Bernie said. "But Canadians are from everywhere. The head of their national research council is here."

"What's his specialty?"

"Administration? I don't actually know. She's been busy." Bernie shrugged. "And the guy they have running this tent is Dr. Chau. He's a measurements and standards guy— extremely detail-oriented, wears loud shirts. He's catching a nap or bringing in more equipment. He likes to take the night shift." Bernie pulled a notepad from his front pocket. "I'm trying to keep track. I need to figure out how to contribute. It's very different here." Bernie started walking towards the tent, bringing Ulz with him. "In New Zealand, we had only the aliens. Our focus was entirely on Wae and Waewae. Biologists, linguists, and behavioral scientists were the core. Here, the engineers are shoving everyone else aside.

"Some of it is my fault. My analysis of the ovoids has everyone looking at them as microscopic brain-scanning cell phones instead of biological cells. But mostly it's that," Bernie pointed at the sky-filling vessel over the farm, before directing Ulz into the staging tent. "We've got a big, hovering ocean cauldron, and we can't stop staring at it. Actually, it's what we wanted to see in New Zealand. I think it's a human flaw. You can have an alien in front of you, but what you really want to see is their spaceship. And this.... It's even more antagonizing. We can see the effect of their technology but not the technology itself. All the tech is still hidden behind the wizard's curtain."

"I see."

"You'll really see after you've been here a day or two. It creates a certain mental frenzy." Bernie pointed at a cooler in the corner of the tent. "Juice is there. The doctor is through there, and I think Paik is with Serese already. When do you want to talk about RNA memory weirdness?"

"Now. Tonight."

"You won't be sleeping?" Bernie asked.

"No."

"Me, neither," Bernie said. "I'm visiting the farm in the morning. It'll be my second walk through the keyhole since I got here, and I'm not ready. I'll sleep after."

"Serese and I are joining you." Ulz pointed at the schedule on the white board which had been updated with blue marker.

"She cut the rest of the morning team," Bernie said. "It makes sense. We go in groups of four now, and she added herself, you and Mike." Bernie stared at the board for another moment. "Did she keep me because I'm me or was it random?"

———— ⟨⟩ ————

Bomani shifted from deeper thought to shading a hastily sketched figure. The struggle to understand how the aliens stepped from star to star was wearing down his pencil. He focused on the EM pulse that preceded their arrival in Wellington. The latest iteration of inadequate equations was the culmination of three days of work sequestered with Sanford in a navy hotel in Pearl Harbor without a computer or a TV.

The grey-haired physicist was on the couch, fading into the tropical upholstery.

"Sanford?"

"Yes, what?" Sanford sat up. "What?"

"Progress." Bomani joined him on the couch and tapped the page with his pencil. "I'm making progress."

Sanford looked at the work, frowning. "If you write the superposition like that, cutback damping kills the process."

"What if it didn't?" Bomani asked.

"But it will. It does," Sanford insisted.

Bomani pointed at the sketch next to his equations. "The field symmetry in this direction—"

"That is not a direction. It's an imaginary axis."

"Fine." Bomani circled the offending parameter.

"It's not fine!" Sanford extended his fingers, as though he wanted to steal the pencil. "The supermodes…. That has to be wrong. The insertion losses would be extreme."

"That problem is lightyears away!" Bomani responded. "We don't know anything about insertion."

"The propagation losses look infinitely worse."

"There is no propagation," Bomani insisted. "The transit is static. *There* and *here* are the same place. The object meets the surface of the space fold. It's *there* and *here*. And then it's *here*. And then *there* and *here* split away."

"And when space and time unfold, the peel off process throws a thermal wave that incinerates the sun." Sanford flicked his fingers against each other.

"No. The splitting energy has to flow back through the node to balance the—"

"Has to? Has to?" Sanford squinted at the page. "It's not in these equations."

Bomani took a breath, planting a hand on the paper, covering his own inadequate work. "But it will be, because it has to be, because the aliens are here, and we still have a solar system."

"It won't work that way unless it's forced."

"So, it's forced." Bomani scrawled an arrow-capped '*F*' in the middle of the page. "There's a better equation and a perfect force. The object transfers and—"

"And the extreme fields turn it into vermicelli," Sanford responded. "That is a textbook spaghettification scenario."

"Is it strange that I enjoy listening to you argue?" Sgt. Malone interrupted them from the doorway.

"Did you let yourself in?" Sanford asked.

"None of these doors lock," Malone replied.

"You could knock," Bomani said.

Malone knocked on the door behind him. "Pack now. We're going to the airport."

"Going where?" Sanford asked.

"To the airport."

"Do we have a choice?" Bomani folded his pages of work together.

"Do you want one?" Malone asked. "You either stay on the ride or you get off."

"Give me a moment," Sanford said. "I need to gather my things."

Sanford left the room, and Sgt. Malone looked at Bomani, waiting for him to push the argument.

"I'm already packed," Bomani said finally. "Do I get my passport back?"

"I can ask," Malone answered. "Spagettification?"

"The distortion of objects caught in a massive asymmetrical gravitational field," Bomani answered. "Physicists make up whimsical terms, so they can pretend they were joking when their theories fail."

"Don't insult Hawking," Sanford called through the open door of the bathroom as he emerged with his shaving kit.

«»

Harry woke in the old armchair with a book about beekeeping in his hand. The living room was illuminated by the floor lamp next to the chair. Estlin had fallen asleep on the couch, and the squirrels had gathered around him. He was breathing erratically, his eyes closed, his arms and legs twitching. The squirrels were all awake and standing tall, watching Estlin from perches on all sides of the couch.

Harry dropped the book on the stack next to the chair. Estlin gasped. His eyes opened with a flickering, blank gaze that was disturbing. The squirrels scattered back, giving their human more room, but staying close and concerned.

"Lyndie?"

There was no response. Harry rose and placed a hand on Estlin's shoulder. "Lyndie?"

With another strong twitch, Estlin's eyes focused.

"You okay?" Harry asked.

"I fell asleep."

"Yes, you did," Harry replied. "What were you dreaming about?"

"I don't know."

"Was it about the Waes?" Harry asked. "It looked a bit rough."

"I don't know." Estlin sat up and dismissed the squirrels with a gesture that was mostly a morning stretch. "Where is everyone?"

"Who is everyone?" Harry asked.

"Everyone. Different people." Estlin looked around the room. "There are people in here all the time. They like to look through my cupboards and make judgements about how much soup I own."

"A group arrived after you fell asleep," Harry said. "I waved them off."

"I'm surprised that worked."

"I have an intimidating smile." Harry flexed shoulders strengthened and damaged by a lifetime of rugby scrums.

"True," Estlin said. "I wonder if they spent the night on the front step. I did really pitch a fit yesterday when I kicked everyone out."

"Good," Harry said. "You needed a break. Do you want to sleep more? Or take a shower? I can hold down the fort."

"A shower. Yes," Estlin said. "What time is it?"

"Five thirty."

"We'll have more company soon," Estlin said. "How many time zones did you drop yesterday?"

"I should know," Harry said. "Do you have coffee?"

"There's tea."

"Unacceptable."

"Avoid the milk. It's gone off. And don't bother making breakfast." Estlin paused on the stairs. "Sorry. Take what you want from the cupboards, but Bernie will bring breakfast. He was with the morning science-nerd team yesterday—he got here faster than you—and he brought waffles. It's kind of crazy. Out there, it's a state of emergency, a scramble-everything-you-need-for-first-contact situation, and someone clearly brought a waffle maker. I got fresh waffles, and I may have demanded more waffles."

Estlin half laughed, and then wavered on the stairs, his expression suddenly sad and uncertain. A silence fell as Harry watched Estlin's wet eyes blink, looking for alien influences and seeing none.

"Take your shower, waffle diva," Harry said. "I'll tip out the bad milk and write a list for Bernie. It looks like no one has even brought you a bucket of crayons to help document the visual communication for us."

"I have a notebook."

"Can I read it?"

"It's on the counter," Estlin said. "Bernie photographed the pages."

"You shower. I'll catch up."

"Okay."

Harry watched until Estlin reached the top of the stairs, and then opened the fridge door and held on to it. Having chased the situation since Estlin and Wae had disappeared in Wellington, he needed to get his footing and not think about the remnant of Yidge upstairs, burned into an alien hard drive.

He dealt with the milk carton and evaluated the near empty fridge. Pulling the notebook off the counter, he decided to read it outside. He'd forgotten about the group that had wandered in during the night and was annoyed to find them on the porch. Four people were occupying the stairs and porch swing, their lanterns shining in the morning light.

"Anything happen out here?" Harry asked the man on the porch swing.

"No."

"We met at the tent," Harry said. "I've forgotten your name."

"Theo Chau. I set the access schedule here." Theo stood. "Can we go in?"

"Why?" Harry asked. "Estlin's in the shower. There's nothing in his fridge. And the aliens you are here to observe are in the tree."

Harry sat next to the door, leaned against the house, and opened the notebook. As he skimmed the first few pages, the atmosphere shifted. Wae had clambered to the limit of the nearest, lowest branch to look at him with bright yellow eyes. The deep blue spikes covering its body were folded flat, giving it a smaller, more contained appearance. Its hands, feet and tail were wrapped around the branch.

"Well, I missed you, too," Harry stood, keeping a grip on the notebook, and crossed the porch. "I have mixed feelings about you abducting my friend, but you got him home safe. I'm good with that."

Harry left the porch to walk under the branches of the tree, looking for Waewae. "Do you want to tell me what you're up to now?" He spotted the other alien higher in the tree and dangling sideways, holding on to a branch with one hand and its tail.

Wae walked backwards along the branch with pointed elbows and deliberate chameleon-like steps.

"Is this another application of stress to watch us react?" Harry asked. "Because I can tell you, everyone is stressed."

Wae stopped, its attention lingering on Harry.

"Is it responding?" Chau asked.

Wae raised its head in a way that made Harry glance towards the driveway. He said nothing, but knew more visitors were arriving as Wae leapt upwards, bounding through the branches to vanish into the canopy.

"Did it respond?" Chau asked again.

"You saw what I saw." Harry heard a rumble from the ice structure. "I think your shift is over."

The ice opened, creating a cloud of mist that hid the process. Bernie emerged from the opening along with Ulz. They were engaged in a scientific argument, Bernie gesturing broadly while Ulz kept his hands clasped behind his back. Harry's opinion of the UN representative rose a notch, which didn't bring it far from the ground because yesterday's efforts had not impressed him.

"Where are the others?" Theo asked.

"Not coming," Bernie said. "Well, others are coming, but it will be Serese and Mike, not Weaver and Saeed. I think Serese took over the scheduling."

"Really," Chau said with the flat tone of someone who may have just been demoted.

"She's added a lot of meetings to the schedule, including one with you this morning." Bernie said.

"When?"

Bernie checked his watch. "Now."

"That doesn't make sense." Chau looked from Bernie, to the house, to Harry and to his team. "Let's go."

Bernie dug into his knapsack and pulled out a camera. "Harry, do you want to swap—where's your camera?"

"Under the tree."

Bernie was perturbed. "You're supposed to wear it." He headed under the tree to retrieve the camera.

"You wanted that camera pointed at the Waes," Harry said. "The Waes are in the tree. The camera is under the tree. What are you complaining about?"

"They're in the tree?" Bernie looked up. "They're in the tree! Ulz, come and see this!"

"Are the aliens—" Ulz joined Bernie, and then ducked and ran away from the tree.

"No, no, don't do that." Bernie raised his hands in a gesture of dismay. "Now, it looks like there are a couple of cocker spaniels up there. That's just wrong."

"I saw a snake," Ulz said. "A constrictor sliding down through the branches."

"Why did they start camouflaging?" Bernie asked Harry.

"They know you want to bother them," Estlin said, emerging from the house, damp-haired and looking better. His t-shirt featured a faded turtle with 'take it slow' printed across the shell.

"Nice shirt," Harry said.

Estlin ignored him. "Did you bring breakfast?" he asked Bernie.

"Yes. Sort of." Bernie dug into his knapsack, pulled out a banana, and held it defensively.

"That's not a waffle," Harry said. "Lyndie said you were bringing waffles."

"Ulz and I worked all night," Bernie said. "We wanted to start early, and it takes a lot of time to go out to the other campsite because of the layers of security. But I have packets of instant porridge and fruit."

"Hold up the banana," Estlin said. "Above your head."

"What? Are they—oh!" Bernie raised the banana, holding it with his fingertips.

Waewae leapt down through the branches, stopping to wrap the six tips of three long toes around the banana and launch itself higher.

"They wanted a banana," Harry said. "That feels like it should be a joke."

"Did you see a snake take a banana?" Bernie asked Ulz.

"Yes," Ulz answered from the safety of the porch.

"That's mean," Bernie said.

"Dr. Lichtwardt and I reviewed cuttlefish neurons and ganglia—"

"Stop," Harry cut Bernie off. "Don't think about cuttlefish brains sliced for study. Not now."

"They're coming," Estlin said.

"Oh! Right!" Bernie covered his mouth and then his forehead. "How do I not think—?"

"The tank is forming," Ulz said. "Excellent. I wrote a list of major discussion points last night."

Harry turned away from Ulz, stepped close to Estlin, and lowered his voice. "Lyndie, you better own this conversation or he'll try to cram a thousand questions into one morning."

The tank looked like a shaft of clear crystal. Harry could see the cuttlefish and waetapu inside, all angled as though swimming downwards. The waetapu swam with webbed limbs and a far greater sway than the cuttlefish. Faint colours flowed across their spikes, matching the patterns the cuttlefish used for communication and camouflage.

"I see them." Ulz pointed at the waetapu accompanying the cuttlefish. "I see them."

"Let Lyndie get started before you jump in with questions."

"How will you start?" Ulz asked Estlin.

"The usual way." Estlin waved at the occupants of the ice tank.

Harry watched as Estlin faded into an absent presence, his eyes tracking images that only he could see. Bernie held two cameras and watched Estlin. Ulz was staring at the waetapu, his nose almost touching the wall of the tank.

Harry waited. He waited long enough that their pocket-world was full of light, and he imagined, somewhere beyond the tank, the sun had freed itself from the horizon. He waited until he knew Ulz had reached the limit of his patience and was about to interrupt.

"Lyndie?" Harry closed the space between them. "Has everyone said good morning?"

"Good morning?" Estlin said, as though this was a completely odd pairing of words. "The brightening. No, I didn't.... good doesn't associate with light levels. They aren't attached to sunlight the way we are. They asked about airplanes. I explained."

"You explained?" Bernie asked.

"A little," Estlin said.

"How do they know about planes?" Ulz asked.

"Just guessing," Harry said. "But they have sharp eyesight, and they're hanging with a species that travels from star to star."

"The planes in Samoa were disruptive," Estlin replied. "The cuttles could feel-hear them. They can feel-hear the distant planes now."

"Do they want the no-fly zone expanded?" Harry asked.

"No," Estlin said. "They're just curious."

"I hope we can have a precise session," Ulz said. "It may seem harsh, but we need to be absolutely certain the cuttlefish know you don't speak for humanity."

"They know."

"It's worth revisiting this specifically," Ulz said. "We need to have a documented conversation about it."

Estlin looked to Harry and said everything he needed to with one eyebrow.

"They need to know you aren't an appropriate representative for mankind," Ulz said. "You haven't been trained or selected or empowered to speak for us."

"You're hitting the point a little hard," Harry said.

"It's necessary," Ulz responded. "Communication is difficult. We should come back to this subject as the clarity of dialogue increases. It should be the first important note whenever different individual cuttlefish or aliens join the negotiations."

Harry detested this idea, even as Estlin nodded.

"It fits today," Estlin said. "It distinguishes your purpose here from mine."

"Are you sure—?" Harry had an answer from Estlin before he could finish asking. He saw the shift in Estlin's eyes and tried to imagine the symbols that would have to be invented and defined to get through what Ulz thought would be a preamble and not a lengthy, complicated conversation.

"What happens now?" Ulz asked.

"We shut up and let them talk," Harry answered.

The concentration in Estlin's expressive, dilated eyes, betrayed the difficulty of explaining to the cuttlefish that the only person who could communicate with them wasn't *qualified* to communicate with them, at least not on behalf of humanity. Harry guessed that Estlin's representation of humanity encompassed everyone, without splits of geography or hierarchy or disproportions in wealth. Did Ulz expect him to explain democracies and dictatorships? Or intelligentsia and inequities in education?

"Do you think he's changed topics?" Ulz asked.

"No," Harry said. "You gave him a real puzzle."

Ulz looked at him without comprehension.

"You started this, now you have to let Lyndie sweat it through," Harry said. "It isn't something he can leave off as an unfinished conversation."

A cold draft crossed the deck, and Harry saw an interruption arriving.

Serese and her security man were walking purposefully towards the house. Harry knew royals and their representatives operated in a world where no show started without them. "Dr. Lichtwardt, did you skip ahead of schedule?"

"What?" Ulz followed his gaze, understood the question, and said nothing.

Serese joined them on the porch. "You've started?"

"Yes." Harry could tell from the flickering of Estlin's half-closed eyes that he was too engaged with the cuttlefish to respond. "Lyndie is telling the cuttlefish that he's not qualified to talk to them."

"That's not what I said," Ulz interjected. "I understand Mr. Hume is a uniquely gifted translator. But he's a *translator*, not a spokesperson."

"It's a delicate and complicated thing to *translate*," Harry said. "As Ulz has started this conversation, I suggest that we give Estlin time to finish it."

It was clear Serese disagreed, as Harry thought she might.

Chapter 4

Estlin felt a warm hand lifting his body from the water. The encompassing hand became a gentle touch on his elbow. He was tangled in ideas and had trouble rising. Serese was close, her eyes full of liquid reflections. It struck him deeply that she was more qualified for this job. She had trained to be her complete self when standing in a point of light. As a principal dancer, for each performance, she absorbed the work of a collective and blended the colours to crystallize an experience and share it. Serese had danced in vast theatres, and knew how to hold a thousand conversations at once.

"Mr. Hume," Serese spoke softly. "Estlin, I'm sorry to interrupt."

He was too close. His eyes were leaking. He stepped away from Serese.

"They know I'm me," he said. "Just me. Not an extension of you or the larger group."

"Good," Serese said.

"They know my connection to my preceders—" Estlin stopped. Preceders was the wrong word or not a word at all, an invention sliding towards a cuttle idea. "Parents," he said, but that was also wrong. It was too small. "They know my connection to my parents, and the generations before them, is broken."

Harry looked concerned. Estlin gave himself a moment to get his words in order, to keep them simple.

"They know I'm me alone," he said. "They ask me to speak to many, not for many."

"I understand," Serese said.

Estlin felt a welling gratitude, beyond a rational level.

"Are these the same cuttlefish that were here yesterday?"

Estlin couldn't answer. When he tried to ask cuttlefish about individual identity, their answers expanded recursively. It was strange, even considering that each cuttlefish tentacle had a mind of its own. The cuttlefish considering their physical *summation of self* to be greater than one wasn't the problem, because attempts to include arms and tentacles and other parts were still too small and finite.

"Estlin?" Serese touched his arm again. "The reluctant one… I'm certain it was here yesterday. I can tell that the other three have different relationships with each other. I can't tell if they are three different cuttlefish or if there is just one new cuttlefish. Either way, all the relationships change."

"Three different." Estlin knew they were different, though he couldn't define or name them. Serese could see things he had trouble distinguishing, even though his access to the visual acuity of the cuttlefish was improving.

"I know you are processing more than you can express," Serese said. "I think you should work through it later, because we still have company now."

"Yes, there are questions," Ulz said. "How long have they been talking to the aliens? Why are they here talking to you? How long are they staying?"

The words billowed red, and Estlin blinked at the flowing colours that indicated signals from the waetapu's ovoids were cranking open his brain.

"Look at the cuttlefish." Serese's response swirled in beautiful circles of grey. "The patterns dancing on their skins. Their shifting postures and positions."

Estlin looked at the cuttlefish, and their curious, excited and wary colours.

"You don't have to ask them any questions," she said. "Just listen for us. We'll all be quiet now, so you can listen properly."

Estlin closed his eyes, took a breath and let himself float. *Was he not listening properly?* The waetapu in the water opened the window to the other side of the ice, but they stayed deep under the connection. Meanwhile, Wae and Waewae spent so much time communing with the tree that he *missed them*.

The cuttlefish that wanted a stone or a shell to squeeze was looking at Serese's arms. It respected her relaxed limbs, as it would respect any pair of strong eels waiting to strike from their dens. The cuttlefish closest to the tank wall followed Serese's dark eyes, reacting to each moment of visual contact as she watched each of them and all of them. The one behind it was engaged in being a particularly loud yellow while holding an attractive posture that made it feel exceptionally large.

The murmuring reluctant one was hanging back, resisting intrusive contact.

Estlin reminded himself to listen, to settle into the quiet needed to hear the hum of a beehive. He found the reluctant cuttlefish was holding a strong thought, while the others were transient thinkers, their perceptions flickering as fast as the patterns that pulsed across their skins.

The reluctant one disliked the box. It disliked the urchin-skinned creatures that swam like seals. It disliked their way of changing shape without changing shape. It disliked their strength. It disliked being pulled and lifted and lowered to spend time with those who lived on the bottom without buoyancy. It disliked the waste of thinking about whether those born without balance or buoyancy could ever dig it from within like a clam from under the sand.

It disliked the thin, dead above-water, which was now *below* and above. It disliked the dry others who crawled where nothing floated. It disliked the diagonal pleat on the front of Serese's shirt. The edge of the light fabric was hanging limply. There was no current to lift it. Still water was dead water, and stillness surrounded the box.

It disliked that they had all followed the urchin deceivers to this dangerous place, knowing their thoughts might be transformed, their *selves* disrupted into a profound decay that could send them all spiraling to the surface to drown.

It disliked the one who split itself to creep through the water, leaving its body in the silt. It disliked the clumsy disembodied shapes it assumed. It disliked knowing that the creeping one's self was broken and shallow. Were the cuttlefish risking their many, while the others below took shelter, offering only one whose tentacles had been bitten off, one who could pass nothing directly to those around it?

The weight of a cuttlefish seeing his difference and disconnection hit Estlin. It sank him, and he instinctively pulled on the link, trying to maintain it. The cuttlefish realized Estlin was under its eyelids. It clenched, releasing a burst of ink. Estlin was dragged with it through the darkened water, the connection too wide to be shaken off by a jet of movement. The cuttlefish spewed a second cloud of ink, which didn't feel like puking at all, except that it was entirely like puking. The tank lifted away like at elevator clouded with black smoke.

Estlin's stomach hurt. Everyone was looking at him.

"Well, that ended badly," Harry said. "You all here?"

Estlin stretched his hands, flexing his fingers. He didn't know how much time had passed. The tank was still rising to where it could open into the shallows of the bucket of ocean above. "I'm here."

"Want to sit down?" Harry asked.

"No."

"What happened?"

"My fault," Estlin said. "I pestered the one that doesn't like gaijin."

"What's gaijin?" Bernie asked.

Estlin dropped his head and covered his face with his hands. "I don't know," he admitted, because he really didn't know where the word had come from or why he'd said it.

"Bad foreigners," Mike answered from the depths of the porch. "Us."

Estlin nodded. "I was listening to the reluctant one. It doesn't like us. It caught me listening to it."

"That's it?" Ulz asked. "It inked all over the place in a panic because you were listening to it?"

"Yes."

"Isn't that why you're here?" Ulz continued. "Isn't that why the cuttlefish came to visit you?"

"Did you run away from Wae this morning?" Harry asked.

"Estlin," Serese interrupted the argument. "What else can you tell us?"

"I didn't ask them anything," Estlin said. "I was just trying to follow their thoughts. The one most concerned about this situation had the strongest thoughts about us. It got my attention, too much of my attention."

"You angered it," Ulz said. "Or frightened it somehow."

"No. It was already unhappy about being here."

"Unhappy?" Ulz asked. "Do cuttlefish feel happiness?"

"It was aware of the tank and us and the waetapu," Estlin said. "It was considering the risks of contact with us and the aliens. Unhappy might be the wrong word, an extra word, beyond its repeated negative assessment of the risks here."

"What risks?" Ulz stepped back.

"Was it worried about the integrity of the tank?" Bernie asked.

"No," Estlin answered.

"What risks?" Ulz asked again.

"The tank isn't frightening because it might fail," Estlin said. "It's scary because it won't fail."

"I want the porridge now." Harry took Bernie's bag, digging into it. "Lyndie hasn't had breakfast," Harry told Serese as he pressed the packets into Estlin's hands. "Why don't you go boil some water."

Boil water while I argue with people, Estlin finished Harry's thought, and found that he was more interested in the porridge than the brewing argument.

——— «» ———

"We can still talk to the other aliens," Ulz said.

Harry ignored Ulz. He knew how important it was to keep his eyes on the target when kicking towards the post.

"We need to document each conversation before we jump into the next one," he said. "Estlin needs a strategy for his next session with the cuttlefish, and we don't know enough to help him."

Serese checked her watch. "It's past ten. Dr. Lichtwardt, Dr. Springer, please go out and document what you can of the morning. I'll meet with you at noon, and then we can brief the next team. Afterwards, you can rest and prepare for your session here tomorrow."

"Oh, okay," Bernie said. "I need to set more cameras under the tree before I go. Ulz can help."

Harry thought Bernie had just preempted any protest from Ulz without recognizing that the UN man was a problem.

"Go ahead," Serese said. "Harry will follow you out in a few minutes."

Harry gathered his arguments as Ulz and Bernie left the porch. "I didn't want Ulz to push leading questions and interpretations at Lyndie. We need to document his first impressions without extra noise."

"I understand."

"I'm needed here."

"Yes, you are," Serese answered. "I'm setting the schedule now. And I won't be scheduling your time with Estlin."

Harry stiffened at the threat, but Serese continued.

"I set the order that gave you unrestricted access when you arrived," she said. "This is Estlin's house. He needs support and continuity."

"He needs protection," Harry responded. "The waetapu do what they want, and they are happy enough to watch us clash with each other. Lyndie's taken all kinds of hits because I asked him for help. I'm glad he's home, but the longer he's with them, the greater the risk to him and everything he has. And most of the threat is what we'll do because they're sitting in that tree."

"What do you think is happening here?"

"Here?" Harry assumed that an accelerated variation of the events he'd experienced in Wellington after meeting the Waes was underway. "It's been four days, right? I bet your allies are in a rolling boil, and your enemies...does Canada have enemies?"

"Not officially," Serese said.

"Expect things to build to a critical mass," Harry said. "And then there will be a bump, someone will trigger an event and players from all sides will press for an advantage. If things re-stabilize without a change in status quo, the cycle will repeat but the bump will hit faster and stronger."

"You managed the aliens in New Zealand," she said. "If you want more responsibility here, we can discuss it tomorrow."

"I'll think on it," Harry said.

"Good. Now, I'm going to ask you to take a walk."

"What?"

"I need to talk to Estlin, and General Stodt wants to talk to you," she said. "I believe you rely on his goodwill as well as mine. Tell Stodt that I expect you back here by noon."

"Please tell Estlin that I'll be back."

"I will," Serese answered. "General Stodt is in zone 10. Go to the communications center in the staging area. There's a secure connection."

"All right," Harry said.

"Let me speak to Dr. Lichtwardt," she said. "Whatever words you want to have with him, refrain. He'll handle one correction better than two."

"Thanks. I'll give Bernie a list of things we need."

"Good," Serese said. "I'm glad you are here."

Harry nodded and walked over to Bernie, who was adjusting a camera tripod under the tree. "Where's Ulz?"

"On his way out."

"You almost ready?"

"One second," Bernie said. "This one is pointed up through the edge of the canopy. I need to set the exposure manually because the auto adjust is creating silhouettes."

"Why don't you change the angle?"

"Because, you see, the way I've set these out, we get an overlapped array of—"

"No, forget it. I didn't ask," Harry said. "How many cameras have you got in here?"

"Many," Bernie said. "Do you think they'd let me put some in the tree?"

"Not now," Harry answered. "Stop fiddling. The light will change through the day anyhow."

"Actually, the scattering creates a diffuse..." Bernie stepped away from the tree, looking over at the house. He tipped his head back and turned in place, looking straight up at the expansive structure above them. "Oceans are where photons go to die."

"I will leave without you," Harry responded.

"It's too bright in here!" Bernie exclaimed. "Can't you see it? There's too much light! We've got deep water above us.

The leaves should be fading from lack of light. Look at these shadows!"

Harry looked at the shadows. They were soft, overlapping, and unremarkable.

"The cauldron has internal structure. The engineers assume it's for mechanical strength, and the thin plates covering most of the surface are to control evaporation. But it's too bright in here. Those structures must be collecting light and piping it through the water…not just piping, duplicating and cascading. If we have full daylight and the cuttlefish have full daylight, there must be an integrated photon multiplication system!"

"That's very interesting," Harry said. "Can we go?"

"Yes, yes." Bernie pulled a scrap of paper from his pocket, adding a note to it as they walked. "When I tell the engineers that the light tunnels above us are energized and amplifying a fraction of sunlight back up to full daylight, they'll take the credit for figuring it out. I mean, they will figure out the details, but—"

"Is that your to-do list?" Harry asked.

"Yes."

"Add a guest book."

"Why?" Bernie asked. "They are tracking everyone who comes in here."

"Does Estlin have the current list?" Harry asked. "If he wants to talk to someone who was here yesterday morning or three days ago, can he look up who they were? Get a guest book for the house. Everyone signs. Date, name, details. It needs to have a 'purpose of visit' column with two choices, *observe* or *interrupt*. People can mark down how they plan to spend their time."

"I'll have to ask—"

"Put it on the list," Harry said. "And Lyndie needs a big pad of paper, so he can sketch out some of what he sees. His notebook is too small. What we really need is that mathematician who draws well. Put him on the list, too."

Bernie fell a few paces behind trying to walk and write at the same time.

Harry was certain Bernie didn't appreciate what a central role he had or how it could make him a target. "By the way, I think the Russian who gave me a ride may come looking for a favor. Getting me here got him on the ground. We don't owe him anything. He was Doctor Pepel in Samoa, and Mister Pechkin on the flight. Don't be surprised if he pops up at random. The Russian approach has been to stand back and watch closely, but they'll take action if anything motivates them to make a play."

Harry stopped and looked at the ruts of the dirt driveway they were following. The ice structure obscured any view of how far they'd come and how much further there was to go. "They should mark this path."

"It was discussed," Bernie said. "But someone vetoed the use of spray paint."

"Chalk," Harry said. "Or stones. Would the path stay open if you knocked tall wood posts into the ground?"

"I don't know," Bernie said. "An opening is not enough. Signals aren't just damped out by the water. They are actively squashed or absorbed by the ovoids." Bernie stopped and held out his hand. "Harry, you should give me your camera."

"I don't have one."

"But I—"

"You got distracted," Harry said.

"Oh, okay." Bernie pulled the camera off his lanyard and turned it off.

Harry was annoyed. "I need to get out, so I can get back as quickly as possible."

"This structure creates a dead zone. They've laid different types of cable down along this path—unshielded, shielded, coaxial, fibre optic—and they rolled them all out again because nothing works. Relays don't work. The call you got in to Estlin must've slipped through before the full structure settled or maybe the Waes deliberately transmitted it. Everyone hates the silence. When you hand over the cards from twenty cameras, no one appreciates all the windows they have into the past few hours because they are starving for the instantaneous present."

Harry caught that Bernie had shut off his camera while they were still standing in the dead zone. "I've missed a few things. What should I know?"

"It's hard to document this thoroughly without ending up with reams of footage." Bernie hesitated. "When Estlin talks to the squirrels, we record bits of broken, half-spoken random conversation. He gets mad at them. Sometimes he asks for their advice. I swear he was talking to a mole yesterday morning."

"He does that," Harry said.

Bernie nodded. "There may be people who listen to those recordings without understanding how he works with the Waes and how they work with him."

"That's why we need you," Harry said. "To keep everyone focused on the right footage, and to argue with people who want to mount a camera in his toilet bowl."

"Right," Bernie said.

"It's an important job," Harry said. "One you have to take without waiting for anyone to give it to you. Got it?"

Bernie hefted his bag of cameras over his shoulder. "Got it."

Harry had bigger concerns than Estlin *seeming crazy*. Estlin's animal magnetism had originated as a cripplingly strong ability to connect with everyone and everything. It had ruined his childhood. He'd only emerged from the murk when trauma destroyed the inner access point that had flooded his mind with invasive sensory noise from people around him. The obvious bleeds, where Estlin knew what those around him were thinking, were dangerous. Whether the Waes were the bridge in those connections or not, it wasn't safe.

"Do you think posts and string would keep the path open?" Bernie asked. "Or we could try bringing in a row of potted shrubs. I think the structure yields more for living matter, but I don't know if it'd be enough to get a signal through the damping field around the ice."

"It's probably a bad idea to mess with what the Waes have set up," Harry said. "You should at least wait until Lyndie has a chance to ask them about it."

———— «» ————

"Gaijin?" Serese asked Mike as they crossed the porch.

"My father is Japanese," he said. "My mother is Canadian. I went to elementary school in Tokyo, where the protruding nail gets hammered down. I was different. I was gaijin."

"He didn't know where the word came from," Serese said.

Mike nodded, and then stepped into the entryway, took a position by the wall and faded into the background. It was one of his many skills. Serese entered the kitchen. The kettle was rumbling on the stove, far from a full boil. A bowl of oats waited nearby on the counter.

Estlin was at the kitchen table, sketching in his notebook. "Where's Harry?"

"He's gone to speak to General Stodt," Serese said. "He'll be back soon."

"Soon." Estlin checked the clock and continued to work on a rough drawing.

"I met Stodt in Wellington."

"He's advising us," she said. "I was surprised when the prime minister called me. Do you find it unusual that I'm here?"

"No." Estlin flipped through the pages of his notebook to look at a penciled set of circles flowing into each other. "You're very qualified."

"What is it?" Serese asked.

"That's what it looked like when you told me to listen," Estlin said. "Sort of. I don't draw very well."

"I don't understand." Serese sat next to him at the table.

"When the waetapu do their thing, words have colours and shapes." Estlin tapped his forehead. "I think a few extra pathways get crosslinked." He looked at her for several seconds, and then pushed his chair back and quickly stood. "Do you want some water?"

"No, thank you."

Estlin went to the sink, filled a glass and leaned against the counter. "Is it a mess out there?"

"A state of emergency was declared," Serese said. "The Caraway and Chief Mountain border crossings are closed. The Americans have tanks parked on the twenty-foot clearcut along the 49th parallel, and their air force is putting on a show. They also invaded, briefly, yesterday, when the Russians landed, but we sorted it out."

"I'm surprised they aren't in here."

"They are here," Serese said. "And if I let them in but you don't, it will be a problem."

"Not our only problem," Estlin said. "Who's coming?"

"I'll give you as much notice and choice as I can."

"And our military is stomping around?" Estlin asked.

"Think of it like the response to the last major flood," Serese said. "The troops are here to help manage the situation, not to point guns at it. I can't give you any details because we want to isolate those of us who are in contact with the aliens from the people responsible for security and governing the country. There is a policy of strategic ambiguity between us and those other groups. I was selected, in part, for my ignorance. I know enough about government and military structure without knowing too much. My constitutional responsibilities and executive powers as The Queen's representative in Canada have been suspended. I can't summon or dissolve Parliament while under alien influence."

"You haven't lost a single drop of power." Estlin took a large baking dish from the cupboard under the sink. He filled it with water and placed it on the floor. A squirrel scampered over for a drink, while others inched closer, forming a rough queue.

Serese watched as Estlin refilled his own glass of water.

"What do you need to know?" he asked.

"Are there more aliens concealed around the globe?"

"Hanging out with other species?"

"In our cities, observing us," Serese replied. "Two capybaras recently escaped from the zoo in Toronto. It's not the first time they've gone for a walk. Last time, they were recaptured in the park. Now, we've got two massive rodents on the loose, and there are no sightings."

Estlin sipped his water. "They may have been snatched by someone who thinks they are alien imposters."

"I understand that the Waes want you to focus on the cuttlefish," Serese said. "And you can only share with us what they choose to share with you. But when you have the chance, please ask them about the capybaras in Toronto. See if it leads to a larger answer about how many observers are amongst us."

"Okay." Estlin placed his glass in the sink. "Are you good at climbing trees? I can lend you a t-shirt if you like."

Serese realized what he meant and rose from the table, assessing her shirt and slacks. "I'm fine—"

The kettle whistled.

"Don't, don't!" Estlin shouted as the bowl fell from the counter. The oats scattered as the ceramic bowl bounced against the floor without breaking. The grey squirrel on the counter leaned back with a momentarily contrite posture, and then sprang down to join the feasting crowd.

"Bastard." Estlin lifted the kettle, setting it on another element as he turned off the burner. "Sorry. I got distracted. Squirrels. They have no retention. If I stop telling them not to do a thing, they go on and do it. Let's go."

Serese followed Estlin from the kitchen.

"We're climbing the tree," she told Mike as she passed him in the entryway. He nodded and turned on the camera clipped to his lanyard.

《》

Estlin walked between low hanging branches and stepped out of his sandals to climb the tree. Serese followed, slipping off her shoes and placing her hand against the tree's trunk. The smooth bark returned her to the childhood realization that every single leaf was breathing. She climbed into the well-spaced and welcoming branches.

"We won't go very high," Estlin said.

It was a relative statement, Serese thought as she climbed. When Estlin found a suitable branch and braced himself into the crook, the ground was distant, but a vast amount of tree remained above them.

Serese spotted a perch and was reaching for it when a flurry of squirrels rushed up the trunk.

"Sorry," Estlin said. "They finished breakfast."

The squirrels continued to flow around her, spreading throughout the branches.

"The Waes make them nervous," Estlin said. "But I'm here, so here they are."

Four small chickadees darted from branch to branch, moving towards them instead of away. The birds encircled

Estlin, spiraling around him, singing, and then fluttered off to the upper reaches of the tree.

"Have you been introduced?" Estlin pointed into the branches above. "Wae and Waewae."

Serese had seen photos and videos but seeing the Waes crouched above them felt entirely different. Their bodies were a vibrant blue with rusty variations in their joints. Their eyes were more closely spaced than what she had seen of the aliens in the water. The Waes were on two adjacent branches. It was hard for her to judge their posture or what made the strength of the connection between the two of them register so strongly. They had their own space, partially defined by a distinct squirrel-free circumference.

"They haven't been answering my questions, but this is your question." Estlin smiled to himself, leaning against the tree trunk, closing his eyes. "Capybaras. Rodents of unusual size."

Serese heard and saw the squirrels shifting positions in the tree, giving Estlin more room. The Waes above seemed to expand, their quills spreading, but it was more like an idea rising, than a porcupine shrugging into a defensive posture. She felt privileged to be in this timeless place listening to the rustling leaves. The contrast between the tree and world outside, where everything was alarming, urgent, and loud, was immense. It was also invaluable and essential...and not how anyone outside expected first contact to be managed. She knew this would make her job difficult.

"The capybaras are not waetapu.... Oh." Estlin took a deep, shuddering breath. "They were born to come. I didn't understand." His eyes opened, damp and unseeing. His face tipped skyward. "The waetapu limit the number of Waes who are born to worlds that are not homes. They are here while they are here, and after, only their remembrances will travel home. It is a difficult destiny to never live amongst the nsangunsangu—the vast trees."

Estlin looked down at Serese to address her unspoken confusion. "The Waes evolved alongside intelligent trees. They are tuned to live and die within that relationship. Being born to be here, with us, is to be born never to climb those branches. The great forest does not travel."

"I'm sorry," Serese said.

The Waes heard her. Their spines contracted as their heads dropped in unison.

"I'm trying to get a number for you, but—" Estlin's eyes closed. "There are more waetapu here. There are *balancers* above us with the cuttlefish—waetapu who live to understand and maintain environments. They create.... They continuously balance the ocean tank."

Estlin shifted his grip on the tree, his eyes lowering and focusing on her. "I couldn't get a number. It might be a group of twelve. I'm not sure. It was expressed in terms of the number of hands needed to accomplish the job. But I don't know if one hand represents one waetapu or a pair or group of them. Or if one waetapu contributes one or two or four hands to the job."

Estlin wiped his eyes and looked at the waetapu, who were climbing higher. "I think we're done. But I'd like to sit here for a moment."

"Of course." Serese reached for the branch above her, stretching her arms and neck. "Thank you."

"Thank you," Estlin responded. "That's the most I've gotten out of them for days. It feels better...and worse. They'll die here." He released his grip on the tree, remaining well balanced on the branch. "Try not to choose a miserable topic next time."

The squirrels began to clamber across the branches and down the trunk of the tree.

"Harry's coming," Estlin explained. "No. He's here. We better get down."

When they reached the ground, Harry stood with Mike, who was pointing into the tree.

"You're kidding," Harry said, loudly, at Estlin.

Serese picked up her shoes and carried them, knowing her presence would control the volume of the argument.

"That wasn't a good idea," Harry said.

"I had Serese with me."

"It doesn't matter who is up there with you," Harry said. "Ever try to catch a fainting person? They turn into noodles. If you decide to fall, you'll smash your face against every branch on the way to the ground."

"I wasn't going to faint," Estlin insisted.

"They've tapped you out more than once," Harry responded. "Mike, please have Bernie add a climbing harness to the list of things we need."

"Two harnesses," Mike said.

"I don't need—"

"Don't argue," Harry snapped at Estlin. "You don't see how hard you wobble every time they end a conversation."

"We'll add harnesses to the list," Serese said. "Estlin, thank you. I look forward to seeing you tomorrow. I have work to do out there with the maddening crowd. If you need me, just ask. *Any time.* Harry, he hasn't had breakfast yet."

"Really?" Harry pointed Estlin in the direction of the kitchen.

Serese placed a hand on Mike's shoulder as she slipped on her shoes. "You were very relaxed about me climbing into a tree with aliens. Thank you. It was an invaluable experience."

"I have to be relaxed about everything in here," Mike said. "I assume the mind-reading aliens will notice if I'm imagining every possible worst-case scenario while you meet with them. It's kind of like trying not to think about an elephant, but I make every effort."

Chapter 5

Estlin stopped on the porch, turning to watch Serese walk along the driveway, a question on the edge of his thoughts. He'd invited her into his tree and spent a few minutes in the branches not braced against the next expected-unexpected hit.

"What happened to the porridge?" Harry asked.

"Squirrels."

"Of course," Harry said. "She's something, isn't she."

Estlin mumbled his agreement and let Harry press him on into the house.

"I spent four years here so focused on beaver incisors that I know nothing about Canadian politics," Harry said. "Are your politicians more honest than everyone else's?"

"The governor general is appointed not elected." Estlin picked up his ceramic bowl, inspecting it before placing it in the sink.

Harry shrugged off a large backpack, dropping it next to the fridge. "She has enough power to create this brief reprieve, but it will be brief. There are a lot of people itching to be in here. The wariness about being crushed or suffocated or eaten by aliens is wearing off. As you make progress, the outflow of confusing and threatening information is going to increase the pressure."

"I know." Estlin leaned against the counter edge, not knowing what to do next. He didn't want to think anymore.

"Want a grilled cheese?" Harry asked.

"I'm out of bread and cheese and butter."

"No, you aren't." Harry pulled open the fridge door and started unloading the backpack.

"That's a lot of cheese."

"Army sized," Harry agreed. "And check this out." He hefted a gallon jug of syrup out of his bag.

Estlin sat and watched Harry fuss with the baby-proof lock on the nearest cupboard, opening it to add bags of porridge, brown sugar, and dried fruit to the shelves.

"Is that squirrel-proof?" Harry gestured at the latched metal bread box, a relic from a previous age, reinforced with a pair of cinching straps.

"Almost." Estlin wondered if Harry's impulses were entirely his own or if the Waes had nudged him along. Regardless, Harry was either preparing him for a long winter or a lot of company.

"Stodt's worried." Harry turned on a burner and slid the frying pan across the stove.

"How can you tell?"

"He probably sits easier commanding than advising. We have the Americans next door, an overloaded Commonwealth airbase, a multi-national UN peacekeeping force, and a lot of random arrivals. He's concerned about how fast it could flash to chaos. And, apparently, you live within spitting distance of several intercontinental missile silos. Congratulations."

Butter sizzled.

"Bernie says the tape delay on the cameras is driving everyone nuts. How much do you hate the cameras?"

"There were cameras everywhere when I arrived in Wellington," Estlin said. "And you know how many people were glued to the live feed."

"Yeah, but it wasn't my kitchen," Harry flipped over the sandwich in the pan.

To Estlin, it was futile to worry about the little red recording lights. As long as no one made him watch any of the playback, he was fine. "The Waes are recording far more than any of the cameras, and their records may live in some interstellar library long after we're dust."

"Thanks for that," Harry said. "You really have the bright side on all this. And your vocabulary is expanding. Want to talk about the *leakage* or ako i te reo Māori?"

"It's happening. What else can I say?" Estlin responded. "If you hang around here, I may end up knowing you better than you want me to. When the Waes jack up my translating skills, they really jack them up."

"We have no secrets." Harry tossed the grilled cheese onto a plate. "If you do learn my secrets, you don't have to share them with me." He placed the plate in front of Estlin. "Eat. You'll feel better."

There was a piping call from outside and a shudder of attention rippled through the squirrels in the kitchen.

"Company's coming."

"Don't be creepy." Harry sat down with his own sandwich.

Estlin decided to double down on his creeping and gather a multitude of small furry perspectives. "Four people. One of them likes squirrels."

"Eat your sandwich."

"He was in here yesterday," Estlin said. "Wanted to pet them."

"Poor sod," Harry answered. "Does he know that squirrels carry bubonic plague?"

"You bastard." Estlin dropped his grilled cheese on the plate. "You said that on camera."

⟨⟩

Serese swiped through a set of photos on Bernie's laptop. Each of Estlin's rough, crooked drawings was followed by a copy with precise proportions and smooth symmetry— or balanced, inviting asymmetry—with single word titles and descriptive phrases in each margin. Serese lost herself in the image titled "Name". In the left margin, there was a question—*The seed of life?*—which she thought made an equally apt title. The drawing was dated and keywords from Estlin were transcribed, but there was no signature.

She turned the laptop towards Bernie, who sat, quiet and contrite, on the opposite side of the folding table. "Who drew this?"

"Bomani. He's a mathematician from the University of Auckland," Bernie answered. "Harry put him on the list this morning. I put the word around and found out that he's with the Americans in Pearl Harbour."

"Is he on his way?"

"I wanted your approval before extending the invitation, but I gave his name to the security-clearance people here, and General Stodt is sending over the background check completed in Wellington." Bernie slid a handwritten list across the table. The items were organized by requester, and followed by notes on sources and when they would arrive. Two items were starred, Dr. Bomani Manda, and a GISAXS spectrometer requested by Ulz.

"What's this?" Serese pointed at the name of the instrument, not wanting to mispronounce it.

"A grazing-incidence small-angle X-ray scattering spectrometer. It is a surface sensitive measurement device that can probe the molecular structure of the water cauldron, as well as the mixture of organic, inorganic and biological molecules in the ovoids released by the Waes. It should provide us with corroborating slivers of information relative to what we are learning directly from the Waes. And, if we break it, there could be a million-dollar bill for the tool."

"So, you didn't request it."

"No." Bernie shook his head, and then broke into an honest smile. "But I was really pleased when Ulz put it on the list after our discussion."

"How hard is it to acquire one?"

"We could pry one out of the nearest surface science lab in Edmonton. It'd fit in a small moving truck. You'd have to give the lead researcher and his top technician a ticket through the gate here to run it. You also have a world expert in exotic water structures at the Canadian Light Source. I mean, the types of structures you only see when you press a handful of molecules together in a diamond anvil."

"Proceed," Serese said. "Have the research financial officer approve the moving budget and insurance. Please print out Dr. Manda's drawings. I want to meet him as soon as he arrives."

"Bomani—Dr. Manda—in Samoa, he was brave." Bernie's head lowered as he stood. He pulled the laptop from the desk, tucking it under his arm as he backed towards the temporary partitions that defined Serese's office space. "I'm sorry, again, about this morning."

"We'll try again tomorrow at 6 a.m.," Serese said. "Bring your updated request list."

"Thank you," Bernie said.

"Thank you." Serese checked her watch. "Dr. Lichtwardt should be here. Send him in."

Ulz entered as soon as Bernie left, taking a seat at the table, opposite Serese. She waited to see which way he would take the conversation. He remained quiet but was holding himself ready to argue. She wondered if he generally expected his authority to be challenged or if he'd listened to her discussion with Bernie from the other side of the partition.

"You ignored my agenda this morning," Serese said.

"We left a few minutes early, but—"

Serese would not allow her concern to be dismissed. "You left without half the team."

"The tank descended on its own," Ulz said. "Bernie and I were lucky to be there in time to observe the start of the communication."

"When I arrived, it seemed like you were undermining the person the cuttlefish are here to talk to."

Ulz leaned forward. "Whatever the aliens are doing, we cannot rely solely on the *visions* of one recluse."

"I understand the problem," Serese said. "The aliens picked a human to talk to, instead of letting us pick for them. They decided to talk to the cuttlefish. And now the cuttlefish want to talk to the human that the aliens favor. How random and wrong-minded. You could fix this right now if given the opportunity. You know exactly how to have a conversation with a thousand cephalopods."

"Sarcasm isn't necessary," Ulz said.

"Do you want leeway because I didn't speak to you directly?" Serese asked. "Everything was on the whiteboard in the staging room. Did you read it?"

"Yes, of course."

Serese knew Ulz had seen the board. She knew he had failed to recognize that a single word could be the plan for the entire morning. Considering that he worked for the UN, this was disappointing. "What did it say under your name?"

Serese let silence grow until Ulz spoke through clenched teeth.

"*Listen,*" he said.

"I'm standing on the pinch point between everyone out here, and the one whose house is under that droplet of ocean," Serese said. "To help everyone, we have to help Estlin. If you have a different objective, if you don't want to work with me and bear some of the load, I'm sure the UN peacekeeping forces stationed in Camp Three will welcome you as an advisor."

"Understood."

This reluctant response was not sufficient. Serese opened her interview book, sliding the pen from its spine. "I'd like to know about your background, and what you want to accomplish here."

———— «» ————

Bomani watched as another airliner accelerated into the clear blue sky. The Hickam Air Force Base shared runways with Honolulu's international airport. Malone had *stepped out for a minute* several hours ago, abandoning them in the secure waiting area. Bomani appreciated the windows and natural light, but watching the steady stream of commercial airliners lift off in the distance made him feel trapped and anxious. He was also hopelessly behind in his understanding of Sanford's evolving equations.

"We're not going anywhere." Sanford realized Bomani's attention had wavered. "I don't know where these equations are going. If I do figure it out, I think I'll be bound to secrecy. I signed a contract in the middle of the night because I couldn't resist the opportunity. But there's no point of knowing this if I can't even tell my cat!"

"Imagine, if this is my last day to work with you on this puzzle," Bomani said. "And I waste it being distracted by possible futures. Sanford, in so much of this I am just catching up, but each day, each hour, I understand a bit more, even if what I understand is how much is missing, and how much is wrong." Bomani spread his fingers out over the page. "Everywhere I need to go is here."

Sanford nodded and carefully thumbed the left page of his notebook over, moving them into the fundamental equations. "There's a certain magic in this configuration. Creating a form where unlike charges attract but do not annihilate each other. You see how this begins. Now, allow some divergence to lower the exchange energy further."

"So, the columns of charge curl?" Bomani asked.

"Splay, not curl," Sanford answered. "There's a budding pattern, and then all hell breaks loose."

All hell was represented on the page by a polite, parabolic squiggle that reminded Bomani of the Hénon attractor. Bomani had not seen the magnitude or importance of that flutter of chaos before.

"And then it cleans itself up," Sanford said. "Vortex and antivortex pairs annihilate. Domain walls develop and do not go away, creating stable folded wave fields."

"You do everything you have to by geometry."

"Symmetry and asymmetry," Sanford corrected. "The multidimensional visualizations are difficult." He dipped his pencil towards the page, offering.

"No. I like this," Bomani said. "Look at the vector star harmonics."

"Yes," Sanford said.

"Fantastic."

"Fantastic?" Sgt. Malone asked from behind them. "It looks an awful lot like math to me."

Sanford put down his pencil. "We've been waiting a long time."

"Military flights operate on a hurry-up-and-wait basis," Malone said. "Livermore Labs decided they wanted you, but while we were driving over here some uppy-up decided you shouldn't go where the extra-big secrets are because you might still be covered in alien pixie dust."

"What?" Sanford closed his notebook.

"They don't trust our decontamination procedures," Malone said. "Don't worry about it. We've got a more important place to be."

———— «» ————

The number of hangers-on crowding the porch had increased, and Estlin could tell Harry was annoyed. The afternoon team had arrived with extra people, extra kit, and an excess of questions. *Where should we put the climbing harnesses? What's the state of your septic system? Can we inspect your diesel generator? Could you spit into this vial? Have you figured out how many aliens are here yet? Can you ask them again? Do the cuttlefish have enough to eat?*

Mercifully, the tank descended, carried by a series of thumb-like struts. The ice snapped like a knuckle popping each time a strut released the load. The tank was crowded, containing eight cuttlefish and the two swimming waetapu.

The reluctant cuttlefish was circling, looking smaller and angrier. Hypnotic cloud patterns pulsed down its flanks, and its mind felt more contracted and concentrated. Given Cloudy's ink-splotch reaction to attention, Estlin didn't want to ruin the visit before it started. Another cuttlefish surged forward, its skin alive with electric-silver spots and lines, and ragged, silver-tipped folds of skin like sparks above its eyes. The darker folds down its back mimicked seaweed fronds.

Estlin's guts twisted as the connection opened, a swirling red-blue-green ink filling his mind. The ink rippled into thin, dark arcs of watery calligraphy moving in surges, pressed by an unseen current. The arcs resolved into multiple copies of the arbelos, the icon that Sanford, the physicist, had used to represent the Waes' method of leaping across the stars.

The ink curls merged into a large, bladed arbelos that flared darkly. The cuttlefish presented a living symbol, a sea monster that wanted to spread, to choke and digest all life within reach.

Estlin flinched back on his heels, his hands grabbing at empty air. "Oh, shit."

"What?" Harry stepped closer.

"It's the conversation," Estlin said. "*The* conversation."

"Bugger. Calm down." Harry paused to take his own advice before he spoke again in softer tones. "You knew it was coming. Be calm and clear."

The swell of questions from others stirred a cloud of coloured silt off the bottom, but the bright sand could not penetrate the ink and settled quickly.

The malignant arbelos twisted and flowed, forming a dark harpoon that stabbed at the thin, clear barrier, the illusion of separation between Estlin and the water. It stabbed again, halting short of the glass, a question demanding an answer. Estlin hated the question. He hated knowing how to answer it. With the fingers of one hand, he tapped the ice-glass, shattering it as he reached through with his other hand, grabbed the harpoon and pulled it into his chest. The hooks sank in and grabbed. The oily coating found his blood stream and it was swept inwards.

The cuttlefish surrounded him, examining the wound, their W-shaped eyes opening like mouths. They tried to understand how to sever and remove the dangerous idea penetrating the human race.

"You see it. You know it," Estlin said. "The harpoon is in my chest, not my finger, not my arm. I cannot cut it out and survive."

He showed the moon illuminated by the Rosetta Burst, and all the eyes that saw and began to imagine. The electromagnetic burst transformed into a net of ideas that caught the world.

The cuttlefish understood that the dangerous idea had entered the body and could not be removed through the simple sacrifice of an arm. A deeper cut would be required to eliminate the bad idea. It was easy to prevent ideas from spreading through intergenerational memory, because ideas were as easy to kill as individuals. The key was killing them before they reproduced.

A shark approached. Estlin, still pinioned on the dark spike, saw its shadow but could not twist to see its teeth. As the shark circled, new eyes opened within clutches of eggs. The elder cuttlefish bleached white, and the young arrived, their small bright skins bursting with the colours of the past. Each little mind was born knowing its environment, its predators, its prey. The living dark spike in Estlin's chest grew hungry. It unfurled. Membranous tissue connected each inky strand, reaching and ready to envelop an entire new generation.

A great wave pushed back the threat. The harpoon edges ground against bone, lifting Estlin, as the threat was pushed away towards a rocky shore. The question remained: If a culling was required, how many individuals would have to die (childless) to eliminate the (threat) idea?

"We don't work that way," Estlin gasped. "Our children don't carry our memories, only what we teach them." Pressed against the rocks, he tried to explain. He showed parents, each with their own suits of colour, and infants arriving as translucent outlines. The children grew, filling with green flecks and sandy golds; more colours being added with time. The colours were transferred from parent to child, and from population to child, and from child to parent. The unrelenting flow of colours between individuals began with the first breath and never ended.

The harpoon was abruptly withdrawn. Estlin slapped his hand to his chest, where there was no wound to cover. He took a deep breath, heard the cracking of ice knuckles, and knew the tank was being lifted away.

"Sit. Sit, now." Harry said.

Estlin obeyed the hand on his shoulder pressing him down.

"You lost a lot of colour when that started," Harry said. "I thought you were going to drop."

Estlin pressed his palms into the ground, looking past Harry to see the tank rising into the light above. He glanced around to find everyone on the porch looking at him with expressions of shocked confusion.

"Absolute silence." Harry pointed at the closest person. "*You*. Strong tea from the pot, lots of sugar. Now." He wrapped a hand around Estlin's wrist, his fingers on the pulse point. "Lyndie, tell us all of it. Every image. Just talk. Don't edit. Don't skip. Don't think. Tell us now before the shakes start."

"Shakes?"

"That looked almost like an electrical jolt," Harry said. "I think it got your adrenalin going, which is fine, but now that you don't need it, your muscles are going to start shaking it off."

Harry was right. Estlin could feel the vibrations starting in his thighs and forearms.

"Talk now," Harry said. "What was the first image?"

Estlin started to talk. Harry squeezed his wrist every time he hesitated or started to think, so he kept describing image after image until he ran out of words because the cuttles had left him in the mud on the bottom.

"What did I do?" Estlin asked.

"You showed them exactly how helpless we are in the face of an exciting idea," Harry answered. "It's okay. Sit up. Your tea is coming."

"Okay? None of that was okay."

The complaint came from behind Harry. Estlin did not recognize the voice.

"The cuttlefish think people with dangerous ideas should be killed? That was insane. Did he just impale himself on a VR harpoon?"

Harry pressed a warm mug into Estlin's hand. "It's okay. Drink this."

"These dialogs should be planned," the complainer continued. "Why would he tell them that we're helpless!"

"You think deceit is possible here?" Harry rolled back on his heels to deal with the speaker. "Fuck off. I mean it. Go away. Come back when you think I won't notice you."

Estlin tried the tea. It was too strong and too sweet.

"Drink it," Harry said. "This is going to create a bit of a stir."

Chapter 6

Harry stood in the kitchen, unsettled. He was ticking to do whatever needed to be done next, but it felt too soon to do anything. He'd manhandled Estlin to the living room couch and backed away to the kitchen, where Estlin's notebook and pen were waiting on the table. One of the scientists entered from the porch. He was tall, bearded, and inhabited a Canadian stereotype, wearing a plaid lumberjack shirt over a T-shirt bearing the skating-beaver logo for a local hockey league. Harry had forgotten his name.

"We should send out the recordings," Harry said.

"They've already gone. Emmet took them."

"Who?"

"The one you told to fuck off. "

"Oh, good," Harry said.

"I'm sorry about that. I should have reacted sooner."

Harry checked the man's name badge: Stanley Troughton, Microbiologist, University of Toronto / Davis Station, Antarctica. Harry decided to pay closer attention to the people around him and their skill sets. This Canadian had jaunted onto a southern ice shelf with the Australians, which meant he was both extremely competent and a certain kind of crazy.

"I've sent half the group out to debrief," Troughton continued, "including two on our long-shift team. When they return, Dr. Chandran and I will go out for a couple of hours."

The stairs creaked as the doctor descended. She was carrying a green knitted blanket that looked as old as the house.

"I don't need a blanket," Estlin complained from the couch.

"Take it," Harry said. "It'll keep this lot from bothering you."

"If I shiver under a blanket, they'll send a doctor in to pester me," Estlin responded.

"There is a doctor here," Dr. Chandran said. "You aren't being pestered."

"Sorry." Estlin accepted the blanket and extended his other hand. "Estlin."

"Adya Chandran." She shook his hand and released it without commenting on the remaining faint tremor. She picked up a kitchen chair and planted it next to the couch. Harry grabbed a chair and followed her.

"We've reorganized into teams of four," Adya said. "Each team includes a medical doctor, a scientist, and engineers with extensive field experience and other specific skills, including a high level of first aid training. Our job is to support you and support the other visitors who come in for short periods of time to achieve specific objectives. We'll work in long shifts—here and out at the staging tent—and document events as much as possible. Stanley's leading the day shift. He prefers to go by his last name. Theo Chau will lead the night shift. We'll do our best not to overcrowd you, but the shifts will overlap because we want lots of information transfer during the transitions."

"Sounds good," Harry said.

Adya waited for Estlin's nod of agreement. She nodded to Troughton, who snagged Estlin's notebook from the kitchen table and joined them. Harry noted his friend's pallor had diminished.

"You know what we want." Troughton held out the book. "You gave us the visual details earlier, but we really need everything you can recall. What you saw and felt. What it meant to you. What you think it meant to the cuttlefish. What went well. What was unexpected. What was difficult."

"The gory details," Estlin said.

"Was there gore?" Troughton asked.

"No," Estlin said. "No red. Lots of inky black. One bone-grinding sensation—that was creepy—I don't know how a visualization had that *vibration*. I didn't actually see a shark, but I felt the shark. Maybe I saw it the way the cuttlefish see it when a shark shadow crosses the skin on their backs. It was frightening because they are frightened. That's why they are here."

Estlin picked up his notebook and blanket, and went to the kitchen table.

Troughton looked to Harry. "Stay with him."

Harry considered making coffee, but he wasn't in the mood for it. He hovered in the kitchen as Estlin immersed himself in creating jagged, ragged drawings. Returning to the couch, he sat and counted squirrels. Squirrels perched on empty shelves and windowsills. A fluffy grey squirrel was crouched atop the robust antique clock mounted on the wall. The clock face didn't make any sense to him. It could be the squirrel had interfered with the clock's timekeeping, but Harry had also changed time zones. He closed his eyes, and, when he opened them a moment later, the clock hands had wiped away an hour.

Troughton entered from the porch. "The rest of the team is back." He handed an envelope to Estlin. "This is from the governor general."

Harry watched as Estlin unfolded the letter from the envelope. "What is it?"

"Questions," Estlin said. "How am I? Do I need anything?"

"Serese would like you to write or record a reply," Troughton said.

Estlin was still reading. "Canada's trade negotiations with China have resumed, and Serese is asking—" Estlin folded the page in half. "I'm going upstairs."

Estlin ascended the stairs, followed by squirrels. Troughton looked at Harry in silent question.

"I think he's gone to talk to a ghost," Harry said.

Troughton's silent question got louder.

"Yidge Lee. She worked with me in Wellington, and she died aboard the Chinese freighter used to smuggle the Waes and Estlin out of New Zealand," Harry explained. "Her remains are here in a little alien hard drive. The Waes made some kind of recording. I think Estlin's going to discuss this with her."

"Do you think he should do that on his own?" Troughton asked.

Harry shrugged and took the stairs. He brushed by the camera on the landing, knocking its lens towards the wallpaper, and stopped outside the half-closed bedroom door. Estlin was in the midst of a conversation, and he wasn't talking to the squirrels.

"Harry doesn't want to talk to you," Estlin said. "No. I know because I asked him."

The reply from the preserved fragment of Yidge was inaudible.

"He doesn't want to talk to you because you aren't you anymore," Estlin replied. "Your corpse is in Christchurch."

Harry found himself straining to hear Yidge.

"Can you read, or do I have to read this for you?" Estlin asked. "I don't know why she's asking how I feel about the Chinese. You were killed by an American. Does she know that? I don't know that she knows. Now I know how to start my reply What about the rest of it? Do you have an opinion?"

The lengthy silence suggested that Yidge had a significant number of opinions.

"Are you sure? Because I.... No. I asked your opinion. I won't ignore it."

Harry knocked on the door, pushing it open. Yidge looked at him, and then flickered out of existence.

"I didn't mean to end your conversation," Harry said.

"I told her that you don't want to talk to her," Estlin said. "I think she's a bit sensitive about it. If a recording can be sensitive."

Estlin walked around Harry to pick up the tripod and camera on the hall landing. He considered its shining red light and dropped it back in place. "Give me a minute. I'll write a note for Serese."

"Right," Harry said. "Do you have any spare bedding for tonight?"

"Hallway closet," Estlin answered.

Harry checked the meagre offerings in the hall closet and decided to request an air mattress and sleeping bag. Descending the stairs, he found Troughton standing by

Dr. Chandran, who was sitting at the kitchen table studying a printed stack of pages.

"Assessments like this are always signed." Dr. Chandran flipped from the last page to the cover and back through the report again. "Author, specialty, accreditation, affiliation. Is this the opinion of a neuropsychiatrist or some other specialist? They clearly had access to Estlin, but when? The missing information makes the whole report garbage."

"Go," Troughton said. "Find out how widely this is circulating. Take the meeting with the Americans and make notes for your counterpart on the night shift."

"I'm going for a walk," Harry said. "I can take Estlin's response to Serese. She wanted to meet about my job description here. I've also got an idea for an emergency signaling system that I want to run past Bernie. And I'm going to scrounge some bedding for tonight."

"Sounds good," Troughton said. "Dr. Chandran will go with you."

———— ⟨⟩ ————

It began with fine patterns created by internal discourse fluttering on the skin confined between the eyes of the reluctant cuttlefish. It expanded across its body, and then spread from body to body. Trios and quintets swam in parallel, harmonizing their patterns to evoke individual, ingrained remembrances from generations gone. Cuttlefish rose from sandy ledges and emerged from tangles of seaweed to join the discourse.

The argument focused on the many shapes of threats and the equally many responses to threats. The blunt-toothed biter could be avoided by being the rock, being the seaweed, or being the sand, and being still. But vanishing shapes and colours were useless against the sharp-toothed biter that did not use its eyes. Becoming the water snake was only useful against eyes and minds that knew and feared the poison. It was important to know when to shelter, when to hide, and when to ink and run.

The polyps of the new threat needed to be identified to know which threat response refined through generations of practice would be effective. But the shape of the threat refused classification.

A frenzy of pulsing colour spread through the water as trios disbanded and septets formed. *The threat* was closest and farthest from the threat of sky-fall water-boil. Times of sky-fall water-boil were few but sharply remembered. Each evoked remembrance was looped, examined, and compared, but each cuttlefish knew that comparing different shock-to-water threats was as wrong as comparing different teeth-to-flesh threats. There were many kinds of bites. Avoiding teeth required a precise recognition and reaction to the shadow of the biter before the teeth were bared.

Sky-fall water-boil threats could not be anticipated or avoided, they could only be endured and survived. A water-boil threat that could be anticipated but not endured or survived...

It was a new and incomparable thing.

The collective settled into the reflective silence of blank skin.

------ «‹›» ------

The staging tent was crowded and lined with white boards. Harry asked for the governor general and found Serese was occupied. He left Estlin's letter and added a note listing responsibilities for himself under the job title of *sweeper*. He found a coffee and searched for Bernie. The scientist was nested at a desk with four open laptops, and Ulz paced behind him.

"I've got a fix for our communication problem."

Bernie started, raising his hands. "Harry! I didn't think you'd be here. I mean, because you can be in there all the time. How's Estlin?"

"He's fine," Harry answered. "I don't have a communication idea as much as an idea for emergency signaling."

"Everyone wants to crank the signal intensities on hardware they've already taken to the limit," Bernie said. "But I don't think the Waes are deliberately isolating the house. I think they're protecting the cuttlefish tank. So, blasting a signal through is risky. I still have no idea how they are holding up that tub of ocean. The engineers have calculated the force required—their number is twice my estimate, but we agree on the number of zeros. We're bringing in more tools. But I'm afraid that even once we can see what's happening with the water molecules, we still won't understand any of it. It's like pointing a bunch of microscopes at something you need binoculars to see." Bernie fingers settled on the desk as he stopped for a breath.

"I think we can rig an emergency signal for the house," Harry said.

"Really?" Bernie pushed back his chair.

"If the structure collects and transmits sunlight, it should work both ways."

"They tried sending all kinds of optical beams through the ocean tank."

"Not through the side. Up." Harry replied. "One big bank of lights pointing straight up."

"Oh," Bernie said. "But without overflights, we'd need satellite—" He stopped. "We have satellites." Bernie was on his feet and ready to jump off.

"Stop," Harry said. "I walked out with Dr. Chandran. There is a medical report about Estlin. She's at a meeting about it. I need to know where."

The locations of the core team members were tracked on one of the whiteboards. This was convenient.

Harry found the meeting room in an adjacent tent and admitted himself, dragging a chair from the wall to the table. He noted the title on the report in front of Dr. Chandran, and reached for it, waiting for her nod of agreement before pulling it over. Harry focused on the report, and not the summary being bluntly presented by a military doctor at the far end of the table. He scanned through the pages of psychological assessment, guessed at its author, and dropped the report on the table.

"Is this Dr. Liev's work?" Harry asked, interrupting the speaker.

"This is a closed meeting," the doctor responded. "Were you invited?"

"I'm Dr. Hatarei," Harry answered. "Liev forced a dose of an experimental drug on Estlin. She combined the drug with a sedative to knock down his connection with the aliens.

Dr. Chandran, I've only skimmed this report. Where is that discussed?"

"It's not," Dr. Chandran said. "Was it redacted from this report?"

"The report is as we received it," the doctor responded. "I don't have any information about treatment, experimental or otherwise."

"The behaviour described immediately followed the experimental drug exposure," Harry responded. "Estlin had an allergic reaction to it. He was covered in hives when I found him on Samoa."

"That's a significant omission," Dr. Chandran said.

The doctor took his seat and made eye contact with each of his colleagues. "I agree."

"This draft was obviously rushed," Dr. Chandran said. "When it is completed to the level where the authors are willing to put their names on it, we can meet to review it. Please supply records from Mr. Hume's time aboard the aircraft carrier. The wound on his hand was treated there."

"I can acquire those records for you," the doctor responded. "You understand that we still have strong cause for concern."

"You understand that you circulated an incomplete, inaccurate, anonymous report and that's the concern I'll have to deal with." Dr. Chandran slid her copy of the report to the centre of the table. "Retract it. Correct it."

She rose and gestured for Harry to follow as she swiftly exited the tent.

"We should get back to the house," she said.

"I want to grab a few things first."

"I should tell our international liaison that I walked out on that meeting," Chandran responded. "The medical team will have to release a written review of that report. Meet in ten minutes?"

"Works for me."

"Good." Dr. Chandran said. "I need a detailed patient history. It takes time and trust to collect one. Is Estlin likely to cooperate?"

"I'll encourage him," Harry said. "If you want to speak to the doctor we had on site in Wellington, it can be arranged.

Estlin agreed to let us gather his medical history. I'll make sure Bernie gets the files we have and a copy of the consent form to you. The report they are pushing is bog roll. But…" Harry considered how to phrase his concern. "We're built with our brains safely sealed in bone. Everything the Waes do bypasses that protection. They are banging open doors in Estlin's mind."

"Let's talk on the walk in," Dr. Chandran said.

"Thanks." Harry checked the time and went to steal Bernie's sleeping bag.

《 》

Bomani sipped short, painful breaths, his palm pressed hard against his chest, trying to shove his heart down to a sensible beat. The problem was that he hated helicopters more than he hated airplanes. The flight from Hawaii had been tolerable, but when they jolted onto a runway at the crowded Fairchild Air Base, Sgt. Malone pushed them down the tail ramp of the C-17 and up the tail ramp of a Chinook. The duplicate rotors didn't give Bomani any confidence, having engines forward and back meant there was more weight to fall out of the sky. He was strapped to a seat without a window, but acutely aware that they were thumping over ragged terrain in the dark.

Sanford was holding out pages, trying to distract him with simplified equations that captured the essence of a topologically-protected, low dissipation energy loop—a perfect set of twists so tightly integrated with a space-bridging fold that it became the fold. The Chinook was too loud for conversation, and Bomani's fingers were locked. Even if he forced himself to lift a pencil, the vibrations would ruin any effort. He counted the seats that lined the cabin walls and arrived at a number that didn't make any sense. He couldn't fathom why anyone would build a helicopter this size.

The rotor blades thwacked air like fingertips slapping the edge of a djembe. Bomani thought of Chladni patterns, the nodes of stillness on the taught skin of a sounding drum. Drumheads were the cousins of spherical resonators, and the sun was a booming sphere. Helioseismologists could *see* the heart of the sun—the structure of its deepest layers—

through acoustic oscillations revealed by surface waves. Discoseismologists squeezed new perspectives on black holes from the vibrational frequencies of their accretion discs. Cosmologists peered back in time, using acoustic power spectra to see the structure of the early universe. The key was understanding how objects resonated. Did the transit node in Sanford's energy loop pin the fold to local space or to a distant point? Were its edges under tension or free?

Bomani heard the helicopter bank before he felt it. He thought about the spectral harmonics of the Rosetta Burst, the chord that rang out of the space fold as an object transitioned through it. *Such music.* He saw the transfer as a manipulation of an otherwise stable vortex core, the tip of a blade slicing through, an annihilation so beautifully and closely avoided that each occurrence left the universe breathless.

Chapter 7

It was quiet when Harry woke in the dark corner of the living room. The kitchen light was shining but there was no murmur of conversation, just the fridge hum and the muffled complaint of the air mattress as he shed his sleeping bag. Either the night shift was being considerate, or something was wrong.

It was 4 a.m. The front door was open.

Four members of the night shift were in the yard, each in their own pool of lantern light, pointing their cameras at the tree. Estlin stood under one of the low branches with his arms raised to gently press several leaves between his hands. Harry had seen that tilted listening-touch when Estlin introduced himself to other species. He walked to within a step of Estlin, who didn't react to his approach. He looked over his shoulder and found Theo Chau was closest.

"How long?" He took the shrugged response as indicating it was time to interupt. "Lyndie, if you start hugging every tree, the loggers are going to lynch you."

Estlin released the leaves, moving at half-speed. He raised one hand to shield his eyes from the lantern light. "How did I get here?"

"You don't know?"

Pressing his fingers into his dark hair, Estlin shook his head.

"Sleepwalk?" Harry asked.

"No." Estlin found the Waes hidden in the branches above, pretending to be a pair of innocent porcupines. "What time is it?"

"Early."

"Manipulative bastards."

"What are they doing?" Harry asked.

"Acting innocent," Estlin said.

A squirrel leapt onto the nearest branch and sat back on its haunches to kuk and chatter at them.

"Fine." Estlin strode off around the side of the house, moving confidently through the dark. Harry followed and found him opening the tap on an elevated rain barrel. The attached hose shot water into an old rowboat. The battered boat was sunk into the earth, its oars long gone, tufts of dry grass rising at its bow.

"Squirrels drink a lot," Estlin said. "If they're thirsty, I'm thirsty. Not really. Just enough to be annoying. I've got another one over by the well head, but it's...." He pointed off into the wall of ice. "Not very accessible."

"What now?" Harry asked. "Want to spend more time with the tree? Being awake might help."

"I doubt it," Estlin said. "I'm the wrong speed."

Harry looked up, seeking stars and finding none.

"I miss the moon," Estlin said.

Harry wondered if his gaze or thought had been read. "If we had a view, we'd be distracted by the number of satellites staring at us."

Estlin's eyes tracked through the branches to the house. Harry followed his gaze and caught the shadows vanishing over the roof line.

"Fuck it," Estlin said. "They've gone back to my bedroom. Let's make coffee."

Theo Chau was waiting for them on the porch.

"Your friend is in the kitchen," he said to Harry, and left it at that.

Harry stepped ahead of Estlin through the entryway. He found the other three on the night shift occupying the kitchen table. Bomani was leaning against the counter behind them. He had a travel bag at his feet.

"Bomani!" Estlin extended his hand. "I didn't know you were coming."

"It's good to see you." Bomani clamped his hands around Estlin's, his smile genuine and bright.

"Want coffee or breakfast?" Estlin asked.

"Coffee. Thank you," Bomani said.

"Got it." Harry went to the stove, where the percolator was waiting. He put his hands to work in the crowded kitchen, aware that the others were listening. It seemed more intrusive than the cameras.

"When you left Samoa, I trusted you were safe, but the uncertainty was difficult," Bomani said.

"I ended up here," Estlin said. "I don't know how."

"I'm glad. I tried not to worry, but—" Bomani shrugged, as though shifting a burden off his shoulders. "Do you have more equations?"

"No," Estlin said.

"Ah," Bomani said. "But you have something complex and impressive for me to draw, yes? When I got here, I met an astonishing woman who talked about my drawings. I was sweating from the helicopter. I could barely reply."

"Serese Saie."

"Yes," Bomani said.

"I saw her dance years ago," Estlin said.

"She dances." Bomani nodded to himself. "Of course."

"I saw her final performances from the rafters of a theatre. It was an easy job—a gift from a friend. A cloud of bats had disturbed a rehearsal. So, each night I encouraged the bats to roost in the warmth of close company, which is not work at all. And when applause filled the space below, they naturally boiled up and out into the night, not down into the noise and light."

"You are a magician," Bomani said.

"No," Estlin said. "Canadian bats are much smaller than the ones in Samoa."

"I saw little of Samoa and less of Hawaii," Bomani said. "And then Sgt. Malone brought us here. Sanford is with him. I was surprised to be selected."

"Lyndie needs some help," Harry said. "Your kind of help."

"I've been talking to the cuttlefish," Estlin said.

"Cuttlefish talk?"

"It's very visual."

"Yesterday, I was a mathematician," Bomani said. "Today, I am an artist."

"Why don't you take this conversation to the cheap seats," Harry suggested, pointing to the battered couch and chair in the living room. He handed Estlin's notebook to Bomani. "There's a lot in here I don't understand. I think you can help us."

Harry found mismatched mugs waiting on the shelf of a squirrel-proofed cupboard. The percolator was now happily bumping and the smell of the coffee was remarkable. One of the trio sitting at the table shifted his chair back as though intending to rise.

"Going outside?" Harry asked.

They didn't answer, but remained seated, which was good enough for Harry. He turned off the burner and filled two mugs. Carrying the coffee to the threshold of the living room, he paused on the edge of the adjacent space, trying not to interrupt the conversation.

"The idea can't be cut from us," Bomani said.

"I did explain."

"It would be pointless to take my life or Sanford's." Bomani shook his head. "Sanford is brilliant, but without him, we will still stumble down the path because we all saw that beautiful light. The irresistible pattern. Everyone knows. And a subset of everyone will spend their lives trying to understand what we've seen."

"I know," said Estlin.

"How will you save us?"

Estlin blinked at the responsibility that Bomani so confidently and casually placed, as everyone present turned to watch him think.

"The cuttlefish aren't wasteful. They don't want a false solution."

Harry wanted to change the topic.

"That could be worse," Bomani said. "True, final solutions tend to be far more brutal than half-efforts built on self-serving conceit." He sank into the couch and pointed to the smallest visitor perched on the curtain rod above the window. "Is the little striped one a baby squirrel?"

"Chipmunk," Estlin answered.

Harry pushed into the room and handed off the coffee.

Bomani took a sip and placed the mug on the hardwood floor, needing both hands to flip through the pages of Estlin's notebook. "These are less geometrical than the last ones."

Harry considered the armchair.

"What's wrong?" Estlin asked.

"The Americans are passing around a malignant report," Harry said.

"Do I want to know?"

"I assume it's Dr. Liev's work, but someone else could have used her records." Harry didn't know if the report reflected some internal crap on the American side or if its angle was meant to game the Canadians. "No one likes that this whole iceberg is balanced on your head."

"No argument here," Estlin said.

Bomani turned a page in Estlin's direction. "This is disturbing."

"Yes, it was," Estlin replied.

Bomani continued studying the pages.

Harry thought about how to summarize the report. "They are questioning your stability and loyalty to the human race."

"Loyalty?" Bomani asked.

"They think he's too aligned with the cuttlefish and squirrels," Harry said. "Which is, of course, crazy and threatening."

"But it's the gift," Bomani said, turning again to Estlin. "Having the ability to align with what is other and alien—it's how you understand."

"Which is crazy and threatening," Estlin echoed Harry with a shrug.

"This one." Bomani pointed at a swirling image spread across two pages. "We should start with this one. They gave me a box of pencils. I'll set up."

Bomani picked up his mug and used the notebook to wave the others away from the kitchen table. "I need this space."

"The report," Estlin said. "Do I care?"

"No," Harry said. "You're home. Dr. Chandran is handling it."

Harry waited until Estlin joined Bomani in the kitchen, and then dropped into the armchair. He glanced at the time, and let his head fall back.

—— «» ——

Sgt. Malone left the latrine, seeking his team. While he approved of the Canadians' multi-camp structure, there were flaws in implementation. For example, he was in the wrong camp. He'd traded Bomani for a tent for the 3rd Reconnaissance Battalion and a square of grass to park the Chinook. He had no gripe because it was an acceptable ticket price for access to the alien house party. Letting go of the mathematician from Malawi also had foreseeable benefits. It could easily lead to Sanford being pulled into the inner camp, and Sanford was an American asset on contract with the Department of Defense. If he moved, his marine protection team would move with him. In the meantime, it was in everyone's interests to keep the physicist working, which only required quiet space, a pencil, and the occasional meal.

He joined Sgt. Pollock and Dewey as they examined an updated site map. Sanford was in the corner of the tent absorbing more signal data from the second Rosetta Burst.

"We're here," Pollock said. "The Rangers are integrated in the perimeter security force. The UN Peacekeepers are here. They're from Bangladesh and Rwanda."

"That's not surprising," Malone said. "The Canadians have trained the Bangladeshi."

"There are Canadian snipers on the ground and in cherry pickers, here, here, and here." Pollock added the details to their simple site map. "There are more in blinds in the trees on the park side."

"We did the same in Samoa," Malone noted, glancing at Dewey.

"They let a surprising number of rounds fly the first few days," Dewey said. "They were picking off small drones before they widened the perimeter and installed other countermeasures."

"What's our presence inside the fence?" Malone asked.

"There's a mix of plain clothes and civilian under a politician's thumb," Pollock answered.

"Does the thumb have a name?" Malone asked.

"Bob Dunne."

"Shit," Malone said. "Really?"

"Politicians." It was a cuss word for Pollock. "When a heavy job comes in, we figure out how to lift it, and they think on how high it could lift them. And Bobby Dunne? No one will miss him if he catches an alien STD.'"

Malone focused on the site map. "Now that we know that the aliens live in a cloud of mind-control cooties, the important people are all staying well back. The League of Nations is forming in Calgary. The bunkers at Malmstrom are full. There's also a complete split between local response and global response."

"There are decontamination stations here, here and here." Pollock tapped the map. "To cover the outflow of people and material. There are additional stations between the camps, but I'm not confident in their ability to prevent carryover of ovoids or the expansion of the alien influence."

"The breeze can carry the ovoids," Malone responded. "If you think the tanks parked on the border are secure, think again. Are they ten miles away? Which way is the wind blowing?"

"East, north-east," Dewey answered from across the table. "But there are local vortices created by the alien structure."

Malone trusted the sniper to know the fine details of wind forecasts.

"The perimeters are practical," he continued. "There are antagonists that we must keep out of this area. But it's like building a wall around a blimp. The fish tank rolled through the mountains to get here. The critters could decide, at any time, to send it along to hover over your mom's house. Any effective security strategy must be mobile and dynamic."

Dewey crossed his arms. "I would feel more dynamic if my M40 wasn't locked up off the edge of this map."

"You need to be a trusted friend to whoever has the keys to the closest locker," Malone said.

"I am very friendly." Dewey accepted the assignment with a flat-mouthed smile.

Malone had a gift for creative solutions to challenging scenarios, but the blimp problem was a brain twister and for the moment all he could do was tread water.

"This situation is unstable," he said. "Disruption is opportunity. If things go kinetic, get on the side of the angels. Be helpful, gather intel, take a soft step inward, don't get greedy."

———— «» ————

Estlin watched as Bomani added a layer of detail with fluid strokes of his pencil. The image depicted newborn cuttlefish carried by an ocean current across the page before him.

"How's Beth?" Estlin asked.

"My friend, I wish I knew," Bomani answered. "I tried to follow when she was sent away from the airfield in Samoa, but it was not possible."

"She's not here?"

"I don't know," Bomani said. "Dr. Liev's actions had consequences. I think she will be kept away, and that will keep Beth away."

"I hope so." Estlin disliked having drugs forced on him, but that assault paled in comparison to Dr. Liev's guardianship of Beth. Exposing a child to the Waes was beyond bad judgement, it was egomania. The medications Dr. Liev's used to dampened Beth's intense abilities had to be experimental. He didn't want Beth to be trapped in a struggle against chaotic, intrusive thoughts and sensations, but being under Dr. Liev's absolute control was another kind of trap.

"The Americans had the Waes and now they do not," Bomani said. "This is your house. Do not invite her."

"I won't." Thinking of Beth, brought back flashes of Estlin's childhood. He knew now that *bad spells*, fragmented memories of burns and shattered bones, were from hospital visits, when he was an open nerve and taken to places full of pain for diagnosis and treatment.

Bomani put down his pencil. "There is more to this picture, but we should work on the pointy one." He turned to the page with the misshapen barbed harpoon Estlin had sketched. "Tell me about this. Was it as cruel as it looks?"

To Estlin's eyes, the sketch was static and inadequate. The blade had flowed, its edges alive and every surfacepulsing with dark colours. He knew the weight and intent of it was lost on the page.

"It was complicated." Estlin turned the page to show the harpoon the moment after it struck, its tip surging into cross-connected channels of liquid. His drawing was more like the network of veins in a leaf than branching coronary arteries. "It was a question and an answer. That part was here." He tapped his chest. "But I could still see it."

"It's what makes the drawings challenging," Bomani said. "When you see with your mind, the insights do not stop at the first opaque surface. We do this as before, a layer at a time."

Bomani added the date to the top corner of a fresh page, and the number of the page in Estlin's notebook that they were working from. "What would you say it's made of?"

"Ink and obsidian," Estlin answered.

"Sharp, glassy fluid," Bomani said. "Is this shape right? Are you happy with it?"

"No."

"Curves are very interesting." Bomani slid a scrap of paper over the main page. "They can be regular or irregular. Soothing or disturbing. Parabolic or hyperbolic. It could be that we should start with a triangle, get the proportions of the points correct and then add the curvature."

"It started out like the shape Sanford sketched."

"The arbelos," Bomani said. "And then?"

"It duplicated and twisted."

"One set of curves," Bomani said, but he sketched an abundance of curves. "Simple here. Now stretched. Stretched more. Bent. Twisted here."

"That one." Estlin pointed.

Bomani began working with the curves, overlaying them.

"This is better," he said. "Having the Waes where there is a tree to climb instead of concrete and steel."

"I inherited the house a couple of years ago," Estlin said. "It's more than I've ever had."

"To the Waes, living in a house isn't more impressive than living in a tree." Bomani's pencil swept across the page. "Is a city more impressive than a termite mound? The termites where I grew up built clay skyscrapers—ventilation towers for underground cities."

Bomani pointed at the sketch. "I'm drawing this as you did with all the barbs aligned with the plane of the page, but at contact it is more three dimensional, yes? Here, where it is spreading through the body."

"Yes," Estlin said.

Bomani kept his eyes on the page, the pencil moving steadily. "It is difficult to leave the place where you were born. There is preparation. There is a price. An individual can't buy a ticket for the flight unless the collective has imagined and invested in the creation of airplanes and runways. Even when you are a few short steps from a seat that can carry you to a distant city, it's all hard. The stars are different, the air is colder, there are different languages and different ways of living. It's a privilege and a sacrifice."

"It's a one-way trip," Estlin said. "For Wae and Waewae, at least."

"Is it an aspect of the bridge?" Bomani asked. "Or is it a choice that they do not return?"

"I can ask them," Estlin said. "I think it is partly biology. They are born for this task and shaped for it."

Troughton stepped up to the table and surveyed the drawing in progress. "Sorry to interrupt. The Chinese ambassador you requested is on his way. Serese will bring him later today. Bernie brought a loaded electric forklift. He's setting up gear in your yard. If you want to discuss it with him, now's the time. Also, your porch has a sag, and we keep piling people on it. Mind if I stick my head under there and have a look?"

Estlin knew the structure under the porch was solid, but Troughton would want to see it for himself. "Go ahead. You can pull the lattice panel next to the stairs."

"Am I going to meet anything in the dark?"

"There's a rat snake," Estlin said. "But it's friendly."

"Friendly?"

"Well fed."

"It eats your squirrels?" Troughton said. "Isn't that disturbing?"

"Circle of life," Estlin answered. "And they aren't my squirrels. They just converge wherever I am because I'm *shiny*."

"Any other critters around?" Troughton asked. "I mean, the kind with sharp teeth."

"There's a fox den out past the well," Estlin said. "She's quite shy. I haven't heard from her this week. She may have been frightened off."

"Well fed," Troughton said. "How big is this snake?"

"It's hard to miss."

"I need a better flashlight." Troughton left the kitchen, heading out through the entry way.

"I should find out what Bernie is up to," Estlin said.

"Go on," Bomani said. "I have work here."

When he got to the porch, Estlin found a big bank of lights laid on the grass next to the house. He ignored the sidelong glances from the two technicians who were deploying the array of lights, and went to Bernie, who was crouched next to a control box. He waited until Bernie tipped back on his heels and spotted him.

"Oh. Hi," Bernie said.

"What is this?"

"Energy efficient LED flood lights." Bernie threw a grandiose gesture at his new toys. "Brand new. Paik requisitioned them from a football stadium in Calgary."

"Why?"

"Harry's idea," Bernie replied. "It's kind of like a bat signal. We think the structures that transmit light down from the sun can also carry light upward. It should be really interesting. Whether or not it works as an emergency signal, the distribution of transmitted light should tell us about the structure."

"It's got a big red button."

"I know!" Bernie said. "The forklift has gone to bring in the battery. It's simple to plug together, but we won't test it until noon. We need to see if the flash is visible when there is full daylight. We also need time to warn everybody about the test. There are a lot of satellites overhead, and we don't want anyone to get alarmed."

Bernie pulled an envelope from his pocket and handed it over.

It contained a brief, polite apology from Her Excellency the Right Honourable Serese Saie, Governor General of Canada. The official stationery had a rich, thick texture.

"I think she worked through the night," Bernie said.

"She'll be here later," Estlin said. "Did you get any sleep?"

"Yes. No, not really." Bernie was vibrating with excessive cheerfulness. "She gave me the question of the day. It's a follow-up on yesterday's question. We want to know about the balancers and how they create this tank. I have some specific ideas. Do I get to climb the tree?"

"No," Estlin answered.

"Oh." Bernie was crestfallen. "Why?"

"The Waes are in my closet," Estlin said. "Let's go."

"Are they sleeping?" Bernie asked.

"I don't care."

"I care."

"They sent me down a flight of stairs while I was asleep," Estlin said. "And they don't sleep the way we do. When they go still, it's like they shift into a different mode of thinking."

"That's sleeping," Bernie said.

"They're awake."

Troughton's hiking boots were sticking out from under the porch.

"Troughton," Estlin said.

Troughton shimmied out. "Your snake is fat."

"I know." Estlin gave him a hand up. "We're going upstairs. Want to come?"

"Sorry?"

"Bernie has a question for the Waes," Estlin said.

As they passed through the kitchen, Estlin gestured for Bomani to follow as he led the way upstairs.

The Waes were curled next to each other on the shelf in the closet, but the bedroom was already painted with an extra layer of brightness.

"They're awake," Estlin said. "I'm going to start with Bomani's question."

"What question?" Bernie asked.

"They don't get to go home. Not in this form." Estlin leaned against the wall. "Bomani wants to know why."

Estlin found 'why' questions hard to represent. 'Why do you only travel one way?' put certainty to something he was only partially certain about. *Partially certain.* That was a cuttlefish way of thinking. There was certain and uncertain and a third option that encompassed both states. He tumbled Bomani's question in his mind to focus on the physical limits of the journey and whether the passageway only permitted flow in one direction. It was a blunt and clumsy question, and he offered it to the Waes to refine.

The room blossomed with their recreation of the question embedded in the response. The currents of the space fold flowed through the walls of the house, stretching out beyond the tree, and Estlin found himself at the centre of the surging standing-wave as it gathered strength.

The physical adaptations the Waes accepted were nothing compared to living cleaved from the natural attachments of their kind, and that was dwarfed by passing through the perfection of the fold in space. Having the seed of oneself pass through the nexus point, the grace knot, didn't require transformation—it *was* transformation. He could see the seed ship move, without moving, like a mote of dust at the centre point of a lightning strike.

And then suddenly Estlin was beneath a palm tree in Samoa as the Waes spread their ovoids on the Pacific breeze to view the night sky and observe the expected and extraordinary, remarkable, intense burst of light from the grace as a vast visitor transitioned through it.

"What do you see?" Bomani asked.

"The Rosetta Burst" Estlin said, closing his eyes as the aurora dimmed, and the Waes clambered out his window. "The one after they arrived, while we were on the island."

Blinking, he found Yidge sitting on the bed next to him, as visible as anyone else in the room, but with no weight or warmth to her presence. "I forgot about you."

"That's rude," Yidge said.

"How do you expect to be introduced," Estlin asked. "Is there a name for what you are now?"

"Yidge Lee."

"I think your parents would disagree.

"Why are there lamps outside?" she asked. "There's enough light for you and the tree."

"The lamps aren't for the tree," Estlin replied.

"We can't hear her," Bomani said.

"Why can't they hear you?" Estlin asked.

"Because the Waes are precise." Yidge stood and walked to the window or the image of her did. "They are connected to everything around them. We pour concrete so that our feet don't have to touch the earth."

"If we're going to have a philosophical discussion, you should let them in on it," Estlin said. "It will save time."

Yidge leaned against the windowsill, casting no shadow. "You think they want an extra signal firing along their auditory nerves? The sight of me already has them sweating."

Estlin waited.

"No introductions?" Her voice gained an extra buzz.

"Stanley, Bomani and Bernie." Estlin pointed at the group lingering by the bedroom door. "This is Yidge Lee. Or a fraction of her."

"Hello," Yidge said.

"Hello," Bomani responded. "You are the dead girl we saw in Samoa."

"The first casualty of the alien invasion," she said.

"It was painful to see you on the island," Bomani said. "It is less so now."

"Good," she said.

Troughton stepped forward. "Can the camera see and hear you or are we sharing one of Estlin's hallucinations?"

"The Waes' device boosts the signal," Yidge said. "The cameras will see something now, but you see and hear much more."

"I don't want lip readers worried about your use of the word invasion," Troughton said.

"It was a joke."

"A joke about your death?" Troughton said.

"Yidge—" Estlin had too much to say and nothing to say.

"Yes, bad choice of words," she said. "Like saying 'bomb' at an airport."

"It's great talking to you," Bernie said. "Direct questions. Direct answers. Can you tell us about the ice structure? How does it work?"

"How would I know?" she asked.

"I thought..." Bernie pinched away the question, and then kept his fingers curled. "Do you know why the cuttlefish are here?"

"Why wouldn't they be here?" Yidge said.

"But what do they want?"

"What do we want?" Yidge asked.

"We want to understand where the Waes came from," Troughton said. "How they got here, why they're here, what they want from us."

"You want a lot." Yidge shrugged. "The cuttlefish have determined that their argument can't be resolved without further experience."

"The cuttlefish are arguing?" Estlin thought of the few cuttlefish he'd met relative to the hundreds of them overhead. He wondered if cuttlefish arguments were violent.

"I think that's the right word," Yidge said. "You convinced the cuttlefish that the idea cannot be easily eliminated. To determine what to do about this, they must understand the idea. Bomani can teach them."

"The idea?" Bomani asked.

"The grace knot," Yidge said. "It's beyond what the cuttlefish have known."

"It's beyond what we know," Bomani answered.

"Yes, but we don't know much," Yidge said. "Compare humans and cuttlefish, which species has been around for millions of years? Which has stronger multi-generational memory?"

"We don't know for certain," Bernie said.

"Yes, you do," Yidge answered.

"Stability. Memory. Flexibility." Bomani said. "Traits a species needs to absorb a shock like this."

"How many of these visits fail?" Troughton asked. "How often do they trigger self-destruction. Have they told you?"

"The galactic odds don't matter, do they?" Yidge said. "Our odds matter, and the Waes haven't calculated them yet."

"That does feel like a threat," Troughton said.

"It's just a calculation," she said.

"Change threatens those who rely on the status quo," Bomani said.

"For most species, the status quo is dominated by the physical environment," Bernie said. "So, change is only a threat if it alters the environment faster than a species can adapt. I still don't understand why the cuttlefish are here."

"We transform our environment. Every species does," Yidge said. "Meeting the Waes transforms us. The knot has knots. Bomani, you'll be useful today. The cuttlefish need a teacher. You understand what they need to learn. It should save some time."

"Is there a deadline?" Troughton asked.

"Bring my projector." Yidge pointed at a coin-sized object on the bedside table. "It will help," she said, and flickered out of the room.

Chapter 8

The road stretched through dried grasslands with gravel tracks meeting the pavement at numbered junctions. A light wind ruffled the grass and slowly turned the tall white blades of turbines planted across the low rolling hills. Huo had a front row seat in the coach bus, separate from the others on the diplomatic mission. He had no friends aboard and within his group only one other had direct experience of the events in New Zealand.

He'd been a peripheral objector to many decisions made in Wellington, but he owned the failure. His flight to Shanghai was diverted to Calgary, because a special request had been made for his presence. If not for that honour, his involvement with the aliens would be over.

The cragged peaks of snow-covered mountains were visible in the distance. He'd flown over those mountains, which had given way to large, cultivated fields with straight edges and the occasional perfect green circle created by central pivot irrigation. From the airport to the bus to the countryside, he had proceeded with no written briefing and no information about their mission. The bus carried delegates from India and Indonesia, making it inappropriate to ask questions.

The only Canadian aboard was the driver, her eyes hidden by sunglasses. Huo wondered how many of these trips she had made and what she had seen, but her demeanor did not invite conversation. The bus slowed and pulled off onto the gravel and grass verge, allowing a convoy of green jeep wagons and trucks to overtake at speed. Huo had not seen civilian traffic since the last checkpoint. The road curved west and he realized the cloud he had seen on the horizon was not a cloud. It was a towering, shining structure that dwarfed the dark line of tents and vehicles along its nearest edge. The world was on a fulcrum, and, whatever lay ahead, he would do his best to reach out and steady the lever.

《》

"I'm not a teacher." Bomani followed Estlin down the stairs to the kitchen.

Estlin stopped at the base of the stairs. "You taught me."

"Was I successful?" Bomani asked.

"You can teach me again."

"I will," Bomani said. "I'll have to if you need to teach the cuttlefish."

Estlin looked at the button-sized piece of alien tech in his hand. "Yidge said this would help."

"If the idea is dangerous, why share it?" Troughton pulled a chair away from the kitchen table, and then didn't sit in it. "The question has to be asked."

"It isn't our idea," Bernie said.

"The Waes should do this," Bomani agreed. "Our work is too fragmented and flawed."

"That's not what I meant," Troughton said.

"They are asking us because the question they have is about us," Estlin said.

Bomani did not see how he could help. "I'm a mathematician not an anthropologist. I don't know what we're going to do."

"Nothing," Troughton responded. "We'll do nothing. You have part of a model that will probably take decades to develop, and we can't even conceive of the technology required to use it."

"Every university will have a course on the Rosetta Burst within the year," Bernie said. "It may seem like nothing outside of those classrooms, but it is the opposite of nothing."

"Show them how far beyond our understanding and abilities this is," Troughton said. "We'll do nothing. It'll take generations."

"That is their concern," Estlin said. "The mistake we might make ten thousand years from now."

"If we last that long," Bernie said.

Estlin turned and headed for the door.

"Too pessimistic?" Bernie asked.

"They're coming," Estlin said. "Bomani, you'll want to see this."

"I'll bring more cameras." Bernie grabbed the closest tripod.

"Be cautious," Troughton said to Bomani. "Find out what they want."

Bomani nodded and followed Estlin out of the house, across the porch and down the steps to the dry grass. A shaft of light led his eyes up to a glistening glimpse of sky to where the ice had vaulted upwards and a chamber was spiraling down, riding the outside rail of a clear crystal staircase.

"Nkhuwuka chala," Bomani murmured.

"You are awake," Estlin responded.

"It's different," Bernie said.

"It's different every time," Estlin answered.

The chamber slowed and settled a few feet above the grass. The tank was cylindrical and small, relative to the two cuttlefish circulating within it. The clear walls became opaque at the thicker base.

"Do they have names?" Bomani said.

"Not the way that we have names."

"Have you named them?" Bomani pressed his fingers against the smooth surface of the tank. It was an unyielding solid, and he pressed harder than he intended, pushing for the expected cold sensation of ice or glass. It felt like the surface matched the temperature of his skin.

"No," Estlin said. "I've met these two before."

The cuttlefish stopped circling, orienting themselves to look at Bomani's hand. One had a dark face, raised arms, and wrinkled skin with white splotches that pulsed. The other had smooth skin, flattened arms, and wide zebra bands moving slowly across its body in sync with the undulations of the lateral fin encircling its mantle.

"Spark and Cloud," Bomani said.

"Where are their translators?" Troughton asked.

"We don't need their translators," Estlin said. "They need ours."

Bomani removed his hand from the tank and looked over his shoulder at Estlin, whose eyes were focused in the middle distance. Wae and Waewae were behind him, clinging to the side of the house above the porch.

"Oh, hello," Bomani said.

The aliens looked larger than they had in the room upstairs. Their limbs were extended, split fingers spread wide, gripping the aged boards. The blue spikes on their arms, shoulders and tails bristled up. The direct, yellow-eyed gaze of the closest one was unnerving. The orange-eyed one was above its partner, limbs tightly bent, and head tilted upwards. With effort, Bomani turned his attention to the cuttlefish and found them just as alien.

"Their eyes." Bomani knew Estlin's descriptions of visual communication were a deceptive simplification. What would the cuttlefish see when one tried to share the perceptions of a human eye with all its in-built distortions and assumptions?

"You need a key," Estlin said. "We see water. They see the current."

"What does that mean?" The images Bomani had to work with were pencil lines projected from incomplete equations.

"Particles of sand shifting in the water shine like dust in a beam of light," Estlin said.

"Cuttlefish can see the spin angular momentum of photons," Bernie said. "Each grain of sand shifts the polarization of the light it reflects and...sorry." Bernie pressed his fingers to his lips but could not stop himself from finishing his explanation. "Where we would see a bright speck as the grain of sand reflects photons into our eyes, the cuttlefish see how the sand transforms the light—shifting its polarization."

Estlin nodded. "It's too much information if you weren't born to see it. But we have a lot to show them. Think in layers. Begin with a current. Or begin with a grain of sand. Movement is more important than shape. Shapes change. Teach them. They are here to change."

"Is that what we're doing?" Bomani asked.

"If we can't forget or eliminate the idea, the cuttlefish need to know more about it," Estlin said. "Spark and Cloud are willing to experience the threat to understand it."

No one had seen the Rosetta Burst directly, only diffuse reflections of the light it emitted. Bomani had seen one picture of the source—blurry butterfly-wing arcs of energy building near Neptune—and he knew the image was a colour-shifted reconstruction.

"I didn't bring my notebook," he said.

"Take this."

Estlin pressed Yidge's projector into Bomani's palm. It was warm from Estlin's hand and had the weight and feel of a smooth, flat stone. It darkened to match Bomani's skin.

Bomani blinked, his eyes hot.

"You just need to float a little." Estlin folded his hand over Bomani's hand, pressing his palm against the object. "See the water around us."

Bright grains of sand appeared all around them, shifting and swirling in a fluid more viscous than the air.

"How did you..." The sand pulsed and twisted with each of Bomani's words.

"Make them dance," Estlin said.

All the grains stilled for a moment in a way that somehow said *quietly*, and then Estlin released Bomani's hand. The grains spiraled into a series of vortices, spinning faster when Bomani tried to clamp down on his thoughts. He stepped back, clenched his hand and then opened it. He simplified his thinking, settling on a long string of zeros. This calmed the water around him, blanking the slate, but communicating nothing.

He looked at the cuttlefish, and the trace of eight tentacles pursed together appeared in the sand. As soon as Bomani saw them, the tentacles splayed out in excitement. He calmed himself until the image relaxed, tentacles drooping downward. The image combined moving grains with grains brightening and dimming and twisting in place. As he noticed this, a surge swept through the image, fragmenting it.

As the sand flowed around him, it curled in eddies that were fascinating and distressing, because Bomani realized the current he created was meaningless. He swept the sand into arcs and circles and, finally, an arbelos, but none of it had any meaning.

Bomani closed his fist around the alien stone, and then opened his hand and offered it back to Estlin. "I am sorry. I don't know how to do this."

"I didn't want to get wet." Estlin ignored the offered stone-like object and stepped toward the tank. "They live with buoyancy. We live with gravity. We feel like we fall or sink alone, but we are always dancing with a partner."

Turning to face Bomani, Estlin closed his eyes and fell backwards, plunging into the tank, leaving only a faint fragment of himself standing on the dry grass. Estlin showed the cuttlefish how whales and water danced with the Earth—each holding the other—the greater the body the greater the grip. The invisible tentacles that held the whales, also pulled stone, shell and bone down to the bottom, and extended beyond the water to embrace the massive colony of abalone that shone in the night sky. The Earth's tentacles curled into the translucent arms extending from the shining disk, as though an octopus had made a home at the center of the distant shells. The sand suspended around Bomani shimmered and surged, defining the boundary between water and air. Estlin's avatar floated, gazing skyward, he reached up to roll the disk, revealing it to be a sphere. He shoved the sphere to Bomani, and it dragged a surge of water with it. Given this gift, Bomani took the story and found the cuttlefish to be apt pupils with many, many questions about the moon.

⟨⟩

Harry found Troughton at the sink doing dishes and walked through the kitchen to look in on the occupants of the sitting room. Estlin was stretched out on the couch. Bomani was in the adjacent chair, sketching in a notebook propped under the shining lamp. Dr. Chandran was with them, quietly occupying a kitchen chair placed near the threshold of the room.

Harry shrugged off his backpack and set it on the floor next to the fridge, mindful of the egg crates stacked on top of sticks of butter. He found a dish cloth in a counter drawer and joined Troughton. "I gather I missed a big show."

"It was different," Troughton said. "Bomani got plugged into the conversation. I thought he was..." Troughton gathered a handful of cutlery from below the suds. "I don't know. I gave permission, and then watched him stand there while the cuttlefish swam in loops. They were skimming the tank wall, flashing different colours. He had them so wound up, and I had no grasp on the ideas he was winding them up with. It turns out it was just a preamble, a two-hour physics lecture about the moon."

"Bernie said it was about gravity and tides."

"Same difference," Troughton said. "I opened the door wide. I don't think we can disrupt their conversation now."

"Why would you?"

"I don't know." Troughton rinsed the teapot and left it on the rack. "But the outside world might want to hit the brakes. I'm not sure what happens if they try to stop the conversation by pulling Bomani out of here. I'm sure there will be some folks that don't like how far I let it go."

"You have to go with your gut," Harry said.

Troughton dried his hands with the hem of his t-shirt. "This job is not good for the digestive system."

"An amazing variety of people will question your competence and decisions," Harry said. "They'll watch hours of video and think they know what it's like to look out this window."

The paint on the wood windowsill above the sink had been scuffed away. The view through the glass softened into light nothingness a few meters from the house.

"In Wellington, I was against locking up our visitors." Harry checked the fridge, looking for a beer he wouldn't find, and started loading in the eggs. "We needed security to keep people out. But there were people who brayed for barred cages, as though our visitors should be treated like zoo specimens. It was all arrogance and foolishness, but they probably think that the Waes walking away proved them right. More locks, more cameras, more armed guards? It wouldn't have mattered. Wae and Waewae are manipulative little buggers. They go where they want to, and they are good at getting what they want, whether the manipulation required is subtle or obvious." Harry closed the fridge. "It was really rude of them to vanish without saying goodbye."

"Do you think they'll do it again?"

"Probably," Harry said. "Best to expect it. We can worry about the Waes, or the cuttlefish, or the global political implosion, but there is a new threat here."

Harry saw Troughton glance toward the living area where Estlin was still lying on the couch.

"Yidge was my assistant." Harry took a seat at the kitchen table. "I knew her. I chose her, and she betrayed me. If the recording the Waes created is true to who she was, she could betray me again. She may have already done it by inviting the Chinese ambassador here." Harry looked at the table, his fingers following the deepest scratch in the wood as he shook his head. "I suggest you instruct me not to damage that man during his visit."

Troughton took the seat across the table. "Estlin invited him."

"Yidge invited him." Harry met Troughton's eyes. "She died in front of Lyndie. He won't refuse her...or whatever bit of her is left."

"Your word, please," Troughton said. "You won't *damage* Ambassador Huo."

Troughton extended his hand across the table. Harry felt a strange relief as they shook hands because the commitment directed his energy towards controlling the boil.

"When the Chinese snagged Estlin, Wae followed," Harry said. "Everyone's got that figured out now. It's easier to catch and confine a human than a pair of camouflaging aliens that like to climb trees. Whatever priorities you have, watching out for him better stay at the top."

"We have security—"

"Don't say it," Harry said. "If there is an issue, it will be in here."

"You want to invite the military in?" Troughton asked.

"No." Harry knew an armed patrol would not make the house more secure.

"Estlin demanded a weapons ban," Troughton said. "The Patricia's have followed it. They want to secure both ends of the gate tunnel. They had a presence here until yesterday, and they are pushing to continue here. I don't know what your thoughts on that are, but I leave the security decisions to others."

"Inexperience or experience?" Harry asked.

"Up North, when I had the watch, I failed."

Harry waited for the rest.

"Polar bears hunt people if they're hungry, and they're all hungry now," Troughton said. "I saw a polar bear climbing the near side of a pressure ridge, and I waited to see if it would catch our scent. When it turned, I waited. When I fired a warning shot, the rifle kicked, and then I couldn't see the bear. The tracks told the whole story. No one got hurt, but I wasn't trusted after that. Too hesitant."

"Experience is experience." Harry was glad to know Troughton had a bone level understanding that inaction or momentary distraction could plunge you into shit. "There's another vulnerability—outside forces can attack your team through their loved ones."

"We know," Troughton said. "My partner was pulled from his deployment. He was on a frigate in the Pacific. You'd think that would be safe. Not exactly safe, but safe from outside interference. But they took him from the ship to a mysterious, more secure location. Dr. Chandran's husband, brother, parents, and kids are together in protective custody. My mom was moved to the Governor General's residence and has her own security detail. She was approached before I got yanked in from a fishing trip because the shortlist leaked before the ink dried."

"Aliens arrived and you went fishing?"

"It made sense at the time. I didn't see the point of hanging around Toronto while idiots were lighting cars on fire." Troughton scratched his beard. "I washed this shirt in a bucket after I got here. Is there any protocol for greeting China's ambassador?"

"Do you have a large wooden club?" Harry asked.

"Right," Troughton said. "What happened in Wellington?"

"You know the Waes showed up in a park?"

Troughton nodded.

"Exotic animals were sighted." Harry decided to trust Troughton. "While I was on the search, the pair that adopted Estlin broke into my truck. I determined that they weren't there to steal my shovel. I introduced them to the prime minister. I will give you my story, but I don't know why they chose me. I may have just parked under the right tree."

Chapter 9

"There is something about us that is like a barnacle broken from the rock," Estlin said.

Bomani placed his pencil between the pages of his notebook and closed it.

Estlin let his attention drift, his eyes scanning the wood joists of the ceiling. The couch was a faded orange remnant that he had picked up for free, but it was comfortable. He'd beaten the cushions with a broom before bringing them into the house, the dust billowing like clouds of krill. "We grow like clams on the bottom…clams that don't know they are clams."

"Okay." Bomani placed his notebook on top of the books stacked by the chair.

Chandran shifted in her seat, observing, as it was her job to observe.

Lying down, Estlin felt slightly afloat. He'd stayed with Spark and Cloud during their visit, pulling ideas together whenever they threatened to unravel. Bomani had started with cautious shapes and ratios, gaining confidence until the ideas flowed and flared. He gave the cuttlefish time to assemble concepts and anticipate revelations, creating the satisfying suspense and reward of any hunt.

"The cuttlefish thought the disconnect was part of my difference," Estlin said. "I never met my father. I barely remember my mother. But that's not what they meant, that would never occur to them. Cuttlefish don't parent, they die before the young emerge from their eggs. It's the other losses that confuse them. We have to learn basic things over and over again—how to see, how to grip, how to eat. And we aren't like seaweed, we are aware of the losses. It drives us to create crutches to compensate for our crippled minds—spoken language, written language, stories, books, songs. We invented paintings, photographs, libraries, schools, and memories written on sticks, because every generation forgets what it should be born knowing."

"Would there be no war or more war if we could not forget the truth of war?" Bomani asked.

"We would *improve* war so it could not be remembered."

"War without monuments." Bomani interlocked his fingers, leaning forward in the chair. "The first casualty is truth."

"There is a risk," Estlin said.

"Always."

"Your equations are dangerous. The cuttles think that your dangerous ideas need to die."

"I know," Bomani said. "Mathematics can be a surprisingly risky field of study."

"I don't know where this is going," Estlin said.

"We'll find out, eventually."

"What if it's a short walk to a sharp drop?"

"Then we dance with gravity," Bomani said. "There is a difference between taking reasonable precautions and pretending to be smaller than you are because there is a risk that you'll be forced down by those who think you should be smaller." He smiled and lifted his notebook. "This book is a reasonable precaution." He showed Estlin a half-finished sketch. "Do you agree with this image? Or did you see it differently?"

"A little different," Estlin said. "Wetter."

Bomani turned the notebook to look at forms on the page.

Estlin could tell he was looking at it the wrong way. "Not a soggy, heavy wet." He raised an open hand. "Lifted. Held."

He watched as Bomani added a subtle uplift to each shape with a few pencil strokes to the shading.

———— «·» ————

Sgt. Malone found his professor hunched over the table in the corner of the tent and suspected that he'd worked past the point of diminishing return. "Do you have enough pencils?"

Sanford looked at him with confusion and glanced at the pencil in his hand.

"Did somebody feed you?"

"Yes," Sanford said.

"Breakfast or lunch?"

Sanford nodded vaguely. "When will Bomani be back?"

"I don't know," Malone said. "The Canadians may keep him."

"There's a knot here," Sanford said. "Bomani's good with knots. I can hear him telling me to think harder. The nodes are dimensionless, but they're still structured. I don't have the tools for this."

"You should get yourself a coffee," Malone said. "More if you're hungry."

Sanford stood, slowly straightening against the stiffness of his joints. "I shouldn't be selfish. Bomani could help with the folding pattern, but if he's with the aliens, that's best for all of us. He asks good questions."

"He'll ask for you if you can help." Malone was confident in his strategy. "The Canadians are feeding everyone. We'll secure your notes, and you'll need your ID."

Malone accompanied Sanford to the mess tent, splitting away from the coffee line-up when he spotted Pollock playing solitaire at a nearby table.

"Want to deal me in?" Malone asked.

Pollock reached under the table and pulled out a laptop. "Dewey's been watching the front door," he said. "Want to see the morning arrivals?"

Malone accepted the laptop and scrolled through the images. "Are those shrubs?"

"Two truckloads," Pollock said. "Unloaded at the gate. They are going to try to prop open the house accessway."

"Do you think it will work?"

"Nothing has," Pollock said. "But I'm prepared to be surprised."

Malone continued through the photos stopping at a mid-sized moving truck. "What's this?"

"Scientific equipment," Pollock said. "An X-ray machine from a university lab. It came with one professor and one technician."

The next image was of a busload of new arrivals.

"Chinese nationals," Pollock said. "Those two are from Indonesia. One is a politically active traditional musician. The other we haven't pinned down yet."

Malone nodded and continued to the next image. "I recognize him."

"Huo Wei, the Chinese ambassador from Wellington," Pollock said. "I'm surprised they let him in, considering the mess."

"No." Malone pointed at the thin man in the background of the photo of Ambassador Huo being greeted by the UN man, Ulz. "Behind him. Do we know who that guy is?"

"I don't think so," Pollock said. "I'll check. Want me to make small talk if he slithers in here for a snack?"

"Not yet." Malone raised a hand to wave Sanford over before he could be tempted into sitting at any of the other tables.

———— ‹‹ ›› ————

Huo accompanied Governor General Serese Saie down the shrub-punctuated path. The scientist who reminded him of a hedgehog was prattling along behind them, explaining adjustments to a light installation. Saie's bodyguard led the way. His features suggested a mixed heritage, but he carried himself with a North American self-regard, stepping ahead when the passage opened, his eyes concealed by sunglasses. Huo was glad that he'd shed his final security minder at the gate to the staging area.

The fog ahead of them dissipated to reveal an auspicious tree glowing in the diffuse light. The jumbled warbling of birds in the branches lifted his spirit as the tension that had built through the morning was released. The farmhouse was further down the dirt track, tucked under the far edge of the tree canopy. The remarkable light revived its grey siding, revealing the coarse grain of the wood.

Bernie split away to greet and join a pair of engineers working on the impressive decks of light. A bearded scientist sat on the steps to the house, waiting for them.

"Ambassador Huo, this is Dr. Stanley Troughton," Serese said.

The scientist did not offer his hand or offer a word or smile of welcome.

"They are waiting," he said, turning away to open the front door of the house.

Serese gestured for Huo to proceed. Her every action carried the distilled power of the artist and the athlete. Even her request to be addressed by the informal, familiar use of her first name contained a power beyond fame. She followed him up the short flight of stairs and into the house.

Huo hesitated when he saw the young woman waiting for him. She appeared far more solid than he expected. He knew the apparition had appeared in Samoa, but to see it was another matter. She was wearing a blue dress with a distinctive floral pattern. The dress flowed with her movements. Being confronted with this illusion of life evoked emotions that could not be categorized, but Huo's years in the foreign service relied on his ability to control his reactions.

He forced his gaze onto the others standing in the kitchen and bowed his head.

"Mr. Hume, I was honoured to receive your invitation," he said. "I hope you are well."

A squirrel descended the stairs, sniffing the worn tiles of the floor. It regarded Huo with one of its dark eyes and scampered away to stand behind Estlin.

Estlin stood with Harry, who silently watched Huo.

"Good evening, Ambassador," Yidge said.

She had Korean features, a New Zealand accent, and a pragmatic bold manner formed by the blended cultures in which she was raised. The perfect match of this unique mixture by the replicant before him was chilling, particularly given that they had last spoken one day before she died.

"Miss Lee, I am glad to see you." He forced the congenial greeting.

"Glad?" Harry said. "Is that how you feel when you look at photos of the dead?"

"I'm not a photo." The young woman's face flickered with anger and argument.

"I'm sorry, love." Harry's expression softened. "But you are a fantastically complicated photo."

Huo knew those seeking technology to defy death would spare no cost to acquire what he was seeing. It was another source of pressure and instability.

"Photos remember a moment," Yidge said. "I remember a lifetime."

"You are a book that can be left unopened on a table."

Hou felt that Harry's words were meant for him.

"Do you know why the aliens saved you?" Huo asked.

"I helped them," Yidge said.

"It wasn't a kindness," Estlin said. "It wasn't out of friendship. The Waes are here to collect information. They collected her while blood poured from her back. It was…painful."

"It didn't hurt," Yidge said.

"Yes, it did," Estlin responded.

Harry opened his hand to reveal a small stone the colour of his flesh. "Yidge, please excuse us for a moment."

Huo watched the frighteningly realistic flow of emotion across her features, progressing to resignation before Yidge nodded and vanished.

"I gave Yidge the quill Wae gave us and sent her around the world." Harry placed the stone on the table with a measured movement that marked the surface as a grave. Huo could see it no other way.

"I know," Huo said. Yidge had delivered sections of the quill to laboratories in Shenzhen and Guangzhou.

"The value of what she carried—her value—required extreme safeguarding," Harry said. "What did I promise would happen to any country that failed to protect her from border to border?"

The words were crushing. Huo hoped the sickness within did not show as he answered. "Exclusion."

"Exclusion," Harry agreed.

Yidge's death had occurred days after she completed her journey with the quill. It was outside the bounds of the agreement that protected her travels. But one could not argue legalities with someone placing personal grievances above the welfare of nations. Huo chose his words carefully.

"Mr. Hume, I am sorry I could not respect your wishes," he said. "There has been a dangerous cycle of impulsive actions and reactions. I regret that I was unable to create the time needed for reflection and understanding before you left the embassy. Miss Lee volunteered to travel with you. I did not even consider denying her. I was saddened and angered, when our efforts to provide secure transportation for the aliens and yourself proved insufficient."

"I was with her when she died," Estlin said.

"We know who shot her," Huo said. "They are here, too."

This truth had no place in the current discussion. Huo knew it as soon as the words were spoken. Estlin took an instinctive step backwards, pinching his hand, his nails pressing into the centre of a knit wound.

"I didn't invite you." Estlin looked at the small object on the table. "Yidge asked for you. What's left of her remembers you. She asked, and so you are here."

He walked past Huo, leaving the room without another word. Troughton and Saie's bodyguard stepped aside, creating a path out the entryway, and then closing the gap between them.

"Lyndie is more forgiving than I am," Harry said. "When I came looking for him, you had your security shove me off your steps. The next time I bang on your door, I expect you to answer for yourself."

Huo knew he would have to be cautious with Harry Hatarei, who stood with his arms crossed, the curling tooth-like patterns tattooed on his forearms biting into each other. The biologist had been intelligent, direct, and pragmatic in Wellington—in action, he had proven to be aligned with Huo's own approach to the aliens. He was an asset who would remain spoiled if the matter of personal honour could not be resolved.

Huo returned his attention to the governor general. He straightened his spine and lifted his eyes. "Here, we must extend ourselves in ways that are difficult. It is difficult to leap forward, as we must, and still be cautious and thoughtful. When we stumble, we must stand again. I am the country I serve and represent. If there is restitution owed, it is mine. But we are needed here, there is no balance without us."

——— «» ———

Estlin raised an arm overhead to grip a branch of the tree as his breath hitched and wheezed. Yidge's death was a sequence of bloody images repeating and repeating. He hoped the Waes wouldn't notice. The meeting he'd abandoned buzzed at the back of his mind, and he retreated further under the tree as Huo and the others spilled out onto the porch. The trunk of the tree filled his field of vision, and he pressed his hand against an ancient wound in the bark.

"Your excellency, I look forward to our next meeting," Serese said. "Bernie, please escort Ambassador Huo out to the staging area. I'll follow in a minute."

Serese projected the words, and Estlin knew he was meant to hear them. He was grateful when Bernie guided Huo away. The rumble of the path opening and closing faded.

"I wasn't very diplomatic," Estlin said.

"You were honest." Serese joined him under the leaves at a careful distance. "Thank you for suggesting Huo."

"It was Yidge's suggestion. I only had one conversation with him in Wellington."

"You wouldn't have given me his name if your instincts disagreed," she said. "Do you need to talk about what happened?"

"No." Estlin turned and pressed his back against the trunk.

Serese gave him time to reconsider this answer before she nodded.

"It's an impressive tree," she said.

"It's dying."

The day he arrived, he knew his squirrel problem wouldn't bother any neighbours, but he mourned for the tree. The copper beech was a vulnerable giant. He had considered transplanting hazelnut saplings—to sacrifice the young for the old.

"When I stay in one place, trees die," he said. "I ask the squirrels not to gnaw its buds or strip its bark, but they don't listen when they are hungry."

"It's different now," Serese said. "The tree is historically significant. It will be protected. It'll have its own budget with Parks Canada."

Estlin's throat constricted at the thought. It was part of a foreseeable future where the house was not his house. He wasn't good at *having things*. He'd always doubted his ability to keep the property, and knew that without his *shine*, the squirrels would disperse and pose no threat to the great tree. But now, the copper beech had its own fame and would attract crowds that would trample its roots to carve their initials.

"I'll add an arborist to the schedule," Serese said. "We can feed the squirrels to alleviate stress on the tree."

"It's not allowed." Estlin flinched at how childlike his protest sounded. "I don't feed squirrels, but I've been accused, fined and evicted for feeding squirrels."

"A lot has changed in a very short span of time," Serese said. "What should we do?"

"Feed them."

"Done." Serese surveyed Estlin's company of squirrels. "Can you tell if there is a sick squirrel here?"

"Mange, rabies, leptospirosis, yes," Estlin said. "If the squirrel is a vector and not suffering, no."

"Plague?"

"Probably not," Estlin said. "But the black death isn't a threat. Basic antibiotics."

"I'll request a risk analysis before I permit traps and blood sampling."

"Sunflower seeds," Estlin said. "Feed them and collect the shells. You can have saliva samples from all of them in an hour. I don't know if it would be enough saliva to work with, I just know that plague is transmitted by bite."

The squirrels scurried around them, spiraling up the tree, and Estlin heard the Waes arrive, leaping from the roof of the house into the branches above them.

"Do we need the harnesses?" Serese asked.

"No," Estlin replied. "They're coming down. They think you have a question."

"I have many."

"One," he said.

"The structure above us is beautiful," she said. "We don't understand how they created it or how is it maintained and transformed. It appears effortless, but it must require enormous power. If they were using the sunlight, we'd be standing in shadow, so where is the power coming from?"

Wae and Waewae settled in the lower branches. They were closer than they needed to be and weren't masking their forms.

"Hello." Serese held the moment with open hands.

At the edge of the tree's canopy, Troughton's team joined Serese's security man. She heard them arrive and nodded at Estlin.

"Structure and power." Estlin didn't know what the ice structure looked like from the outside, but photorealism wasn't needed for the visual elements he created for the Waes. He started with a shaded box. Casting off the outer casing, he dove into the dark unknown within it. Raising a blue lantern, he illuminated a small pocket of salt water, like the dim view before a deeply submerged camera. The light flickered, revealing glimpses of dark forms and movement, including the visitors circling him. He directed his insufficient lamp at his questions to illustrate his curiosity and lack of understanding. He tried to pass the imagined lamp to Wae and felt an unexpected resistance.

He tried again, concerned that he was stumbling against the Waes assertion that they were observers and collectors, not communicators. Wae ignored the dim lamp and turned on the sun. It seared Estlin's assumptions. The ice cauldron held more than water, cuttlefish, and their favorite snacks. A fragment of ocean floor was above/below them with rock outcrops rising through sand and columns of seaweed.

The balancers appeared, the pair rising from the depths to circle each other with slow strokes of their long limbs and wide, flat tails. Their eyes were midnight blue and dark egg-shaped structures were clustered on their shoulders. They tasted the water with the palms of their hands—judging the temperature, salts and dissolved gases—and then they spread a cloud of bright dust, which assembled into vertical spirals. The spirals warmed the water, creating a buoyant column that rose, leaving the net of dust behind, as though it was tethered to the bottom. Above them, solid plates parted allowing the warm water to meet the air at the surface.

Estlin focused on the energy heating the water, driving the circulating current. He visualized the dust spirals, brightening them, adding threads that pulsed with the same golden hue. He left the thread ends loose, drifting in question.

The threads curled through the water to catch their ends on the dark lumps on the shoulders of the balancers. From there, they braided into ribbons that spiraled into the depths. Estlin followed them down to where the ribbons burrowed into the sand. He tried to excavate one of the pulsing threads, but the grains slid through his fingers. He wrapped his hands loosely around one of the ribbons and felt no heat or threat. He tightened his fist and yanked. The ribbon looped his hand and yanked back.

His face hit the sand. The grit passed through his eyes and teeth, and he bashed downwards through layers of rock, ice, air, grass, earth and more rock. He was surrounded by a convergence of bright ribbons. At the center of the bundle, within the rock, two great beasts were slowly moving. Wider grey ribbons reached even deeper, seeking warmth, gathering it up into hard hands. A small black lump was pressed into a foggy grey stone. It was pressed and pressed and pressed until it became clear and colourless. The purified gem shattered into fine bright dust, and the smallest grain was transformed into a bright blue wisp. The wisp was passed into the hands of one of the massive waetapu. It held the wisp, which brightened and folded, smaller and smaller, until the hard hands pressed together. Brightness surged up through the ribbons, and Estlin was shoved away through the rock.

He caught the briefest glimpse of another pair working beneath the rock before he was flung into the air and over the house to fall down into the tree branches.

Estlin's lungs ached. He wondered if he had stopped breathing. It felt as though the tree was wavering beneath his hand as the Waes climbed away.

"You ask interesting questions," Estlin said.

"Are you okay?" Serese asked.

"I think they are burning carbon," Estlin said. "Does that make sense?"

"We burn carbon," Serese replied. "It must be a clean fire, we haven't detected—"

"Not fire," Estlin said. "I think they burn carbon the way a star burns carbon."

"I don't understand."

"I saw one of the pairs that maintain the cauldron," he said. "And then I went below, in the earth, where there are four who push carbon together and feed energy to the balancers above. Four with hard stomachs...sorry, hard hands and star eyes."

"Star eyes?"

"Sending out light rather than receiving it," he said. "I think they gather geothermal energy and use it to fold atoms. They fold atoms in the way that the atoms want to be folded, even as they resist being folded. There's a resonance."

"Ma'm, you asked me to remind you of the time." It was Mike, still standing just beyond the lower branches of the tree.

Serese's look of annoyance faded to acceptance. "I'm sorry," she said. "There is a meeting I can't avoid."

Estlin understood, though the world of unavoidable meetings felt impossibly distant from his house.

"Please send Bomani's drawings to me. Actually, that's not your job." She turned, raising her voice. "Troughton? I want first view of the next set of drawings."

Troughton agreed as he approached.

"Take care," Serese said to one or both of them, striding off to where Mike waited and proceeding from there without pause.

"Something new?" Troughton asked.

"Yes," Estlin said.

"Anything more to do here?" Troughton asked.

"No."

"Want to go back inside?" he asked.

"Yes." Estlin had no words to spare because deep behind his eyes he was trying to hold on to the shape of a fold that could fuse atoms and the colour of the fire released.

Chapter 10

Bernie brought Ambassador Huo to the workspace he had eked out, a semi-private pocket behind a pile of empty equipment crates in a tent linked to the staging area. Ulz was already there, occupying the only chair, which was centered between the monitors.

"There's a pattern here," Ulz said.

"Have you met Ambassador Huo?" Bernie asked.

"Yes," Ulz said. "Serese has me greeting people at the gate."

Although Serese had invited many of them to use her first name, Bernie felt Ulz's tone was disrespectful.

Ulz adjusted the magnification of the footage he was reviewing. "There are distinct cluster sizes and movements. I'm hoping the tracking software will help visualize it."

"We have a meeting in an hour," Bernie said. "Which is soon considering the checkpoints."

"I set an alarm," Ulz said. "We have time."

"What are you looking at?" Huo asked.

"It's like a murmuration of starlings," Bernie said. "Whirling flocks were studied by the Romans to divine the moods of the gods. Now, they are studied to understand distributed decision-making processes, so we can try to recreate them in drone swarms."

"I do not understand," Huo said.

"This is enhanced satellite footage from yesterday," Ulz said. "These are cuttlefish shadows."

"The cuttlefish spend a lot of time settled on or near structures within the tank," Bernie added. "But yesterday, they all went swimming, all at once."

Ulz split the images on his screen, showing a series of frozen frames. "Little clusters and bigger clusters, almost always odd numbers. Multiple clusters whirling around in synch with each other. Individuals moving from cluster to cluster. More cuttlefish engaged. The whole formation was expanding and contracting, and then they suddenly dispersed."

"Was there movement of the water in the tank," Huo asked. "An artificial current?"

"I don't think so," Ulz said. "But we don't know."

"We think they were having an argument," Bernie said. "Estlin said the cuttlefish had an argument, so we decided to look for it."

"I have access to good tracking software," Ulz said.

"For inanimate objects," Bernie countered. "We should be looking at the methods used for schools of fish."

"Cuttlefish aren't fish," Ulz said. "And, as far as I know, no one has observed or interpreted the movements of herring having an argument."

"What if it is simply in their nature to swim together?" Huo asked.

"All of them," Ulz said. "All at once?"

"Yes," Huo said. "Like the starlings or a swarm of bees."

"But there are patterns," Bernie said.

"There are patterns in the movement of leaves on a tree," Huo said. "They move with the wind. They move with the sun."

"Exactly," Bernie said. "The movement is driven. It's purposeful. It's meaningful."

"It's natural," Huo said. "When a river smooths a stone, it's erosion, not an argument."

"But the pattern—" Bernie pointed at the screens, thinking that they should show Huo the moving images that Ulz had frozen.

"I believe you will find patterns everywhere," Huo said. "Meaningful patterns that are worthy of attention. But an argument is an exchange of words. Arguments are built on constructs of language. Humans argue. Cuttlefish don't have words to argue with. Cuttlefish swim together because they swim together."

"Swarm," Ulz said.

Bernie tried to find a diplomatic way to respond. Since the Waes arrival, he'd been accused of anthropomorphizing on a daily basis. "Their intelligence may be different, but it is intelligence."

"I didn't say they lacked intelligence," Huo said. "Their nature is different than ours. A bird does not sing because it has an answer. It sings because it has a song."

This silenced Bernie.

"I can find my way to the meeting space," Huo said. "I should collect my notes and perhaps find a cup of tea."

"The good cafeterias are further out," Bernie said.

"I will find one." Huo nodded to them both before edging out past the wall of stacked equipment.

Bernie watched him go, and then turned to the monitors, searching each frozen frame that Ulz had selected.

"He's right," Ulz said. "I was looking for the motivator within the movement. It could be outside it. We need a wider view. What did Estlin say to them before the argument started?"

"He told them that the ideas we've taken from the Waes can't be cut from us."

"That's grim," Ulz said. "I don't know how to factor that in. We can only monitor all activity and try to investigate swarm events in real-time."

"We should go," Bernie said.

"Yes, but I have another idea," Ulz said. "Lichtwardt means *light watcher*. I track the flickers from objects in orbit, but my name comes from those who kept signal fires on the coast of Germany. We received your intense pulse of light. Now, you must set it up as a blinkgerät—like an Aldis lamp—to flash messages in Morse code."

"Yes. Thank you. Yes." Bernie checked his watch and dashed away looking for Paik.

———— «》 ————

Harry watched Estlin and Bomani work at the table, each with a sketch pad and pencil. It wasn't going well.

Estlin scribbled slash marks across another page of incomplete efforts.

Bomani lifted his pencil, waiting.

"I can't describe it." Estlin pressed his fingers against his right eye. "I can't draw it."

Harry found the latest sketch disorienting—worse than the usual distorted scrawls. "Need sharper crayons?"

"No." Estlin closed his eyes.

Bomani turned the pages in his book. "We could refine the wider view."

"No."

"Or choose another detail," Bomani suggested.

"No. Serese wants to see the fire."

Bomani kept his pencil in contact with the page—awaiting direction.

"I'm sorry," Estlin said. "It's wrong. The dissonance. I can hear how wrong this drawing is…. It's screeching, and I can't fix it. Trying to makes my fingers itch."

"Get the broad strokes down," Harry said.

"There are no broad strokes." Estlin flipped his pencil into the air and let it clatter to the table. "It can't be pulled apart. None of the lines have ends."

He stopped, his head tipping to one side, listening to the silence. "I should water the squirrels."

Estlin turned his back on the work and walked out of the house. Harry followed him.

———— ‹›» ————

Mike followed Serese, walking to her right as the tunnel opened at the edge of Estlin's property line. The Princess Patricia's infanteers were standing guard in their pixilated woodland camouflage which stood out against the dry grassy landscape. Two of his team were also there, waiting to relieve him. Serese's status could have accelerated them through the outbound security checkpoint, however she took her place in line.

The UN man, Ulz Lichtwardt, was ahead of them, distracted from the outward journey by a large piece of inbound equipment accompanied by two new faces.

Mike automatically checked the colour of their ID badges and tuned in to Ulz's conversation.

"Why is the GISAXS considered a spectrometer rather than a diffractometer?" Ulz asked.

The technician didn't answer. He didn't have to because Ulz piled on further questions.

"How much time do you need to set up? Does it have special power requirements? Did you have to remove the X-ray shielding to get it through the scanners here?"

Mike fractured the second, catching flashes of confusion and tension as the grey-haired man glanced at his underling for direction. Adrenalin surging, he signaled his partners and felt Serese peel away, responding to a hand on her elbow, a body already between her and the potential issue as he stepped forward. "Sir. Step away—"

The man closest to the spectrometer turned to face the instrument and the world broke.

———— 《 》 ————

Ulz's blood was painting the dry grass. The slices in his leg burned.

I have eighteen seconds, Ulz thought, because he recognized arterial spray. Each heartbeat sent out a pulse of blood. It should have been alarming. *Shock,* he thought, and reached out to cover the wound. The fingers of his hand were mangled and useless. He felt a surge of tremendous anger that his fingers were useless when he had so little time. He used the heel of his palm to cover a fraction of the wound, blood pouring from his chin as he leaned forward. He hadn't phoned his mother or sister—not since leaving New York— because of the security embargo on personal calls. They didn't know he'd been left behind or that he'd caught up.

The tree sheltering the farmhouse came vividly to mind—the twist of its trunk and the expanse of branches. A great white oak lived by the waterwheel near his mother's home in Blaubeuren. He could hear rain beating its leaves as the buckets of the waterwheel filled and poured. He was cold and the screams around him were muffled, as though he'd been shoved underwater.

———— 《 》 ————

Harry felt a push through the soles of his feet. He looked over at Estlin, who seemed frozen in place. A low-pitched thump rolled across the yard. "What the f—"

Estlin slowly turned and a split second later was sprinting across the yard. The ice billowed back at an alarming rate.

"Troughton! He's running!" Harry shouted toward the house.

Troughton jumped off the porch.

"He's off the path!" Harry pursued Estlin into the long dry grass, losing him in the fog rolling off the shifting ice. He kept a low driving stride, ready to tackle any shadow or glimpse of his friend. He didn't know if they were running towards danger or evacuating from under it.

Harry's foot hit a rut in the grass, and he stumbled, tumbling against the earth. Troughton nearly ran over him, slowing just enough to grab his arm, pull him up, and push him on in the right direction.

The ice parted and Harry was blinded by the sun. The staging tent was off to his right, its sidewall shredded. He scanned the scene, trying to make sense of it. There was twisted metal, clumps of earth and blood.

Troughton reached Estlin first, grabbing his arm. "You can't be here."

Estlin barely shifted in response.

"Lyndie!" Harry pinched Estlin's ear between his fingernails.

Estlin tried to pull away, confusion in his eyes.

Harry held tight. The air was full of grit and sounds that scraped the base of his animal brain. "Go back to the house."

"I don't—"

"Go back to the house, now," Harry said. "Troughton, take him."

"I can triage." Troughton's eyes were scanning the nearest breaks and bleeds.

"Right," Harry said. "I'll take him. Do what you have to."

Harry kept a grip on Estlin's arm, marching him to the start of the driveway and waving off the soldier who considered stepping into their path. As the ice tunnel formed around them, Harry took a breath, and then another.

"You can't do that," he said. "Never again."

Estlin pulled his arm away.

"Anyone who saw you out there might decide to set two explosions," Harry said. "One to draw you out, and one to hurt anyone who would stop them from taking you. Everyone knows that if they get you, they get two aliens for free. Do you understand?"

Estlin surged ahead, cursing under his breath.

"Lyndie!"

"I understand."

"Are the Waes still at the house? Is something else coming at us?"

"They're up the fucking tree," he said.

Dr. Chandran was waiting next to the big red button connected to the array of lights.

"You should get out there," Harry said. "Explosion in the staging area."

"This job comes first," she answered. "Estlin?"

Estlin tried to walk past her.

"Hey!" Harry snapped. "Don't waste her time. She is needed."

Estlin stopped.

Chandran had her fingers on his pulse point. "Why did you run?"

"I didn't run," Estlin said.

"You ran."

Estlin's fists clenched. "I didn't know I was running."

"And now?" she asked. "Are you having impulses that you can't control?"

"No."

"Your pulse is racing," she said.

"I am angry," he said. "People are bleeding out there."

"And the Waes, are they angry?" she asked.

"They don't get mad at crap like this. They get excited." Estlin pulled his arm away and went to the tree. "What the fuck was that?"

"Doc, you're needed," Harry said. "He's fine."

"I have one job," she said.

"He's fine," Harry assured her. "I'll get him inside."

"Why send me?" Estlin shouted at the Waes. "The dead were dead. There was nothing for you to steal. You don't need me to open skulls for you!"

Estlin was surrounded by a surging horde of agitated squirrels. Harry had to shuffle his feet to avoid stepping on them as he tried to get closer.

"Their wires are in deep," Estlin said. "They're in so deep that I see the world sprinting by and my brain doesn't even consider asking my feet to stop." He turned his attention to the branches above. "What the fuck is wrong with you? You don't push me to where bombs are going off."

Dr. Chandran exchanged a long look with Harry.

"Lyndie! Go inside." As he reached out, a squirrel scrambled up his leg intending to use his arm as a jumping off point. Harry shook it off with instinctive, excessive force.

"The others are already inside," Dr. Chandran said.

"Get in the house," Harry said. "We're flipping the deadbolt."

Estlin ignored him.

"You ask. I choose," he shouted. "If you play me like a puppet, I will quit this mess and vanish."

"Stop barking at the tree," Harry said.

The Waes dropped from the tree to roof of the house and ambled along the peak.

"We need to go inside."

Estlin turned his glare on Harry.

"The doctor is needed."

The words registered and Estlin silently brushed past Harry on his way to the house. As Harry turned to follow, Chandran touched his elbow.

"Clean that wound." She pointed at the rash of broken skin on his forearm. It was a shallow scrape from his fall in the grass. "Get Estlin to help you."

————— «◊» —————

Bernie's hands were stinging. He looked at the scuffed palm of his left hand and the similar scuff on the back of his right hand and wondered how that had happened. He was sitting on the ground, his ears ringing.

"Bernie, how you doing?" Sgt. Malone appeared from nowhere, kneeling, reaching out to support Bernie's neck. "You bang your head?"

"No," Bernie said, but the sergeant's hands were already moving across his scalp searching for bumps.

"Any broken bones?" Sgt. Malone asked.

"No."

"I'm going to press your sternum and your belly," Malone said. "Yell if you've got anything to yell about."

Bernie had no complaints. "What happened?"

Malone ignored the question, looking over his shoulder, and then directly into Bernie's eyes. "Want to stay here or get up?"

"Up," Bernie said.

"Good." Malone offered no assistance. "On your feet. Take it slow."

He slung an arm across Bernie's shoulders a moment later, setting them in motion.

The security checkpoint had been blown apart. Bent tables and equipment were embedded in the ground, and the explosion had shredded the closest tent. Three bodies were covered. Ulz was a few feet further away, dead on the grass, surrounded by medical debris from the efforts made to save him.

"Don't look," Malone said. "See the tent? That's where we're going."

Bernie focused his eyes on the ground. Malone steered them around a sharp-edged fragment of metal. Bernie recognized the piece of casing and startled back. "The spectrometer. Spectrometers don't blow up."

"It wasn't an accident," Malone said.

Bernie wanted to lean over and empty his stomach, but Malone was holding him in place.

"Where did it come from?" Malone asked. "Who brought it in? I need to know."

Bernie swallowed, sucked in a breath, and threw up the information instead, as much as he could think of, as quickly as he could.

Chapter 11

"I don't know what he saw," Serese said. "Mike had the others hold me back. He approached the table. It didn't seem urgent, just…. He's cautious. Then he shouted. I heard the warning, not the words. I turned. I didn't see any flash. Dust was driven into my eyes, and I was punched to the ground."

The interviewer had introduced himself, but she'd forgotten his name. She pressed her fingers against her ear and looked for his ID tag but it was twisted.

"We have four dead and eight injured," he said. "Dead are Warrant Officer John Duggan, Dr. Lichtwardt, and the two bombers."

Serese reached out and turned the man's ID tag around, checking the photo against the face before her. He stopped talking and looked at her more closely.

"How is Mike?" Serese asked.

"I saw him before he was evacuated," he said. "Cuts, concussion, broken fingers. He was conscious, but not coherent."

"It happened quickly," Serese said. "I don't know what Mike said or how he signaled his team. They put themselves between me and the blast."

"I read your written statement."

"I had to wait in the…. I was waiting for the doctor," Serese said. "It was the only work I could do. I'm sorry it's so thin."

"It was helpful," he said. "It was consistent with the footage we have."

Serese tried not to think of this quiet man watching footage of people being shredded frame by frame. "Thank you."

"If anything occurs to you—anything at all, from earlier today, from yesterday, anything out of place—report it. Every detail helps."

"Thank you." Serese felt that she should have more words. She stood when he did, looking deeper into the tent as he beckoned the next person to be interviewed.

Bernie was hunched at a table with a blanket over his shoulders, a pen awkwardly pinched in his fingers. She approached and found he was recopying his list because there was blood on his list.

"Add sunflower seeds." Serese sat next to him. "Are you alright?"

Bernie folded his bandaged hands together and tucked them under his chin. "I'm not sure where I'm supposed to be. I slept. I had a nap in the tent with the... the others. The doctor shook me awake, but I was just having a nap."

Serese placed a hand on Bernie's shoulder. "I'm glad you've rested."

"You have more things for the list," he said.

"Are you willing to go back to the house?"

Bernie nodded.

"I think familiar faces are best," she said. "But Estlin was asking your question before this happened. I think we may need an engineer in a specific field to help understand the answer."

Bernie glanced around the tent, recognizing Serese indirect choice of words. "What did he say?"

"They burn carbon like a star."

Bernie stood, his pen dropped to the table and rolled. He caught it before it could fall and sat, pulling his list close. "How did that come up?"

"You asked."

"Oh," he said. "You need a physicist, not an engineer. There was one in Samoa—a friend of Bomani's. Estlin has met him."

"Get him," Serese said. "Now."

———— «◊» ————

Adya Chandran's shift had ended. She'd washed the blood from her hands, filed reports, and prayed. She knew she should rest, but followed the path to the house, the work ethic of years of medical practice compelling her to round on one more patient. Two of the night shift sat on deck chairs next to the red alarm button, another was leaning against the side of the house.

Harry was sitting on the porch swing, illuminated by a hanging lantern.

"He's angry," Harry said.

"How are you?" Adya asked.

Harry twitched at the question, as though it were a bewildering non sequitur, finally he raised his bandaged elbow. "It was a good suggestion. Got him grounded for a moment."

"What happened?"

"I should ask you that."

"I don't know much," Adya said. "The investigation has just started."

Adya joined Harry on the porch swing.

"He wanted to confront the Waes." The swing creaked as Harry leaned back.

"And you're out here."

"He wanted to go storming upstairs," Harry said. "I stopped him."

"I understand, but—" Adya gestured at the door.

"I stopped him in his own house."

"You could apologize," she said.

"No."

"Because you weren't wrong."

"Do you know how many times he's been pinned down, punched, bound and drugged since this started?" Harry asked. "That can't be how we handle things. I'm here to prevent that type of crap—not press him against the wall until he does what he's told."

"He was very agitated," Adya said.

"That's what they do. And when they agitate us, he's the one who gets shoved." Harry kicked off and let the bench swing. As it swung forward, he got up and let it propel him away, across the porch and down the steps. He kept walking.

Adya rose and entered the house. She found her teammates in the kitchen. Everyone was ignoring the shift change tonight. Bomani was at the table, working with the new physicist, a professor near retirement age, who had been pulled through the staging area earlier at some speed. Estlin was propped sideways on the couch in the next room, hands on his knees and his head tipped forward.

"How is it out there?" Troughton asked.

"Settling," Adya answered. "Is he sleeping?"

"No," Troughton answered. "No one is."

"Privacy, please," she said. "Doctor. Patient."

Troughton considered the request, glancing at the cameras around them.

"I know it doesn't exist," she said. "Humour me."

"Let's go admire the dark." He waved Emmet and Saeed towards the porch when they hesitated. "Bomani? Sanford?"

"Can we finish this?" Bomani asked.

Adya nodded.

"I'll send the others out to sleep," Troughton said. "Leave this to the night shift."

"And you?" she asked.

"I'll wait for an update from you," he said.

Adya watched Troughton step out, and then joined Estlin on the couch, checking the hour reported by the clock.

"How many dead?" Estlin asked.

"Four," she said. "Including the two who brought in the bomb."

"And?"

"Ulz Lichtwardt and John Duggan. He was with the Princess Patricia's."

Estlin turned his face away. "It looked worse."

"It was worse," she said. "Several others were evacuated with significant injuries."

"What a stupid thing." Estlin pointed upwards. "This is all stupid."

"What is?"

"Having aliens in my house," Estlin said. "Someone trying to blow it all up."

"Do you plan to sleep tonight?"

"Are you planning to offer me pills?"

"No," Adya replied, although she had considered it.

"I'm not going to let the Waes trip through my nightmares. They are intensely interested in violence."

"You'll have to sleep sometime."

"Not tonight."

Adya watched as Estlin shifted around on the couch, planted his feet and pushed his toes into the floor, leaning forward.

"Harry didn't want me up there earlier. He was probably right."

"Will you tell him that?"

"I don't know if they understand the difference between asking and forcing."

Adya waited, sensing Estlin had more to say.

"The Waes have so much range" He tipped his head back to face the ceiling. "It doesn't matter if I'm in the room with them or down here."

Adya realized Harry had only blocked a staircase, and all of them had assumed Estlin was resting. "Did the Waes anticipate the explosion?"

Estlin looked at her. "I don't know. I haven't asked them about it. But I know they aren't surprised. They are here to watch us react to the stress they create by being here, and they already know we like to blow shit up." Estlin's fingers tapped a rhythm against his knees. "I felt wrong before it happened."

"What kind of wrong?"

"Restless," he said. "I wanted to be outside. I went outside."

"And then you ran," Adya said. "How did you feel when you stopped running?"

"Detached."

"Physically detached, like you were outside your own body, or emotionally flat?"

"Both. But it's a different kind of splitting." Estlin raised one hand, turning it palm up and then palm down. "I don't know how to describe it. And I don't know how to get them to understand. I tried to push them. How else could I ask about them pushing me? But I can't push them, and when I tried, it all flipped around. It was like flying backwards, like being swept into the air before you decide to leave the ground. Except you have decided, and somehow the clock is broken in a way that puts everything out of sequence."

"You are working with aliens," Adya said. "Think of our interactions with other species. Throw a ball for a dog. Where do you draw the line between making a request and triggering an instinct to get the response you want?"

"When they are manipulating our perceptions, when I engage with them, if it requires thought—drawing memory into a visualization—it can be challenging to interpret their responses, but they have the frequencies right. When it requires action, it goes off the rails. It's not even on the rails to start with..." Estlin shook his head. "You end up holding out a banana without a single thought about why it's in your hand or where you picked it up from. And I think that the way they understand consent, if I've taken action, if I'm running across the field, I have consented."

"We have parallel neural pathways," Adya said. "I'm not talking about the autonomic nervous system. This isn't as simple as your spine yanking your finger away from a flame. There are multiple paths within the brain. When they want action, it could be that they bypass the part of you that reflects and records things into memory. Depending on the part of the brain they access, you could consent without your long-term memory being engaged, leaving no record of the request or the thought process or the decision."

"You think it's part of how they ask us to do things," he said. "An unintended consequence, not a deliberate manipulation."

"It is possible," Adya said. "It depends on what part of the brain they are sending signals to."

"Benefit of the doubt."

"Yes."

"It's still creepy."

"Yes," Adya agreed. "But it has happened to other people—conscious or unconscious actions are taken that ultimately benefit the Waes. I don't think it's specific to you or your atypical autism."

"I don't have autism."

Adya wanted to have this conversation and knew to wait and listen.

"I am *atypical*," he said. "There may be a structural difference in my brain. And I'll agree it presented like autism when I was young and sensitive. But I wasn't struggling to process signals from my own senses, I was being overwhelmed by input from other people's senses." Estlin's hands flexed into fists. "When my connection to other people burned out, everything changed. I was still different. I am different. But I don't think of it as autism… unless I'm somehow a very rare colour on the spectrum."

The records indicated that Estlin had been hospitalized for months after his mother was killed when he was twelve. Adya wondered if the catatonia had been triggered by the emotional trauma of witnessing her death or if his minor injuries had caused a cerebral microembolism.

"The trick that the Waes use to push me around, I need to find a way to talk to them about it," Estlin said. "If they want me to run, they have to ask properly."

"Is it dangerous?" Adya asked. "Does it feel dangerous?"

"It doesn't feel at all. Not until afterwards."

"Do you think they would run you off a cliff?"

"No," Estlin said. "But I've been dreaming. In my dreams, I fall upwards."

———— ⟨⟩ ————

Malone checked his watch and knew he'd find Pollock in the cafeteria. His upgraded ID had a new stripe. He'd traded Sanford for a band of bright blue. Green would have been better, but he'd wait for the next opportunity.

Pollock was sitting with Dewey. Malone grabbed a glass of water and joined them.

"You're back," Pollock said. "Our asset took a walk without an escort?"

"Access to the house wasn't an option for me," Malone responded. "We'll get his footage and notes."

"Did you see the corridor?" Dewey asked.

"It rumbles," Malone said. "Are we listening for it?"

Dewey nodded. "So far, every transit we've recorded appears in the shared activity logs. The pitches were higher when the squirrel man dashed out after the blast."

"The crater was forty yards from the tank wall," Malone said. "Did they want mayhem in the camp, or did they want it to put a dent in the structure?"

"The blast wasn't big enough to bring it down." Dewey said.

"We don't know that," Malone said.

"Hell of a splash if it happened," Pollock said.

"If that was the objective, they would've tried harder." Dewey responded. "Bigger bang. There wouldn't be corpses for the Canadians to pick over for biometrics."

"Our radicals bought or hacked deep enough to find that shipment," Malone said. "Did they exploit an opportunity or create it?"

"I'll find out who asked for the X-ray system that blew," Pollock said.

"It was Ulz," Malone responded. "I don't think he expected to die, but someone may have encouraged him to ask for the equipment. Ulz made the request. Bernie Springer took the request to Serese Saie, and she approved it."

"The bomb was in a transformer box," Pollock said. "Something that would appear to be a normal add-on bolted to any European equipment that is plugged into the grid here."

"They got past dogs and swabs," Dewey added. "So, perfect seals and the surfaces were parts per billion clean. There are inspectors with drills and screwdrivers everywhere now."

Malone looked to Pollock. "Dig up what you can on equipment. What's here. What's coming. Who's requesting gear."

"In progress," Pollock replied.

"No one blinked when the wrong pair of faces came through the gate," Malone said. "Who else is here that shouldn't be? Or do you think they used that weakness only once?"

"We haven't talked about motives," Dewey said.

"Perturb and observe," Pollock said. "It's what the aliens are doing to us."

Malone disagreed. "Someone expects that kick to work to their advantage."

"It worked for us," Dewey said. "We stepped in. We weren't the only ones."

"Insufficient motive for the risk." Malone preferred to think on his feet but stayed at the table. "Who would push us that hard now?"

"The pressure is rising," Pollock said. "Everyone is sharpening their knives. I asked about it yesterday and hit a wall, fucking compartmentalization."

"Can't blame them," Dewey said. "We're in here covered in alien mind-control powder. I don't trust us either."

"Assume it wasn't us," Malone said.

"The Chinese are pretending we didn't humiliate them in Wellington," Pollock suggested. "That could drive a lot of stupidity."

"Wrong timing," Malone answered. "Their ambassador went to the house today. Why risk a lock out?"

"It was the Swiss," Dewey said. "They're tired of being neutral."

The laugh helped Malone break the frame that split the world between America's enemies and allies. "Banks aren't neutral, they're immoral."

"This circus is mobile," Pollock said. "Ignore that the little fuzzies invited themselves to the squirrel-man's house. They leapt here when missiles smacked the runways in Samoa. If you think that's how it works and want to see them jump off this continent, maybe go further northeast—"

"It's too unpredictable."

"It might not matter where they end up if you hate where they are enough."

Dewey swiped his palm across the table. "The Russians loaded one precious Kiwi on a plane, and the Canadians let them land in an uncontrolled area. Who knows what they off-loaded."

Malone knew the crowd that dismissed Sanford because the physicist was from a lesser west coast university were utterly galled that a M□ori biologist from the underside of the world had a lead role in first contact. Some idiot stateside had sent out a directive to discard Harry Hatarei on a runway in Samoa, imagining that the Kiwi would eventually swim home never to be heard from again. "Did you talk to your Canadian friends?"

"Yes and no," Dewey said.

"Go fishing," Malone said. "Find out if they asked Dr. Hatarei about his traveling companions. And I want the satellite footage."

"Got it." Dewey stood, grabbed his empty glass, and carried it off to the dirty dish bin.

Pollock's fingers found a spoon on the table. "I met our new second lieutenant this morning."

"How'd that go?"

"Full dress uniform and he looks about twelve. He would like you to arrange a meet and greet between Senator Dunne and the aliens."

"I don't have that kind of leverage," Malone said. "Did you suggest that he pull his own lever?"

"I did." Pollock tapped the table with the spoon, the smile lines around his eyes crinkling. "Imagine staging a grip-and-grin photo op with aliens under the tank full of cuttlefish."

"Does Dunne know that the space critters digest with their palms?" Malone asked

"That does raise the stakes on a handshake. High potential for a dramatic photo." Pollock set aside the spoon. "The lieutenant also had some suggestions for you."

"Suggestions?"

"Not orders. Not yet," Pollock said. "He suggests twice daily face-to-face sessions with you to discuss the situation. He suggests 07:00 and 19:00."

"He knows how long it takes to transit between the camps here?"

"Approximately." Pollock shrugged and leaned back. "Some people have shitty jobs."

"Ass kissing jobs that we don't want," Malone agreed.

"I suggest that we help second lieutenant Rupert acclimate."

Malone nodded.

"I can take meetings that conflict with your visits to the staging camp," Pollock said. "Rupert will understand the priority, and I prefer walking to sitting."

"Starting tomorrow?"

"Tomorrow," Pollock agreed. "It would be a midnight update if you went now."

Malone decided to use his upgraded pass. "They are reconfiguring the staging area. I'll go assess the changes. I *suggest* you update Rupert on Sanford's access and check the transit time at this hour." He waved at Pollock and left the table.

The crescent moon illuminated patchy clouds and the faintly gleaming tank. The breeze was damp. The staging area had been reshaped to exclude the blast area. Tents and tarps protected the bomb site from the weather, but Malone glimpsed the forensic analysts working in pairs. Additional fencing created a new security post preceding a narrow approach from another angle.

Several tents had been repositioned and racks of hazmat suits were shoved together and abandoned in the space between tents. Sampling buckets collected the light rain and the runoff from the tents. Malone considered taking a look at the staging area beyond the gate, but his attention was drawn by someone stepping into the shadows of a narrow space between the tents. He followed on instinct.

At the end of the narrow passageway, the junction with a crosswise tent was filled with stacked equipment, creating another narrow squeeze space. He rounded the corner confidently, and had a split second to realize his quarry had vanished. The blow to the back of his skull filled his eyes with white sparks. Malone staggered forward as the fucker who'd hit him made contact again, increasing the speed at which he pitched into the ground.

He lost a few seconds in the black or the grey, dragging shallow breaths through clenched teeth. He had to get his shit together because the threat was sharing the air with him. His eyes sparked when he tried to lift his head, but he persisted, propping himself up on one hand.

"It's very annoying."

Malone agreed, but couldn't trust his voice. It felt like one of his eyeballs was wandering off.

"I arrived yesterday."

Malone tracked the voice to the speaker, who was crouching close by in the deepest shadow available. It was the viper who had followed the Chinese ambassador. He spoke with a Baltimore drawl. Malone was certain the man had spent time stateside, perfecting the accent.

"I know," Malone said.

"I was there when the explosive was brought in," he said. "I saw nothing. I walked next to those men and did not see the threat. It's annoying."

"I saw photos. I focused on you."

"The aliens have chosen small, soft countries." The shadow shifted. "They choose people who do not appreciate the danger."

"It's challenging," Malone agreed.

"You were in New Zealand. US Special Forces. Do you know who blasted the hole in the ground?"

Malone hated this game. "No."

"True capitalists are sociopaths," the viper responded. "It is hard to understand their motives—or very simple. The younger man used a string of identities. He flew to Edmonton from Montreal. He flew to Montreal from Rome. He arrived in Rome from Munich. He took a train from Regensburg to Munich. He landed in Regensburg on a private jet. That was careless."

"I'm sure…" Malone shifted onto his knees, this stole an extra breath from him. "I'm sure, the billionaire is…shocked that a deranged acquaintance…borrowed his jet."

"Young billionaires can be too generous with their friends," the viper agreed.

"It's a problem," Malone agreed. "Will it get bigger?"

"Impossible to know." The viper leaned closer. "I think they were attempting to provoke the aliens, so we can all see the threat and prepare to respond. Given what's coming, risking our only direct source of information was insane."

"What's coming?"

"The sky is falling," he said. "They don't want to ask the translator, but fear will change that soon."

"What?"

"There is a new light in the sky. Two lights, actually. Moving fast. Coming here."

Malone considered what to do with this information.

"Tell your physicist." The shadow stood. "He can get the message to the house. The source of the recent disruption will be eliminated. But anarchists inspire each other. Please be vigilant."

As the other walked away, Malone let his head sag.

"Vigilant," he muttered to the grass, and considered vomiting. He planted one foot, grabbed his knee to steady himself, and rose. The wobble wasn't bad. He fixed his posture by force of will and set off, wondering if little bits of alien were falling in the light rain.

Chapter 12

Estlin didn't remember falling asleep, but his dry mouth suggested that he'd managed a few hours rest. He pinched the grit from the corners of his eyes and was glad Bernie wasn't around, trying to collect the dust in a vial.

"What was that?"

"What?" Estlin rolled over.

"You were dreaming." Harry filled the armchair. His sleeping bag was rolled up on the air mattress by the wall. "It looked like you were working on something in your sleep."

"Nonsense dreams," Estlin said.

"What kind of nonsense?"

"Nonsense."

"The cameras are all keen on dreams," Harry said.

Estlin imagined that someone, somewhere was responsible for watching hours of videos of him sleeping in order to transcribe summaries of each twitch and murmur. He stretched out again to stare at the ceiling. "I dreamt I was a house."

"A house."

"You asked." Estlin tried to pull together the patchwork fragments of the dream. "I was a house. And I was climbing a rockslide." He raised a hand to suggest the incline, but knew it hadn't been a rockslide. It wasn't like clambering over jagged scree, but it wasn't a unified rock face or cliff either, more like the dusty summer scar from a winter avalanche.

"You were a house?" Harry said.

"I was big. I had windows."

"And you were climbing. How does that work?"

"It didn't involve hands and feet," Estlin said. "But it did take effort. That's all I can say."

"Where were you going?"

"Nowhere," Estlin said. "There was a slope, and I was on it."

"Want to offer an interpretation?"

"No."

Harry snorted.

"What?"

"Just nonsense," Harry said. "You need to eat. Wash. Find another shirt. I'll grill something."

Estlin stood, looking upwards with his eyes closed to reduce the number of visual overlays. He wondered if the Waes had woken him or just knew he was awake.

"Cuttlefish?" Harry asked.

"Cuttlefish," Estlin agreed.

"They can wait while you have a slice of toast."

Estlin didn't argue. He wandered into the kitchen and struck a flame on the burner under the kettle. Bomani had someone helping him scrutinize the set of ugly drawings.

"You were on the plane," Estlin said. "The day this started. How long ago was that?"

"I'm Sanford."

"The professor," Estlin said. "Sorry I forgot your name."

"They said you needed someone to talk about carbon fusion. There are actually several different processes. Each one releases different amounts of energy and has a unique set of products. Your sketches are hard to follow, but they suggest a known but improbable process. Actually, all the processes are improbable outside the conditions in a star. But if we can pin this down, I can think about it. I'm already thinking about it, and how one type of folding could have led to another. A steppingstone to the space fold that I think created the pulse, the Rosetta Burst, when they arrived. Can I ask—"

"Not now." Estlin turned off the burner. There wasn't time for tea or fusion reactions. He added a 'sorry' because he didn't intend to be dismissive or cruel. The rumble above them grew obvious. "They are coming down. Bomani, do you have the projector?"

"Projector?"

"The little whatsit."

"Yes," Bomani said. "It's funny. When I put it on the table, it turned into speckled stone."

"It does that," Estlin said, but noted the object's current bright pebble disguise stood out against the table rather than blending in with the surface of the wood. "Are you ready?"

"For what?"

"To show them your Rosetta fold, curve, burst thing."

"I should have thought about this." Bomani turned to Sanford. "Any suggestions?"

"The counterweight lift-bridge is a useful analogy, but they don't have bridges."

"And they live with buoyancy not gravity," Bomani responded. "There is an internal balance with respect to a fluid environment."

"Be glad that their eyes can see above the water," Sanford said. "Imagine where you'd have to start if they'd never seen the moon or the stars?"

"That's a useful thought." Bomani picked up the pebble-like device on the table. "If they were from the depths and did not know the stars above, I would begin another way."

"You can't explain an interstellar transport system without a universe full of stars in the backdrop," Sanford said.

"I can't?" Bomani rolled the pebble between his fingertips. "They know about nets and currents and buckets of water. The first simple description we would think of is a discontinuous jump from one point to another compared to the normal tedium of moving continuously through space. But the fold is not discontinuous. Think about swimming or sinking compared to riding a swift current. Or moving from the past to the future, when they wake up small, with old memories and new eyes."

Estlin realized that his immediate workload had just dropped dramatically. "Go ahead," he waved Bomani toward the door. "I'll be there in a minute."

He opened the fridge.

"What are you looking for?" Harry asked.

"Anything." Estlin failed to find anything, closed the fridge door, and then opened it again.

"Are you being stubborn?" Harry asked.

"Yes."

"Interesting."

Harry joined him at the fridge, placing a hand on the top edge of the door, holding it open. "Sit down. Let's see if you can last five minutes."

Estlin sat at the kitchen table and immediately felt the pressure rise. Harry tossed an apple at him. It was a welcome distraction. Crisp, tart, unexpected. He took a second bite.

"How is it?" Harry asked.

"Tolerable." Estlin's knees were vibrating. "But there is definitely a push."

Estlin took another bite of the apple, but knew he wouldn't get any further. He held the apple and waited.

"Two and a half minutes," Harry said.

"That's enough." Estlin rose and tried to ignore the immediate sense of relief. He gestured for Harry to proceed and paused in the doorway to remember the taste of the apple. "It's not stealing," he told the squirrel on the table. "I left it there for you."

The squirrel remained happy with its daring theft and beat Estlin to the door.

He crossed the porch, skipping down the few stairs to the grass where Bomani faced a tank that held only Spark and Cloud.

"He started without you," Troughton said, no judgement in his voice.

"It's better this way." Estlin blinked as whisps of colour deepened and brightened. He smiled. Spinning to catch Harry's eye, he pointed at the pattern.

Harry shook his head, indicating that the forms Bomani was creating weren't being broadcast to all eyes. Estlin looked more closely, and then looked through the pattern into the tank where he saw rhythmic echoes and fragments of shapes playing across the skin of each cuttlefish.

"What is he doing?" Troughton asked.

"Folding," Estlin said, because Bomani was folding the current generation into the next generation. He was connecting the current generation, to the previous one, and the one before that, and onwards through a sequence of folds across decades, and then centuries. The folds collapsed, twisting into a single fold that directly connected an ancient ancestor to the present. It felt like the first science fiction story ever told to a cuttlefish. New patterns blossomed across their skins as they embraced the story, repeating, examining and retelling it to each other.

The time fold was a fantastic 'what if...' to imagine. The cuttlefish expanded their retelling across the projected display. This was an act of imagination, distinct from the reality of the Waes arrival. To the cuttlefish, the Waes weren't any stranger than the creatures that rose from the ocean's depths or plunged in from the air. They also weren't the first to scoop a swarm into a tank and haul them away.

As new colours were blended into the folding pattern by the cuttlefish, Estlin knew Bomani had what was needed. The imagined time fold could be reimagined into the idea of a spatial fold, and then the details could be handled one at a time.

Bomani turned, or at least his awareness did. The net of ovoids around him were so energized that Estlin could see the space Bomani created for him.

"Swim with me?" Bomani asked.

"Yes," Estlin said and allowed himself the pleasure of joining the conversation with a splash.

———— «» ————

Malone accepted a palmful of painkillers from Pollock. There were five pills in three colours and he swallowed them without question, chasing the collection with juice, hoping the sugar would also help.

"You think we're about to lose a billionaire?" Pollock asked.

"I don't think it was a forewarning," Malone answered. "I think they already won a Darwin Award."

"Let's hope they died quickly and alone," Pollock said.

"Accident or overdose?" Dewey shrugged off Pollock's sharp glance. "It'll make the news."

"An American billionaire." Malone kept his eyes on the table. Everything was a notch too loud. "Young, reckless."

"Hell no," Dewey said. "Did we just get primed for an assassination within our borders?"

"The billionaire isn't important." Malone was glad Dewey didn't say the name that sprang to mind. He needed to drop a lid on the conversation and get to the last hill of words.

"Do you think it was an *official* unofficial contact?" Pollock asked. "The one party or a faction in state security?"

"I don't know." Malone didn't care if the viper was following a directive or improvising. He knew he should be assembling scenarios from each foundation, but instead he wondered if anyone had watched him get his bell rung, and who might be watching and listening now.

"He wants me to tell Sanford," Malone said. "There are two bright objects—in space—accelerating in our direction."

"Bright, as in big?" Pollock asked.

Dewey leaned in. "Invasion size or extinction size?"

Malone was too tired to worry about the crap that everyone would worry about. "What would be the point?"

"Logic is not required," Pollock said.

"Extinction is extreme," Malone answered.

"Well, I don't like us, and I'm human." Pollock shrugged.

"That's hurtful," said Dewey.

"You're tolerable," Pollock answered. "But you're a sniper. You love your scope more than anyone on the wrong side of it."

"Emotion has nothing to do with it," Dewey said.

"Yes, it's all math. E equals M C, click, boom," Pollock said. "And we have evidence that the aliens are good at math."

"Assume that we aren't facing instant annihilation," Malone said. "Fear is fuel. This whole place is about to ignite."

"We'll think on it," Pollock said. "I'll take the next meeting with second lieutenant Rupert. You should crash for a while, unless you want a trip to the med tent first."

"No."

"Dewey, wake him for concussion checks," Pollock said. "We'll wake you if Sanford wanders out from under the tank."

"They owe us the latest video files," Malone said. "Tell the Canadians that we need Sanford for an in-person report now."

———— «» ————

Troughton leaned against the kitchen counter and listened to Sanford and Bomani argue in the adjacent room, though, objectively, they were aggressively agreeing with each other on most points.

"You confused them." Sanford circled the small room, stopping in front of the old clock on the wall.

"They caught the concept," Bomani said.

"Unmuddling space and time will be challenging." Sanford steadied the clock with one hand and pulled down on the chain to lift the pinecone shaped weight.

Watching the long draw on the chain, Troughton realized that the pendulum had nearly wound down.

"I think they got a fairly sharp view of it," Bomani said.

"But the geometry—" Sanford adjusted the other clock weight.

"Is another conversation," Bomani said. "The next conversation. And we have to muddle time and space even more if we want them to understand the dynamic coupling in your bridge."

"What?" Sanford turned to Bomani.

"Space and time are flowing in opposite directions in the transfer node."

"That's impossible," Sanford said. "Space-time is too stiff."

"Too stiff?" Bomani spread the fingers of his raised hands. "You already pretzeled it!"

"That's not how it works."

"We don't know how it works. We only have theories. But it's what your equations suggest." Bomani deftly grabbed the air in front of him, twisting his hands together so his thumbs pointed in opposite directions.

Sanford stared at him. "That gesture. Your hands changed directions six times. Why?"

"It's your knot."

"I need to see it again."

Bomani showed him. "It's missing the—"

"I know. I know." Sanford stood silent and still for several seconds. His eyes widened. "Dynamic coupling and your perfect force."

The argument-agreement moved to the kitchen table, where notebooks opened and pencils were pulled from pockets. Harry was at the stove scrambling a dozen eggs in a cast iron pan. A pot of beans was simmering with three empty cans on the counter next to it. Estlin wandered into the kitchen, filled the kettle and offered to make toast. Troughton recognized that it was time to bring in his team for the collective meal. He turned and found Emmet standing close behind him. The young engineer was a polymath whose technical skills exceeded his social awareness.

"Supplies have arrived," he said.

Troughton followed Emmet to the porch and saw the electric forklift vanish as the tunnel closed behind it. The loaded pallet was blocking the center of the gravel driveway at the edge of the open space.

Saeed came around from the side of the house. "The septic system is in good shape. Mr. Hume gave me the name of the tech who helped with the refurbishment last year, so I have all the details now. I'm still bringing in chemical toilets. The flow of people will increase, and it's not appropriate to have everyone traipsing into the house."

Saeed Musa was the quietest member of Troughton's team, and the most effective at accomplishing whatever needed to be done. He was an engineer with the Canadian Forces disaster response team, officially on leave and out of uniform to serve as part of the first contact support team. While in university, Saeed had won a bronze medal in middleweight wrestling, and Troughton, still in high school, had watched every interview with the humble Olympian.

Saeed pulled the work gloves he kept tucked through his belt. "We should bring those supplies to the house," he told Emmet. "I'll re-use the pallet to send a load out."

"I'll help," Troughton said, joining them. "Lunch will be ready soon. Saeed, please mark off a drop point for future deliveries."

The pallet was loaded with hockey bags. Saeed made quick work of the straps and pulled the first heavy bag off the pallet, letting gravity take it to the ground. The strip of masking tape across the bag declared that it contained 60 kg of sunflower seeds. There was a second bag of sunflower seeds with an added "Please read instructions" label, and the other bags full of hazelnuts, acorns, walnuts and birdseed.

Troughton pulled the first hockey bag across the yard, its wheels dragging whenever the compact earth of the driveway yielded into a sandy rut. He shoved it against the side of the house under the eaves. Saeed followed and they returned to the pallet for more bags.

Emmet was still there. He had an open bucket at his feet, a clear plastic sheet wedged under his arm, and a page in his hand.

Troughton dragged another two bags over to the house and went back for more. Saeed did the same, and then grabbed the empty pallet, ignoring Emmet who appeared to still be studying a single page.

"The sunflower seeds come with instructions," Emmet said.

"Follow them," Troughton answered. "And then come in for lunch."

Troughton stacked the last bag and joined Saeed, who was holding two of the folding chairs from the stack next to the house. Troughton picked up two more chairs.

"He lacks certain instincts," Saeed said, nodding towards Emmet.

"I know," Troughton answered.

——— «» ———

Serese had writer's block. The pen in her hand would not touch the paper as seething, spitting shock and anger blotted out the sympathy she needed for the blank cards before her. She had requested the cards far too soon because she knew decontamination and other restrictions would slow their sending. She put the pen down. Returning the cards to their box, she placed the box on the folder of names and details, and pushed them to the left edge of her desk. She had survived, even thrived, through a series of grim meetings, making necessary decisions. Now, the simplicity of her mismatched chair and desk—the idea of sitting at it opening a card or a file—was threatening to undo her.

"I was wrong," Bernie declared as he entered. "I thought it was amorphous, but its crystalline and amorphous. There are fine alternating layers. Crystalline for the strength and a high-density amorphous structure for compressive and decompressive flow, so the structure doesn't fracture."

"I don't understand," Serese said, though a part of her mind was applying choreography to the words.

"It's like Kevlar. Those fibers have a crystalline core and amorphous shell. Any crack that starts in a crystalline layer terminates when it hits an amorphous layer. And then the hydrogen bonds in the crystalline layer can reform, healing the trillion tiny stress fractures that prevent a spiral break."

"Is it important for me to know this?" Serese asked.

"No. But, yes." Bernie swallowed and sipped a breath. "We got another GISAX. I didn't ask for it. I mean, the last one blew up. I didn't even think to ask for another one, but the science community is really angry. Two of their own were left dead on the roadside. It's a matter of honour. They pried the nearest instrument out of a lab, and the company flew their techs in to take it apart and reassemble it for the security inspection. And they essentially broke it in half to point it at the ice for me."

Bernie was smiling and didn't seem aware of the tears on his face. Serese knew it would be important for her to prepare further cards to convey her condolences and thanks to the team and community that helped send him flying into her office. Bernie caught her shift in attention. He looked at the box on her desk.

"Important part," he said. "Right. Sorry. We were running the first scans. We only got one dataset and the signal vanished, so we shifted the beam and it happened again. And they wedged in a borescope camera to get a magnified look at what was happening. As soon as they turned on the beam again, an ovoid arrived and it ate all the X-rays."

Bernie's smile and fingers opened in an expression that said, "*See. Very important.*"

"I don't understand," Serese said.

"That's how this whole thing works," Bernie waved at the sky. "I mean I knew it, but seeing it is something else. The ability to efficiently transform and move energy around—capturing it and releasing or transmitting it on a microscale, but in a way that is directed and reactive and has macroscale results."

"Bernie, please."

"Everything is waves—X-rays, visible light, the heat from your body radiating in the infrared," Bernie said. "The ovoids can absorb these waves, store the energy, transform it and re-release it. They can individually capture and release X-rays or work together to capture and create microwaves. But waves are energy. An ovoid can transmit power to other ovoids, but if it releases energy at a wavelength water absorbs, it can melt and move ice."

Bernie bounced in place. "I'm saying that the waetapu never had to build a fire to keep warm. Technology that we build around a central power cell, they would approach from an entirely different angle. Completely distributed."

"That's important," Serese agreed. "What's next?"

"We keep learning," Bernie said. "We got an ovoid under the X-ray beam, but it's absorbing the X-rays instead of scattering them. The techs are pulling the filters out of the instrument to hit it with the bremsstrahlung—the broad band X-rays, not just peak wavelengths."

"What do you need?" Serese asked.

"Nothing," Bernie said. "Nothing. I just came... I came because it's exciting."

"I want tea," Serese said. "Please join me and share all of that again."

Chapter 13

The meal on the stove was warm and waiting, the burners off. Troughton watched Harry stack plates and cutlery on the counter as the group gathered. It made him wish for music because the diverse mix of people in the rustic kitchen reminded him of house parties in Toronto. The notebooks had been cleared from the table, and there was room for the two folding chairs he carried. He set them down, and the overhead lamp above the table swayed. As he registered the movement and what it might be, the entire house jerked sharply.

Troughton dropped onto the vibrating floorboards and pulled himself under the kitchen table. He grabbed the table leg as it started to dance and knew the old structure would either flex through the shake or burst into a million splinters. He thought of Matteo, and the poem left pinned to their fridge the morning he flew out for deployment. Bomani scrambled under the table from the opposite side, wrapping his arms around his head, elbows out.

The rolls had a rapid frequency, but the intensity didn't build. The house creaked and shed dust. The plates hit the floor and fractured. And then it stopped. Troughton silently counted seconds.

Bomani shifted to look at him. "Earthquake?" he asked.

"Felt like a quake," Troughton replied. He hoped it was an earthquake because he didn't want to guess what it would feel like if the Waes' dome had shielded them from a missile attack. Troughton lost count of the seconds passing, but decided it was time to move.

"Any injuries?"

Estlin, Sanford, Adya, Bomani, Harry and Saeed sounded off in a smattering of "No's".

Emmet appeared in the doorway. "Was that an earthquake?"

"Everyone outside now!" Troughton ordered.

He got to his feet and watched Bomani gather his notebook and drawings. Adya had the emergency backpack. Troughton followed Estlin out the door, grabbing the climbing harnesses from the hooks on the wall of the entranceway. The team was waiting, gathered a few feet from the house.

"Where are the Waes?" Troughton asked.

"The tree," Estlin said.

"No climbing. We only go up if we have to," he said. "Was it them?"

"I don't know."

"That was close." Troughton knew quakes from a year in Tokyo. The shimmy had immediately followed the first jerk— without any delay or rolling of the earth. "It had to be them."

"Unless it was us," Saeed said.

"It was them," Estlin said.

Troughton could imagine the threat response this would generate. "You have to tell them we are terrified of earthquakes. Tell them that earthquakes make the things we build collapse and crush us. Tell them that inducing earthquakes near a supervolcano, doesn't just alarm you. It alarms everyone around the world."

Troughton tried not to think of the catastrophic potential of destabilizing the Yellowstone caldera. He turned to the rest of his team. "Emmet, run the passage now. Stop at the last marker and hope you meet someone coming in... otherwise, baby steps and back up if the air smells wrong. We have no injuries. Report that and stay out there unless you are ordered to return. Saeed, inspect the generator, batteries, fuel and power lines, and then check the house. Exterior structure only. Sanford, sit next to the big red button. If an aftershock creates any need for assistance, punch it. Bomani, set up a table next to Sanford. Keep working."

"Do you think the load points for the tank shifted the earth?" Bomani asked. "There's a lot of weight above us."

"We'll ask," Troughton said. "Everyone stays out of the house. If you left something important inside, I'm telling you it's not that important."

He wondered if the beans were salvageable or if the pot had filled with dust and debris from the rafters. He looked towards the house. A hint of movement made him brace for another shake, but all was steady. The shifting shadow revealed itself to be the rat snake emerging from under the deck. Conversation died away as everyone watched the snake slither towards them and then glide onwards to the right edge of the driveway. The ice rumbled, lifting into a low corridor to let it pass.

Emmet looked at them in question.

"Go," Troughton said. "Tell them I'll send another runner out when we have more information."

He turned his attention to Estlin and found that he was still following the snake. "What?"

"Nothing."

"What did it say?"

"Loosely translated: *Fuck this noise.*" Estlin looked off to the driveway again. "I agree."

"Sorry. You have a job to do." Troughton kept one climbing harness and passed the rest of the tangle to Adya. She dropped all but one and prepared it for Estlin.

"Don't climb unless you have to," Troughton repeated himself, as he tightened the straps on his harness. "And don't make any mistakes when talking about earthquakes and volcanoes."

Adya stepped into the third harness, shortening all the straps to fit her slight frame.

Harry dismissively pushed the remaining two harnesses around with the toe of his shoe. "Don't climb."

Troughton agreed, but he wanted Estlin in the harness. He wanted a tether. He wanted to set the rules: no wandering, no running away. The full scale of the responsibility he'd accepted hit him.

"Lyndie, stop." Harry stepped between Estlin and the tree. "Did you have any warning that was coming? A hint you couldn't recognize until now?"

"Nothing."

Troughton considered evacuating Sanford and Bomani. He glanced at Adya. She looked at him as though she could see his mind was scattering. She lifted her chin and with a flick of her eyes she directed his attention to Estlin.

"Asking or telling?" Harry demanded.

"Asking," Estlin answered.

"That's right, questions first," Harry said. "What's the question?"

It's obvious, isn't it? Troughton barely held back the words.

Estlin looked at him, his expression distant and calm. "No, it's not."

Adya looked up into the branches. "They're already here, aren't they?"

"Closer," Estlin said.

Troughton spun around and found the Waes in the lowest branches, closer to the ground than he'd ever seen them.

Harry stepped closer to Estlin. "Are you asking them about actions or intentions?"

"They're the same colour, Harry." Estlin said. "I'll give them an empty box. They'll fill it. They can fill boxes and boxes. They don't get to break my house."

Or the planet, Troughton thought.

"It's safer if I start with a smaller question," Estlin said. "A local question."

"I agree." Troughton was glad to have his voice again, but from the glaze of Estlin's eyes his approval was barely needed. "Cameras."

Adya righted the fallen tripod nearest her. The other cameras surrounding them were still standing, red lights shining, though some of them had shimmied into different positions. Troughton checked the camera on his lanyard. He heard Estlin's breath hitch, and then rasp from his lungs as though he'd been punched.

Harry leapt forward and put his body between Estlin and ground, grabbing the straps of his harness. He grunted as Estlin's weight hit him, controlling the drop, rolling back and then over, pushing his friend onto the ground beside him. "Fuck."

Adya stepped in, crouching to place her fingers on his wrist. Troughton joined her, reaching out to assist, but stopped short of touching Estlin.

"He's breathing." Adya repositioned Estlin's limp arms, rolling him into a recovery position. "Pulse is steady."

"What happened?" Troughton asked Harry.

Adya tapped Troughton's hand, pointing with her thumb. Both Waes were on the ground, close and creeping forward, their spikes bristling. They were too close, and Troughton was on his knees, leaning over Estlin, off balance.

"Hie!" Harry was on his feet and blocking. "Get back in the tree. Climb to the sky."

Yellow-eyes rose on its hind legs, standing still as a statue as orange-eyes slowly backed away. It appeared to transform into a shambling raccoon, though the mask was unconvincing given the other alien standing in plain view. As it climbed backwards into the tree, its partner leapt into the canopy with shocking velocity and strength.

Harry crouched next to Adya. "They've done this before. They should fucking know better now. Last time, he was only out for a few seconds. It hurt him, but it didn't hurt him."

"Did he wake spontaneously?" she asked.

"I pinched him," Harry answered. "Want me to—"

Adya had Estlin's hand. She pinched the skin between his thumb and index finger.

Estlin's fingers twitched. He pulled his hand free and shifted his forearm to cover his closed eyes. "That was stupid."

He took a tightly controlled breath, lifted his head slightly, and flinched. "I'm going to lie here for a minute."

"Good idea," Adya said. "Can you show me your pupils first?"

Estlin lowered his arm and squinted at her. Troughton saw his pupils respond to the light.

"Thank you." She sat back to address Harry. "Critical questions only. As soon as he's sitting up, I get five minutes for a concussion assessment."

"Seems like they kicked you in the head again." Harry pointed at a trace of blood on the corner of Estlin's lips. "Was that like last time?"

"My mistake." Estlin hooked a finger into his mouth, dragging it along the inside of his cheek, checking the damage his teeth had done.

"Their mistake," Harry said.

"My mistake. The only scale they had was my house."
He covered his eyes again. "I imagined my house shaking.
I turned my house into big empty box with clear sides, and
then I opened the lid."

"That was the plan." Harry's tone was encouraging. "It
was a good starting point."

"Fuck you." Estlin let his arm drop away from his eyes.
"How much information do you keep in your cranium?"

Troughton considered one and half liters of folded grey
matter against the volume of a house.

Estlin propped himself up. "They compressed everything
they siphoned from Yidge into a marble with room to spare.
Offering them a big glass box to fill is asking for a stroke.
That was stupid. I should have imagined a tiny box. A grain
of rice. A grain of sand. A thread of information slowly
spooling. I asked them to drop a house on my head."

"It's still their mistake," Harry said. "Not yours."

"Will you let Dr. Chandran assess you?" Troughton
asked. "Harry and I will give you some space."

He was glad when Harry nodded in agreement.

"Let the Doc do her job." Harry patted Estlin's shoulder
and walked away.

Troughton followed Harry across the yard. "We can get a
couple of chairs. What else will he need?"

"A glass of water to wash down whatever pill the doctor
offers," Harry said. "Time for the pills to kick in."

"What happened?"

"You heard. Information overload," Harry answered. "He
asked. They answered."

"Is he going to have a pile of information for us when his
head stops spinning?"

"I doubt it," Harry said. "When he got zapped in Wellington,
it was like a short circuit. He didn't get to keep any of it. This was
a different kind of question, but I'll bet that he either has nothing
or not enough to trust. He was seconds into it when he dropped."

"I was fiddling with the damn cameras," Troughton said.

"Don't kick yourself too hard. I was barely fast enough to
keep him from eating dirt." Harry picked up a pair of folding

chairs and then put them down again. "He risks that every time. And we pretend he has a choice."

"Should I get Bomani to try with the stone?" Troughton realized the communication device was likely still in the house.

"I think that would be a really bad idea," Harry responded.

Troughton agreed but he couldn't think of any other options. "We need to know what that was." He knew every measurement and model possible would be applied to the quake and none of them would decrease the level of alarm. The energy release would be discussed on the scale used for atomic bombs.

"Don't worry," Harry said. "In a few minutes, Lyndie will be back on his feet. He'll pretend he has a choice and he will volunteer."

Troughton realized how hard and fast he'd pushed Estlin after the shake when no push was necessary. He reconsidered his role.

Saeed joined them. "No critical damage. I've shut off the gas and water for the moment. I'd like to go into the house."

"Can I help?" Harry asked. "I could use a job." He nodded over to where Estlin was now walking slowly with Adya. "Do you think Lyndie will need me in the next twenty minutes?"

"No." Troughton picked up the folding chairs. "Please inspect the house."

《 》

The shaking stopped. Bernie uncurled, releasing his grip on his head. Serese was standing over him in her usual, composed and stable stance. She placed her teacup on the nearest table as others rose and scattered off to their duties.

"Your hand is bleeding again," she said.

Bernie found a splash of red seeping through the gauze wrapping his palm. He'd lost his balance on the first jerk of the ground and had tried to grab the corner of the table on the way down. "What happened?"

"We're going to find out."

"Okay," Bernie agreed. "Do you think they are—"

He dismissed the thought. The waetapu's structure was strong and elegant down to the molecular level. He didn't want to reimagine the earlier bomb as a prelude to a greater assault.

The thought snapped at him again because humans were stupid, and he knew that one of his worst-case scenerios could pound the earth that hard. If a deliberate zap of interference, like the one used in Samoa, had disrupted the Waes' array of ovoids, the center of the structure could have collapsed, crushing the house and everyone in it. He didn't want to believe it or speak it.

"I need the latest satellite images."

"I'm sending you to the house to deliver information to our team."

Shit! Bernie thought, because he didn't want to swear in front of Serese.

"If that was the Waes, I need you to figure out what they did and how they did it."

Shit! Shit! Bernie thought, both palms damp with sweat.

"Okay?" Serese asked.

"Okay." Bernie folded his hands together, using his thumb to apply a painful level of pressure to the scrape across his palm because he needed it to stop bleeding.

"We're going to the staging area," Serese said. "Shout requests at people along the way."

She took off at a jog.

Bernie scampered to keep up, and then stopped himself to called across the tent to his closest colleague. "Paik! Satellite images. Please! Bring them to the gate."

———— «» ————

Bomani sat in the dust next to the array of lights with a notebook braced against his knees. Sanford was sitting in a chair next to the control bank and its big red button.

A squirrel bolted out of the house, carrying an entire slice of toast and closely pursued by two other squirrels. The toast edge hit a tuft of grass and barrel-rolled the squirrel as it fractured. The squirrel continued at full tilt with the remaining half of its bounty while the others battled over the portion left behind. Another squirrel scrabble broke out on the porch.

"What am I working on?" Bomani asked.

"We're lucky the house didn't fall on us." Sanford shifted in the chair.

"We're lucky to be here." Bomani watched Estlin circuit the yard, walking with Adya Chandran, staying away from the tree. The shifting earth was one more risk wedged into a pile of risks—not to be ignored, just part of a vast equation that already contained more improbability than probability.

"Excuse me," he said, and left to join Estlin and the doctor. He exchanged a glance with Adya, seeking and receiving permission to walk with them. Her hijab was the gentle green of growing things with a feathery pattern in yellows and blues along the edge.

Estlin had his head tipped forward, half-closed eyes focused on the ground.

"My friend, I saw you stumble," he said to Estlin. "How are you?"

Estlin gave him a glance, dismissing a question that Bomani knew had been asked too many times.

"I'll be fine," Estlin said.

"Good," Bomani said. "I'm glad your house didn't fall down."

Estlin stopped and looked at him. Bomani had seen the shine of tears held in Estlin's eyes before and didn't know if what he was seeing was pain, emotion or alien influence.

"I've had some strange dreams," Estlin said. "It's easy to think that everything is about the Waes, but I think my dreams are about losing the house, because I know I've already lost it."

"Why do you say that?" Bomani asked.

"It's not really mine now," Estlin said. "If the Waes left tomorrow, this would still be the first house they visited."

For all the uncertainty the aliens generated, Bomani couldn't find a shred of probability that this perfect place would remain Estlin's home.

"I inherited this place from an uncle," Estlin said. "I don't remember him, but we must have met when I was a child. He was a recluse. I think he may have had a problem like mine. Not squirrels. But some kind of trouble."

Estlin resumed his walk, and Bomani followed with Adya.

"When I signed the papers, I knew I wouldn't be able to keep it," Estlin said. "I only had a photo and the surveyors map. I didn't know what shape the house was in or how quickly the property taxes would wipe me out. It was always temporary. It just felt different. I like this house. They do not get to knock it off its foundation." Estlin changed their collective direction, putting them on a path to the tree. "Bomani, I could use some help."

"It's why I'm here."

"I just made a stupid mistake," Estlin said.

Bomani tightened his grip on his notebook. "Mistakes can be very informative."

"I knew right away what I'd done wrong," Estlin said. "And now I'm wasting time."

Bomani looked to Adya for a medical opinion. She took in a long deep breath with a gesture inviting Bomani to slow down and notice the pace of his own pulse.

"We have time," Bomani said.

Harry emerged through the open door of the house. He came straight down the steps and across the yard, carrying the speckled stone pinched between his thumb and first finger. Bomani realized he had forgotten it in the house and reached out, thankful to have the needed object.

"How can I help?"

"I need a new question," Estlin said.

"Algebraic, geometric or statistical?" Bomani asked.

"Oh, I'm wrong." Estlin's fingertips tapped together. "I'm trying to think of a way to stitch bits of geometry into volcanic pressure. But this is about probability."

"The space between impossibility and certainty." Bomani rolled the speckled stone between his fingers and felt it warm to his touch. "There is an equation for expectation."

"Show me," Estlin said. "We have time."

Chapter 14

The jagged crack was four to six inches wide with finer branches splitting from its edges. It crossed the path on a near perpendicular track. Bernie pulled a tall blade of grass from the edge of the path, fed it down the crack and met no resistance. He figured the deep black would swallow a flashlight beam. What he really needed was a plumber's scope.

He checked the number on the marker behind him and it indicated that the crack crossed the midpoint of the long driveway. It felt different being alone in the corridor. The curving white surface over his head hummed as it waited for him to move. He hummed back, and wished that he'd listened more carefully on previous trips instead of expounding on random things and arguing with Ulz. He wondered how many steps behind Ulz he'd been when the detonation occurred. There must be an equation for it—for the decay of explosive force, the distance between death and a smattering of scrapes. He had a new bruise on his chin, which he found in the mirror in the staging tent. Serese had caught him staring at it and gently encouraged him onwards.

The camera hanging from his neck was dedicating twenty-four frames to every second that passed. It had watched him play with the blade of grass. He considered adding some analytical commentary, but didn't want the moment transcribed for even greater scrutiny. He stepped over the crack and quickened his pace, grateful when the fog before him dissipated to reveal the house.

Harry, Troughton and Saeed were waiting, and he closed the final distance as the ice wall rumbled down behind him. The hug was unexpected and more affection than Bernie had ever received from Harry. The joints in his back and shoulder popped audibly, and Harry immediately released him.

"I heard you got a little blown up," he said.

"A little," Bernie admitted.

"How are things out there?"

"Scary?" Bernie swallowed nervous laughter. "The quake startled everyone. The seismologists are arguing about the magnitude because it was a surface event. So, alien weirdness, not a normal quake, about 6 on the Richter scale, and higher on the other scale.

"There's a break in the earth midway up the path. It's about this wide, like a crack in lake ice. I think someone should follow it. They might end up popping out somewhere on the perimeter, but I think they'll end up on a circuit that will bring them back to the driveway." Bernie swept his finger around, pointing away and then through himself, drawing a ring that included everything around them. "I think it might be a very interesting crack."

"That is interesting," Saeed agreed.

"Want to take a look?" Troughton asked.

Saeed nodded. "I'll take our video of the shake and let them know that the house is intact."

"Tell them that Estlin tried to get a quick answer," Troughton said.

"They'll want your footage of the knock down."

Troughton pulled the card from the camera hanging from his lanyard and handed it off, replacing it with one from his pocket. "Can you be back in two hours to take out our next report?"

"Sure. Stay safe." Saeed left them, waving over to Adya and gesturing his request by lifting the camera hanging from his neck.

"Knock down?" Bernie asked.

"Same as Wellington," Harry said. "When he asked the wrong thing and took a blast to the brain."

"He's okay now?" Bernie looked across the yard. Estlin and Bomani had a pair of lawn chairs on the grass in front of the porch and were surrounded by enthralled squirrels.

"He's shiny," Harry said.

——— «» ———

Estlin caught himself slipping deeper into the chair. He had drifted into the furry collective. Their attention wasn't love. It wasn't even about him. It was like a place with the perfect temperature, the perfect light, and the softness of a den.

"Are you broadcasting?" Bomani asked.

"No more than usual," Estlin said.

"They seem particularly attentive."

"They like your equations."

"Really?" Bomani looked at the furry faces around them.

"No."

"And you?"

"I have enough." Estlin pried himself out of the lawn chair. "You have the Waes' widget and know how to start. You've spent enough time trying to teach me. It'll sink in as you go through it again."

"I'm not climbing the tree."

Estlin was still wearing the climbing harness, one thumb unconsciously hooked in the belay loop. "We're close enough. No climbing required. Want to lie under the branches? Harry will be happier if my head is on the ground."

"That should be safe." Bomani closed his notebook, his pencil folded into it, marking the current page. "Whatever that shake was, they wouldn't harm the tree."

"Hm." Estlin hadn't thought of the potential root damage. The earth around the tree appeared to be undisturbed. He kicked at a tuft of grass with his toes and found it to be solidly anchored.

"It's not just precision," Bomani said. "It's attentiveness."

Estlin entered the shade of the beech tree, chose a spot and stretched out. The ground found the knots in his neck and shoulders. He shifted, trying to find a comfortable position.

Bomani sat next to him and leaned against a low-slung branch. "They didn't break your house."

"True." It was funny that, under the circumstances, this could be considered a deliberate kindness.

"The squirrels really do love you."

The scurry of squirrels had moved with him, taking to the low branches to surround them. *It's not love*, he thought.

But whatever the attraction, it was enough to quell their territorial instincts most of the time.

"You're short on words." Bomani had Yidge's stone-that-wasn't-a-stone between his fingertips. "What do you see?"

Nothing, Estlin thought. He looked up at the leaves. *Everything.*

"Yidge?" As soon as he spoke her name, she was standing over him. "Why does the tree look so... brilliant?"

"It always looks that way," she said.

Estlin realized that light from beyond the visible spectrum was adding layers of astonishing clarity to the branches above him. "Not to me."

"Well, that's true." Yidge smiled. "If I told you that the network of ovoids on your eyes were feeding your optic nerve a few extra signals, would it ruin the magic?"

"No."

"It's a gift. Enjoy it."

"So, they're sorry?" Estlin knew that was the wrong word. The Waes were not sorrowful creatures.

Yidge crouched next to him or at least her image did. "How's your headache?"

"Better." Estlin didn't think there could be a connection. Extra colours should create headaches, not fix them, and he'd taken the pills offered earlier.

"Relaxation helps," she said.

He remembered that it had been her job to be helpful. She'd brought him a toothbrush. She'd brought him a shirt.

"Yidge." Estlin's vision blurred. "I'm sorry you died."

"You should have a nap," she said. "Leave this to Bomani."

"Okay," Estlin said.

It shouldn't be okay, Estlin thought. But as soon as he said it was okay, it was okay very quickly.

———— «◊» ————

Bomani considered whether he should ask the others before attempting a solo conversation with the Waes. Estlin was sleeping soundly. It was needed sleep, even if the transition was unnaturally quick. He did not want to initiate a discussion that would result in someone prodding Estlin awake to confirm that he agreed with the change of plans.

The others had set their chairs in a row at the edge of the canopy, as though waiting for a parade. They were discussing the situation at a stage whisper.

"It shouldn't have surprised them, but I think it did," Harry said. "The Waes immediately dropped out of the tree."

"Did they stridulate?" Bernie asked.

"That's a fancy word." Troughton had the seat on Bernie's other side.

"I just learned it," Bernie said. "They can shriek by scraping their spines together, like bugs, really big bugs."

"I haven't seen that footage," Troughton said.

"There's no footage from Wellington," Bernie said. "The cameras were out. But I have an audio recording."

"They were silent," Harry said. "No shrieking."

"No, right, of course," Bernie said. "Whether it's a defensive display or an alarm call, there would be no point. I mean, they're the ones that caused the problem."

"He's asleep," Bomani said, so quietly that only Adya heard him.

She nodded once. Yidge also gave him a nod of encouragement, and then faded away. The Waes remained high in the branches, motionless, but visible due to their distinctive colour.

Bomani closed his eyes and closed his hand around the stone. He tried not to think about supervolcanos. He wanted to keep it as small as one house and one expectation. Would the house remain still or would it shake again?

He imagined a basic finite state machine, a coin operated turnstile. A system with only two states, gate locked and gate open. His attempt to project this intangible idea wavered, like he was flowing forward and backward between fragments of the idea, even as he was trying to visualize each separate element. Bomani opened the notebook. He knew his pencil could help him and that Estlin would appreciate the record. He started with two states and two inputs. Transitions were either forbidden or guaranteed. Pushing against the locked gate did nothing. And if the gate was unlocked, adding a coin did nothing.

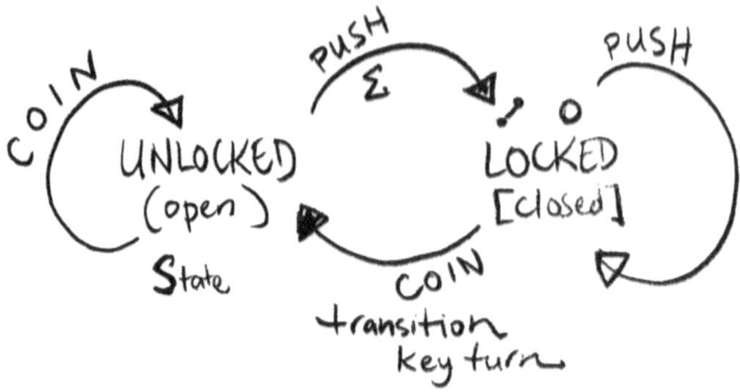

The right action had to meet the right state. Locked gate, apply coin to unlock the gate. Open gate, apply push and re-lock the gate. The little system with its pairs of states, triggers and transitions didn't require text, and it didn't require an introduction to turnstiles used by bipeds who had also invented tickets and train stations.

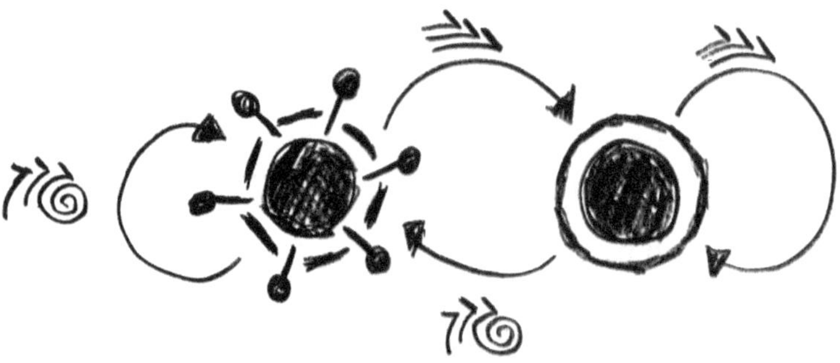

This was a first step towards the real question. What state was the house in and what state might it transition to next?

Bomani created a Markov chain with earthquake-driven transitions and transition probabilities that could be tuned from improbable to unstoppable. The house could shake and return to stillness, but if it was shaken to the point of collapse it would remain a pile of kindling with no transition path back to a standing structure.

Whether or not the Waes appreciated his concern, they liked his diagram. Every state, transition and trigger sprang to life simultaneously, the animation diminishing stepwise until it was reduced to one state, the other arrows and elements fading away, leaving a simple, clear message.

The house would not shake again.

Bomani absorbed this reassurance.

The Waes shifted from the mundane "house collapse" conversation to a bright and shining question of greater interest — the likelihood that a leaf would fall from the tree. The leaf question depended on many factors, sunshine and rain, day length, temperature, soil and wind. The animation included trigger probabilities and transition durations. The single leaf became thousands of leaves, patterns flowing and breaking until it appeared that what happened every autumn would not happen at all.

The squirrels were the next topic. Squirrels sleeping, waking, walking, sniffing, scratching, eating, drinking, running, climbing, jumping, resting, and hibernating. The Waes presented actions as states of squirrelness—the location changes associated with running and jumping were immaterial. Each squirrel-state was connected to numerous other states, and there were even more triggers for transitions. The diagram rapidly expanded into three dimensions like a popcorn kernel bursting off the page. Bomani's pencil couldn't keep up.

The horde of squirrels became a single squirrel sprawled on a branch, a patch of lichen beneath its palm. The story-state of the lichen should have been simple, but the lichen had more states of being than the squirrel—more modes of growth and reproduction, and limitless interdependencies. It had a host (tree) and was a host (micro-animals), and the lifespan of the lichen was greater than the leaf or the squirrel, creating a vast, incomprehensible, colourful scheme.

The colours faded and the Waes returned to the sketch of the house cycling in its lifeless stillness, which now appeared to be so simple as to be almost a lie because, in every moment, everything was moving on multiple axes and multiple scales. A new image emerged and quickly swooped back and forth across the page to create another beautiful closed loop.

"You dropped your pencil," Estlin said.

Bomani blinked and found his fingertips pressed against an empty page. "You're awake."

Estlin propped himself up with his arm, and then shifted into a sitting position. "What did I miss?"

"Not much." Bomani found his pencil on the ground and picked it up. "Your house isn't going to shake again."

"Good."

"I got that answer quickly." The tip of Bomani's pencil was broken—or had it worn down? He flipped through the pages of the notebook to where the drawings declined into bare scratches with the occasional scrape of grey. "And then things went off on a tangent."

"That happens," Estlin said. "What came up?"

Bomani dug the metal pencil sharpener from his pocket and put it to work. "Squirrels and lichen. But it came around to the tree and house in the end. How long does lichen live?"

"Forever," Estlin answered. "Not forever. It can burn. The squirrels will eat it if they get hungry enough. But it doesn't age."

"That's interesting. I've never thought about that."

"What did you draw?"

Bomani flipped to a pair of pages where he knew his broken pencil had climbed up and down an infinite number of branches. He knew it was the tree, dwarfing the house that was beneath-behind-beside-within it, and he knew that every branch his pencil had failed to draw represented more than a woody limb of the tree.

"I don't know. I drew a lot. But at the end, the final image felt like a correction or clarification." Bomani turned the page again and used the side of the pencil lead to lightly shade across the imprints on the final blank page. "At first, I thought it was because I had only drawn the house and not the tree and house together." Shading across the simpler, final drawing, revealed the fragmented light inverse of the curves, but it was enough to bring the image rushing back to his mind. He redrew it and showed Estlin.

"What's that?"

"I don't know," Bomani said. "Everything and nothing. I couldn't capture it. There was a scale problem. But this was the critical part of their correction. It was clear that they weren't going to rattle your house again, but representing this as stillness was incorrect." He returned to the first drawings. "It could just be that on the grander solar-scale and on the finer molecular-scale, everything is moving." Bomani looked at the fuzzy circles-in-circles on the page, which failed to capture the house and the tree and the squirrels and the lichen and everything.

"Did you find out why they rattled us?" Estlin asked.

"No." The communication had veered so completely that Bomani had lost all the other questions he and Estlin had discussed. "Sorry. Do you want to try asking now?"

"Not really," Estlin said. "And there's no time. Spark and Cloud are on their way down."

"When?"

"Now."

"Now?" Bomani had an idea on how to start the next conversation with the cuttlefish, but he hadn't discussed any of the details with Sanford.

"Soon." Estlin looked over to their audience in the row of chairs. "Where did they get sandwiches?"

"We should eat." Bomani stood, extending his hand to help pull Estlin to his feet.

"Saeed brought lunch." Harry pointed at the open bag of sandwiches and snacks. "What's the verdict?"

"The house won't shake again," Estlin said. "And the cuttlefish are on their way."

"Details, please." Troughton was standing with Saeed, who was swapping out the battery and memory card on the nearest camera.

"Bomani, details?" Estlin said. "I have none."

"Wait," Troughton said. "Why?"

"He slept," Bomani answered.

"You had a nap?" Harry asked.

"Sort of," Estlin said. "The Waes know how to push the off button."

Bomani chose a sandwich. "I thought they were fixing your headache."

"It is better," Estlin answered. "Bomani had a good visit with them. He has drawings."

"Dr. Manda." Saeed stepped forward. "May I photograph the pages of your notebook?"

"Not yet." Bomani changed his mind and offered the book. "Go ahead. But it won't make sense to anyone without more notes, and I'll have to redraw some of them. My pencil broke and I didn't notice." Bomani looked up to where the ice structure was simultaneously opening a vaulted channel to the sky and lowering the pod of water that formed in the process. He grabbed a sandwich. "Sanford! I have questions."

The physicist responded to the call, abandoning his post by the big red button. He pointed at the transforming structure above them. "That's remarkable."

"Are they coming down for another lesson on the Rosetta Burst?" Bomani asked.

"Yes." Estlin was pouring water into an empty container. He put it on the ground for the thirstiest squirrels.

"I want to start again with gravity and the structure of stars," Bomani said. "Sanford, how big is the sun relative to the moon? I only need rough numbers for scale."

"Volume or mass?" Sanford asked.

"Mass," Bomani answered.

"About 27 million times," Sanford responded. "The volume difference is greater, maybe 65 million times. The hydrogen plasma at the surface of the sun has an incredibly low density, like the air at the limit of our atmosphere. The density increases ten or twelve orders of magnitude from the surface to the core. The moon's just a rock—no atmosphere, no extreme density change—but on average the moon has higher density than the sun. It's just one of those weird true things."

"Cuttlebone has a density of about 0.6 grams per cubic centimeter." Bernie was hunched in a nearby chair with a sandwich in hand. "If you want a physically intuitive density scale for the cuttlefish, compare water to the lightest part within them, the porous, air-filled bone they used for lift, one compared to point six."

"And the core of the sun is 160," Sanford added.

"Thank you." As Bomani ate, his literal visualizations were replaced by the Malawian flag, with its red rising sun, follow by flashes of bright chitenge. He imagined fabric printed with brilliant colours, patterns that he could create, transform, overlay, merge, and fold.

Chapter 15

Bright sunlight illuminated bands of blue in the wall of ice as the tank of cuttlefish slid down. Troughton loved the colour, associating it with the dense, ancient ice of glaciers. The walls of the smaller tank were opaque. He knew they would clear by the time it touched down, but for the moment there was no way to tell how many occupants the tank carried.

Troughton was glad that Saeed was back. He had an expeditionary spirit, alert to what was needed for the team to collectively achieve what was required, however well- or ill-defined the objective of any given day. There was a hefty red bag at his feet, the white lettering declaring it to be an EMT Trauma First Aid Kit.

"What's this?" Troughton asked.

"Present for Adya," Saeed said. "Given the shake, she's doubling the first aid kit we have on-site. I prioritized carrying it in. The Governor General wants you to consider reducing the number of people here."

"What's your opinion?" Troughton said.

"We're already a skeleton crew," Saeed answered. "Nothing's changed for me. Dr. Chandran is very committed, but deserves a conversation with you. Emmet's out. That's an acceptable reduction. Harry's not going anywhere. Bernie's a lateral thinker. If he's inclined to stay, I'd fight to keep him. The Americans have decided to pull Sanford out. Whatever their reason, there's no point arguing."

"And Bomani?"

"Essential," Saeed said. "You won't find another with his mix of expertise, and yet..."

"What's up?" Troughton asked.

"The earth cracked. They want to reduce our numbers. But I'm told they've prioritized getting a Canadian with Bomani's skills in here. They have a short list."

"Odd priority." Troughton didn't actually find it odd. All high-level committees had at least one embedded sociopath ready to find a target to devalue. Given that his team was full of targets, it was a fucking cliché to find Bomani, from the heart of Africa, at the top of the list. Such problems always required an active response. "How good are your drawing skills?"

"Acceptable," Saeed answered.

"We need to keep the numbers down, but we also need to make sure that those in critical roles have support and back-up," Troughton said. "I'd like you to shadow Bomani. Adya and I will have to cover some of your other jobs. When things have stabilized, we'll discuss whether we need to backfill your position."

"I'd like to follow-up on the house inspection first," Saeed said. "I've got a checklist and a gas leak detector."

"Do that now," Troughton said. "I'll keep an eye on this conversation, and then I'll go out with Sanford. While I deliver the latest recordings, I want you to dig into Bomani's notebook. Copy the diagrams. Question them. Show what you can bring to it."

Saeed acknowledged this with a nod, pulled his work gloves from his belt and set off to the house. The creaks and thrums of the shifting ice structure ended as the tank settled above the grass. Its walls were now clear and revealed two cuttlefish and their pair of swimming translators. The open column above it admitted a beam of direct sunlight as Estlin and Bomani stepped forward.

———— ‹‹ ›› ————

Estlin dove after Bomani and the cuttlefish, swimming towards the horizon moon with easy, effortless strokes. They passed through the hazy deep-blue threshold of air and into the black, star-filled sky, following a current of light until the orb filled their eyes. Splashing into the fine grey sand and heaps of shining broken shell, he twisted to swim onwards, pursuing the brightness back to its distant source. From Earth to moon to sun, Bomani led them, diving into the core of the star, where the heat and pressure folded and fused hydrogen, converting shavings of mass into energy.

The sun was a kinetic collage of billowing bright fabrics. Within the chaos, compatible patterns found each other and rippled in harmony. The patterns merged and brightened, the transformations illuminating the surrounding mass of printed swatches, igniting new harmonies.

The colour storm pushed Estlin to the verge of laughter. Bomani caught him by the wrist and pulled, directing him back to the surface. They swam through the aura, the cuttlefish bursting ahead, spiraling around Bomani. They jetted across the solar system, swiftly shifting from quantum folds to the expanse of a massive space fold. It rested like a quiescent cuttlefish half-buried in the sand of a starfield. It breathed like a living thing, slowly growing, waiting with patient stillness, holding, until it burst with light while, within its core, mass moved without moving. Bomani pulled them into the center of the fold. The humour and wonder of the journey froze away, overwhelmed by a reaction that scratched like an anxiety attack. Estlin couldn't feel the ground beneath his feet. He couldn't feel his hands clenching. He was trapped in an impossible, distant place, with lungs too small to breathe, his heart in an inefficient stutter, its rhythm broken. The cuttlefish were with him, ready to ink and run.

"Bomani, stop." Estlin's eyes were full of water, blurring his view of the ground. The air tasted thin. "Stop. You can retell when we are less rapid brightness." He pressed his fingers to his lips. The words were wrong and yet they were absolutely correct. His brain wasn't diving, he could only find wrong words.

"I understand," Bomani said.

Estlin gestured his thanks. Spark and Cloud settled, brightness rising and fading in slow waves across their backs, their bellies pale. Estlin stepped back and lost his footing, as though he'd gone off a curb. He fell into Bomani, but was solidly caught, and placed back on the even earth. A clear, crystal filigree extended around the tank and lifted it upwards. The crystal bands chimed as they broke and reformed, creating a progression of ringing tones.

"I don't think the idea was alarming," Estlin said. "It was the idea of the idea. The threshold ahead."

"There's time," Bomani said.

"A little time," Estlin agreed. Time was a mix of yellow and orange, which ribboned up into the tree. Everything around them crystallized, as though filtered through another perspective, making every edge sharp and allowing you to see the bottom and the top of every leaf at the same time. "There is something more."

"I see," Bomani said.

Estlin felt very small, which was okay because what the Waes wanted to share with them was subatomic.

———— «◇» ————

Serese's mind had wandered. She didn't know how much of the daily highlight reel she'd missed. Most of it, likely. She reset it to start again and closed her eyes.

There's something about us that is like a barnacle broken from a rock.

She imagined that complete sentence as the title of a dance piece. Who would move first, the company or the soloist? How many colours would be combined to create the blues? Would it sing like wet fingers stroking a glass harp or thump like muscle and bone striking taught skin?

"It is an interesting thought." Huo was standing in the doorway.

"Sorry?" Serese said, which was Canadian for *you have interrupted me and I wish you would fuck right off.* She paused the footage. "Can I help you?"

"It's interesting," Huo said, "to think that our greatest difference is how quickly we forget. That centuries of rapid change, which we call progress, is not just the product of intelligence and invention, but relies on a gap in memory."

Huo entered her office taking the seat in front of her desk.

"We can unlearn as fast or faster than we learn," he said. "Allowing each generation to race ahead to glory or catastrophe, not bound by the constraints of the past. The Waes are like the tip of a thorn, piercing our arrogance. We can react with aggression or see something new in the drop of blood that rises—that we have an unexpected defining feature: We forget."

"Which drives us to build theatres and libraries," Serese said.

"And burn them to the ground," Huo answered. "When the spark of a *new idea* is threatened by the record of its past failure. Even when records survive, and the language they are written in survives, there is the risk that we will believe that we have advanced beyond our own nature and cannot fall into the traps that have collapsed past civilizations."

Serese had studied the origins of dance, back to the earliest markings on rock walls. She had seen artifacts sifted from the sand, enigmatic fragments of altered bone and stone, as early marks of self-awareness—of emergence—not signs of a collective failure of memory.

"I find it strange how many people consider Mr. Hume's circumstances as evidence that he is anti-intellectual or that he has rejected society," Huo said. "His difference is fundamental. Therefore, even when he stands next to us, he lives in a different environment. His past should not be seen as a list of failures. He left many academic institutions, but in each case, I think the beginnings are more important than the ends. He has lived in many places, in many different ways, and suffered many rejections, but I don't think he ever rejected us. It may be remarkable that he holds no malice over his circumstances, however, I find this to be the case. It could be that this is like looking for malice in the heart of a wild bird, and I should not be surprised at all."

"I appreciate your perspective," Serese said. "Do you have advice for the challenges ahead?"

"There is a crack in the earth." Huo's tone was even. "Have you told him of the other approaching concerns?"

She knew that he was referring to the open secret.

"I was late to learn of them myself," he said. "I do not feel the delay was beneficial."

"Soon," she said.

"Thank you." Huo rested one hand on the desk. "I understand that some time was needed to quantify distant signs in the sky."

"The new illustrations are clearer and yet are viewed in many ways," she said.

"Very many ways," Huo agreed. "I have written a note. It is not official. I wanted to share my personal thoughts with Mr. Hume. I hope they are helpful."

It was a single page with a single fold. Serese opened it and read. "I will send it with the package going to the team at the house."

"Thank you," Huo said.

Serese watched the ambassador, waiting for him to rise from his seat and depart. He did not.

"I'm sorry I must bother you with one further matter," he said. "A member of my delegation was expelled from the site."

"Yes," Serese said. "Do you require an explanation?"

"No," Huo responded. "Some react poorly to the psychological stress of this situation. He was isolated from the rest of our delegation. It is unfortunate that we did not recognize this as a sign of his distress. I understand that he was rude to your soldiers when he was asked to leave. We appreciate your assistance in identifying his illness and wish to assure you that he is being transported home. Thank you, again, for your consideration and goodwill."

"No problem," Serese said. "I hope his health improves soon. I understand that he left with a sore stomach."

"Yes," Huo said. "It is unexpected that someone selected for his international experience could have such a bad reaction to local food."

"I am certain this experience will improve the screening of your delegates in the future," she said. "You can also submit any special requests to the cafeteria. We are doing our best to accommodate everyone."

—— ‹›› ——

Malone was in the grey space of wakefulness when the LEDs strung from the ceiling filled the tent with cold blue-white light.

Pollock planted a chair next to the cot. "On the scale of zero to very concussed, do you remember what happened yesterday?"

"Yesterday?" Malone rolled onto his back. "How long did I sleep?"

"Long enough," Pollock said. "They finally relayed the directive to bring Sanford out of the house. You missed an earthquake, or did you wake up for it?"

"What?" Malone sat up.

"It was a small quake," Pollock said. "Want painkillers?"

"No." He found his boots next to the cot. He couldn't remember taking them off.

"The viper is gone." Pollock continued the update. "The Canadians are polite, but if you cross them, they will kick the shit out of you. After your encounter, someone asked the creep why he was creeping and he didn't answer nicely. They carried him out strapped to a stretcher."

"Good," Malone said.

"It was handled quietly," Pollock responded. "And we got a ping on the photo we flagged the day he arrived. He was a *cook's assistant* on the cargo ship that booted out of Christchurch. He must have hidden like a rat rather than resisting when our team extracted Estlin and the aliens."

"I'm surprised the Canadians didn't keep him."

"They have bigger concerns," Pollock said. "The crack from the alien earthquake encircles the house. We don't have a conclusive depth measurement yet."

"Crack?"

"The crack across the driveway," Pollock said. "It seems like an acre of earth just broke off in place."

"Crap," Malone said. "They're going to lift the house. Forget getting Sanford out. We need to get in there."

"I don't know about that," Pollock said. "After the shake, a snake slithered out on this side, and a fox ducked out the back. The crafty critters are not sticking around for whatever comes next."

"A fox?" Malone pulled on one of his boots. "Alien-sized? You know they can look like anything."

"I know. Everyone knows," Pollock said. "It ducked into the nearest thicket of trees and down into a gully. Someone really should have thrown a net over it."

"If it was a visitor, no net or dart would have made a difference," Malone said. "You don't snag them unless they want you to."

"It was confirmed that Hume had a fox on the property. While it was leaving, a few rabbits wandered in."

"Wandered?" Malone said. "They were granted an access portal, like the birds."

"Right. It was the opposite of wandering," Pollock agreed. "I don't know why we get one fixed doorway, while other things can hop in through the side."

"How many rabbits?"

"Don't know."

"Someone was counting," Malone laced his left boot. "Local rabbits or suspicious rabbits?"

"Suspicious rabbits?" Pollock rejected, and then accepted this idea. "I will follow up on the rabbits. Where do you think the house is going?"

"No idea." Malone pulled on his other boot. "On the island, Hume said he had an argument with the aliens about swimming. I think they invited him to take a dive in the South Pacific. He thought it was a cuttlefish thing, but we know the aliens landed out there somewhere."

"It's a deep ocean," Pollock said. "In other news, Second Lieutenant Rupert would like you to know that our push to get Sanford to the house has interfered with efforts to establish a true American presence there."

"My push? The Canadians asked for him." Malone said. "Were we supposed to refuse?"

"That is the question," Pollock said. "Rupert wants the chain of command engaged prior to any further action."

"This conversation is aggravating my concussion," Malone said.

"Noted." Pollock stood and kicked his chair back to the tent wall. "FYI, Rupert has clearance to be in here. He's just trying to avoid alien cooties. And he knows about the two inbound UFOs. He took that news without a blink."

"Seriously, how long did I sleep?"

"Get up," Pollock said. "Grab a snack. You and your magic pass need to go wait in the staging tent to sweep Sanford back to us. You know how quickly the professor can be distracted by blank space on a white board."

Chapter 16

Estlin could smell the tree, the grass, and the earth. He blinked away bright traces that reminded him of the ceiling of the Temple of Heaven.

"That took a while." Harry was occupying the nearest lawn chair. "Want to tell us what it was about?"

"It was complicated," Estlin said.

"What kind of complicated?"

"It was very…" Estlin tried to find a red-gold spiral-stepped word. He looked to Bomani for help.

"Technical," Bomani said.

"Unexpected." Estlin pushed his fingers into his scalp, trying to hold in images. He knew Bomani would want to cross-check every detail.

"Why did they—?" Bomani didn't finish the question.

"I don't know." Estlin felt like the Waes wanted or needed his trust, which was worrisome given that they already had a crushingly deep bucket of ocean balanced over his house. The beautiful, warm *thing* they had shared with him had every colour, curve and texture in crisp focus, because it was the only way to see it, because a passion flower was more than the sum of its petals and parts.

Bomani shook his head and open his notebook to a blank page.

"We need time," Estlin said.

"You had time," Harry said. "Enough time that Troughton considered interrupting. Did you hear us discuss it?"

"No," Estlin said. "That would have been bad."

"Bad," Bomani agreed.

"You didn't get a break," Adya noted. "And we hadn't seen that level of *absence*."

"It was about energy," Bomani said. "I think we need to draw our way to words."

"Yes." Estlin stepped close to Bomani and considered the blank page. "Two diamond pins."

"Pyramids," Bomani said. "Perfect pyramids."

"Mated with a wedge-ring surrounding the point at which they meet," Estlin said.

"That was carbon in carbon," Bomani said. "I think it was graphene encased in diamond."

"The ring was—" Estlin searched for a word. "Alive."

"An X-ray absorber-emitter," Bomani said. "A switch."

"The diamonds weren't perfect."

"They were perfectly imperfect," Bomani said. "The point of each pyramid had an impossibly small imperfection, creating two microscopic, atomically flat surfaces pressed together."

"How do they—"

"I don't know," Bomani said. "Focused on an area that small, the pressure you can create with the force from your fingertips is enormous."

"And the whole thing was shining."

"It was an optical resonator," Bomani said. "Light confined in a cavity. A standing wave reflecting back and forth, gaining intensity. Perfectly phase matched photons."

"Built to shine inwards not out," Estlin said. "Everything brightened, and then it crashed into the center, and then it flashed."

"I think they used the intensity dependent non-linear responses of the diamond," Bomani said. "If you push enough light through certain materials, you can shift the refractive index. Imagine changing the focal point of a lens without needing to change its physical shape."

Bernie and Sanford closed in on Bomani as he sketched, watching the images unfold.

"What is it?" Bernie asked.

"A diamond anvil used to build up heat and pressure," Bomani said. "It is also a laser cavity, able to build and hold an intense beam of light until an atomic layer at the interface of the diamonds at the centre of the structure shifts from transparent to opaque, instantaneously absorbing every photon to create an extreme temperature spike."

"That's beautiful," Bernie said. "The optical equivalent of quenching a superconducting magnet. Flash-bang."

"You're describing a microscale carbon fusion reactor," Sanford said. "It's impossible. It would fly apart before you could achieve the extremes needed to—"

"It can't," Bomani said. "The heat is dumped in faster than it can escape, and the thermal conductivity of diamond drops as the temperature rises. At the centre point, the electrons are ripped off the carbon atoms generating a plasma. The ionized atoms want to fly apart but they are mechanically and electromagnetically forced inwards by the second structure. There is an electromagnetic twist and the carbon ions at the interface fold into each other."

"They burn carbon like a star," Bernie said, stepping back from the others. He took another step and clapped his hands to his face, as though they could press down the hot flush rising in his cheeks. "I forgot my blood pressure medicine."

Estlin walked through them all. He waved Harry out of the lawn chair, picked it up and dropped it next to Bernie. "Here. Sit down."

Dr. Chandran joined them.

"Sit for a moment," she said. "You'll be fine."

Bernie obeyed.

"Why did they tell you this?" Saeed asked. "Why now?"

"He asked earlier," Estlin said, deflecting attention to Bernie.

"I did?" Bernie nodded. "I did."

"We need to work," Bomani said.

"Document it. And then teach." Troughton pointed at Saeed. "I'll take the latest footage out. Sanford you're coming with me. Bernie, I'll bring you your pills."

"I can't go," Sanford said. "Not now."

"It's not my choice, and it's not yours," Troughton responded.

Bomani placed a hand on Estlin's shoulder, disengaging them from the argument. It was an easy thing given the speck of starlight still burning behind his eyes. The table across the yard was waiting with its many coloured pencils.

〈〉

"I can't go," Sanford said, even as he followed Troughton. "This is critical."

The tunnel thrummed as it shifted around them.

"The message was clear," Troughton said. "We were ordered to bring you out."

"I need to stay," Sandford said. "They would agree if they knew."

"You are the only person who can explain that to them," Troughton said.

Sanford knew this to be true, and if he delayed, it might become even harder to convince Malone to let him go back to the house.

"Bomani and Estlin need time to draw out the idea." Troughton offered this as consolation.

"I should have asked more questions." Sanford looked at the smooth structure flowing over their heads. He thought about how few people had the opportunity to experience this walk, even once.

"Diamonds have exquisite properties," he said. "They have a near-magical role in quantum technology. They are used in magnetic sensors—the kind that can read the signal from a single neuron. Complete transparency across visible wavelengths. Extremely high thermal conductivity. Low thermal expansion. Extreme radiation hardness. High melting point which increases under pressure. Density that increases when it melts."

"And we use them for rings and pretty things," Troughton said.

"Because they are magical," Sanford answered. He thought of Millie's diamond. It was resting in a closed box in a closed drawer. He decided that it belonged on the kitchen windowsill, where the morning sunlight would find it. He lengthened his strides to catch up to Troughton.

"I'll need a copy of Bomani's notes," he said. "With the geometry and the wavelength, I can estimate the energy capacity. The laser damage threshold of diamonds is enormously high, but there is a limit. I could assume probable angles based on the crystal structure, and then I'd just need a rough idea of the length of the cavity to start. And if the center point instantly turns into a wall that all the photons smash against, the discharge time will also depend on the length of the cavity and the speed of light in the medium. Photons fly at half their usual velocity in diamond."

"Why tell us?" Troughton asked. "Why now?"

"It's a clean energy source," Stanford said. "The microscale system Bomani described would be self-limiting. It's not explosive. There's no radioactive waste. It could save us."

"I don't think they are here to save us."

The ideas spinning in Stanford's mind slammed to a stop. Imagining alien motivations was beyond him.

"They like Estlin's tree," he said. "They could care about the forests."

"Give us more power, and we will do more of what we do." Troughton's pace slowed. "Dig deeper. Build higher. More power means more people. More food, more tools, more trinkets. It doesn't have to explode. Every army will race to plug into this kind of power."

"They shared an idea, not the hardware," Sanford said. "There's nothing to plug into. It could take hundreds of years to get halfway to a prototype."

"We've never had that kind of patience." Troughton stopped in the middle of the path. "We're fucked. To keep this situation stable, we have to continually convince everyone that we are sharing everything. We get accused of hold backs and deep fakes every day. What happens if we try to clamp down on this for a minute? Even if only to avoid the confusion created by the real-time release of fragmented, incomplete information?"

Sanford wondered if it was even possible.

"If we are absolutely transparent, our allies will take it as a betrayal because we should be smart enough not to share this kind of crap," Troughton said. "Everyone else will insist that any gaps are secrets we're keeping. You were there. Will your keepers let you share your thoughts with the Russians and the Chinese? What about the actual declared enemies of the States? Your silence will drive conspiracy theories about suppressed information. It will tip the scale."

Troughton turned to face the house. Sanford wondered if he was considering going back.

"The specs for a fucking microscale fusion reactor," Troughton said. "Are the Waes trying to create a crisis? Is there some other un-fucking-fathomable motivation for them to throw this at us now?"

Troughton didn't wait for a response, he turned again and continued marching through the ice corridor. As Sanford followed, he tracked back to Estlin's answer, and considered the potential truth in it—that the Waes had shared the details of the fusion reactor simply because, somehow, Bernie had asked.

《 》

Serese washed a pill down with the last dreg of cold tea in her cup. Her right hip was angry. It hated deskwork, and muttered threats of more serious pain as she stood. *Medicate and move.* It was time to walk until the stiffness surrendered. When injuries forced her transition from dancing to arts administration, her walks had created windows for conversation, and let her feel the energy of an entire art centre and sense when it shifted. The Governor General gig had a grander scale and over the last two years she'd walked through cities, towns and remote communities from coast to coast to coast. As she left her office, she felt the push-pull—the need—to get back to the house.

She turned in the direction of Bernie's nest of computers and equipment. She wanted a burst of his enthusiasm, but knew it wouldn't be available because she'd sent him to help Estlin. Serese found someone at the center of Bernie's deck of screens. They bounced out of Bernie's seat as she approached.

"You need to see this."

Serese glanced down at the security pass to cheat. When she saw a written name, she could visualize it as the header of a biographical summary and remember key details from the page. The materials engineer led a neurotech start up. "Hello, Dr. Paik."

"Bernie, I mean, Dr. Springer, asked me to monitor everything while he's at the house," they said, making a quick adjustment to their glasses and turning back to the screens. Their chunky glasses had clear yellow frames that complimented their warm skin tone, and their long hair was pinned in a low bun. "Dr. Lichtwardt had a program tracking the cuttlefish in real-time. I can't access it directly, but it's still running, and it sends out automatic notifications which are copied to Bernie. Look at this. It must be important. It must be."

Serese waited for a conclusion as clusters of numbers crawled across a black screen.

"What is it?" Serese asked.

"Do you want to see the raw footage?"

The screen filled with shifting shadows viewed through the semi-opaque covering of the tank, each marked with a bold black dot. The cuttlefish were dancing. All of them.

"When was this recorded?" Serese asked.

"This is now," Dr. Paik said. "I checked back, and yesterday, there were two updates. Now, it's sending alerts every two minutes. This is only the second cuttlefish event we've observed. Bernie called the first one *the argument*. I think because he had an argument with Dr. Lichtwardt and the Chinese ambassador about it right before things blew up. But he didn't see that one in real time, he backtracked through the satellite images to find it."

"What does it mean?" Serese said.

"We don't know."

Serese focused on the swirling shadows, and the feeling that they generated.

"Stay on these screens," she said. "I want you to print out a summary, and copy the most recent updates to a hard drive. Do it now. I'm going to pick up one page from my office, and I will stop by here on my way to the house."

"I'm supposed to pack all this for the shift to Camp C," they said. "But I'm resisting. If I shut it down, I don't know if Bernie will be able to restart it. Dr. Lichtwardt's program was new. There's no documentation. He didn't...he didn't have time."

Serese flipped over a printed map of the site and wrote "DO NOT MOVE ANYTHING" on the back of it. She added her signature and placed it on the stack of computers.

Chapter 17

Bomani had the skills for curves and symmetry. He could capture complexity, clockwork actions and dynamic shifts, but the spirit in the latest images needed an artist not a stenographer. He glanced at Estlin, who leaned over the opposite side of the table, choosing coloured pencils—green, purple, and grey.

"I can't draw it." Bomani heard the pain of this confession in his own voice and gripped the edge of the table to keep himself from backing away.

Estlin drew with careless speed. He turned the first page to show Bomani the broken lines and blocks of colour. It was an ugly sketch, but Bomani recognized the blast of beyond-purple light hitting the back facet of the diamond like a hammer. The thermal shock compression was conveyed with a few bands of grey.

Estlin peeled apart the pad of paper and tossed half of it across the table, forcing Bomani to catch it.

"Fill the pages," he said. "It's a race."

Estlin continued to create ugly shapes with ugly colours.

Bomani chose a thick black marker, throwing the cap away. He sketched fragments of structure and created movement through thumbnails in numbered sequences. He ripped page after page from the pad, heaping them face down on the table. He drew without colour, without clarity, without notes—and Estlin still won.

While Estlin flexed his fingers and shoved his pages into a rough pile, Bomani created five more drawings. Flipping over his stack of ugliness, he went through it, adding titles to each page. He dropped his pen, knowing every image would need to be redrawn and redrawn and redrawn.

"It's a lot," Estlin said.

"Yes," Bomani agreed.

"It was like a confrontation with a profound painting," Estlin said. "They wanted us to see every stroke of the brush and every colour, and it was breathing."

"I saw," Bomani said. "I saw, but I don't have the tools." With curled fingers, he hit the left side of his chest, creating the paired hard-soft thumps of a heartbeat.

"We need a musician." Estlin pointed at the pages. "We get lost in what we see."

Bomani thought of Sukarnotritapurnoma, the physicist he'd met in New Zealand who framed everything in frequencies, harmonics and rhythms. For Su, the Rosetta Burst was music.

"We have enough." Bomani took another pad of paper from under the table, clear on his job—to draw everything with as much detail as possible in hopes that when Su saw the collection of images, he would be able to hear it.

"Good," Estlin said. "I'll get you a glass of water."

— «» —

The corridor opened, and Troughton felt a drizzle of light rain. Chief Warrant Officer Lacey of the Patricia's infantry was in the staging area, and she offered a nod of acknowledgement as Troughton passed her. Chain link fencing, tents, and tarps surrounded and covered the scars of the bomb blast. Troughton followed Sanford into the staging tent and found Serese already there, sheltered from the rain.

"This is Sgt. Malone," Serese said. "He's here to meet Sanford."

Sanford launched into an argument with Malone as he was swept away by a doctor for the required physical. Troughton sat on the nearest bench, waiting his turn, and Serese took a seat on the bench opposite him.

"How are you?" Serese asked.

He felt like she should have asked a more important question. He fought the impulse to skip over answering because he'd already learned that Serese expected a specific response to any question she asked.

"Rattled," he said. "Walking out, I interrupted Sanford to go off about *concerns*. Sorry." He lifted the camera dangling from his neck that had captured all of it to be shared and picked apart.

"It can be disconcerting," Serese said, "to know that there will be a permanent record of how human we all are."

"The latest session with the Waes was about small-scale fusion reactors," Troughton said. "Bomani and Estlin are drawing it up."

Serese opened the folders that she held on her lap and handed him a page.

"There are two objects flying towards us from the Rosetta Burst."

There were successive images on the page showing fuzzy white dots marked with arrows to emphasize their movement against a static starscape.

"How soon?" he asked.

"I haven't been told," she said. "But the tax collectors have started to seize private bunkers."

"You need answers from Estlin."

"Everyone does."

"I'll take this in as soon as I've had my turn with the doctor," he said. "I'm fetching something for Bernie."

"I'm going to the house," Serese said. "If you want to take a short rest, now's the time."

"No." Troughton didn't feel like there was any time at all.

"We'll go together," Serese said. "The cuttlefish are swarming. I have the details from Bernie's team."

"Troughton!" Sanford burst through the tent partition pursued by Dr. Critoph and Malone. "There are two UFOs. We need to ask Estlin about them."

"We know." Troughton showed Sanford the images. "We're going to tell him now."

Sanford recognized that he was being excluded. "Can I—"

"No." Serese stood. "We are limiting the number of people at the house. Submit an access request. It will be evaluated as soon as the current uncertainties resolve."

Dr. Critoph gestured to the medical area. "Dr. Sanford, I will be with you in a moment."

Sanford reluctantly returned to the partitioned area, where Malone waited for him

"Troughton, I'll be at the gate," Serese said. "Join me when you are ready."

"Are you returning to the house?" Dr. Critoph asked Troughton.

"Yes."

"Dr. Chandran requested supplemental supplies." The doctor handed over a red shock-proof hard case. "Medications. Her list, our additions and an inventory sheet."

"Do you have anything for Bernie Springer here?"

"Yes. There is a supply of prescriptions and regular medications for everyone currently on site. Given that you all rely on a doorway that the aliens control, I should have had this covered sooner."

"Thank you." Troughton said. "Could you quickly poke me in the eye? I'd like to get straight back to the house, but the nanotech freaks asked my team to support their ovoids-from-eyeballs study."

"No problem." Dr. Critoph pulled a tear sampling kit from his pocket. "We'll skip the blood tests this time. Have a seat."

A minute later and damp-eyed, Troughton left the tent. He found Serese disagreeing with her security and the Patricia's about whether this was the best or worst time to refuse an escort.

"Troughton is going with me," she said. "One of us will come out with a report within the next two hours. I'm extending the hold on forklift transfers to the house. I'm extending the hold on new visitors. The night shift is to wait here on standby. If there is any turnover tonight, it will happen one by one. While I am in, Chief Warrant Officer Lacey has deciding authority on whether any new information is vital enough to warrant a messenger immediately bringing it in."

"Yes, Madam," Lacey accepted the order.

Troughton looked at the waiting pallets. "I've got a hand free," he said. "What can I carry?"

Lacey split the binding on the nearest load and pulled free a hockey bag. "Water treatment and testing kits. Toiletries."

Troughton hefted the bag. It was bulky, light, and flagged for Saeed.

"What's in that one." Serese pointed to a yellow backpack. The first in a row.

"There was a request for vegetables," Lacey said. "Sweet potatoes and carrots. It's lower on the priority list."

"I'll take it." Serese helped herself to the pack, quickly adjusting the shoulder straps and hip belt.

"I think you have the heavier load," Troughton said.

"I'll let you know if my hip complains," Serese answered.

⟨⟩

Estlin downed a glass of water and filled it again. He set it on the counter and leaned over the sink, staring out the back window at nothing. His hands were steady, but he felt shaky.

"I am not fragile," he said to himself.

"I agree," Adya said. "But you need to eat."

Estlin decided not to acknowledge how violently he'd startled at the voice behind him.

"I ate." He couldn't remember what was between the slices of bread he'd consumed earlier.

"That was hours ago," she said. "And the brain consumes more energy than any other organ."

Estlin hesitated. Anything from the cupboards would require effort.

"Orange juice and a granola bar," Adya suggested. She proceeded to the fridge as though he'd agreed. "It's been a busy day."

"Not done yet." Estlin heard the sliding jangle of the descending tank and felt a dull sadness. He ignored the feeling, hoping the orange juice Adya poured for him would make it go away. He drank it, rinsed his glass, and used a palmful of water from the tap to wash and cool his face. "Could you bring some for Bomani? Spark and Cloud are coming."

"We have to figure out a way to distribute this workload," Adya said.

"Bomani has most of the heavy lifting now."

"I'm not sure that's true. He works with a technological assist that they don't seem to offer to you."

"I don't know why. I don't know why they like my broken brain."

"Broken?"

"Cracked at least, given the leakage."

"I think it's worth discussing more when there's time," Adya said.

"Yes." Estlin appreciated the future tense. "Thank you, Dr. Chanthan."

Saeed was standing in the doorway, ready to interrupt them.

"I know." Estlin smiled for Adya. "This should be interesting."

He followed Saeed out the door and skipped down the steps. Bomani was waiting on the grass.

"I wondered if you were coming," Bomani said.

"Adya is bringing you orange juice," Estlin responded. "Take a moment and drink it."

The tank had the usual volume, but had a wider base which touched the earth at several points. The greater structure had hollowed behind it, framing the display.

Spark surged forward and back, carried by rippling pulses of its mantle fins. Its tentacles and arms were pursed together. Cloud's tentacles flared out drawing Estlin's attention. It was holding itself in the centre of the tank with a greater physical presence than on its previous visits. There were no accompanying translators in the tank, and Estlin knew that Wae and Waewae were high in the tree.

Bomani showed Estlin the device from the Waes. It now appeared as a white pebble.

"What should I do?" he asked.

"Listen," Estlin said.

The story of the cuttlefish was told in a series of vignettes: a satisfying sparring session, a swift swim with the swarm, a rewarding hunt, a long stillness. It took time for Estlin to realize that they were sharing cuttlefish completeness. A day in the life and an answer.

"I don't understand," Bomani said.

"The will of water cannot be denied," Estlin translated, "whether it flows or folds in waves or falls to stillness. The dark *water* above the above, speckled with shining velella, is the same. The swarm remembers what it has always known.

The will of the vast dark water is its own, whether we choose to swim in it or not."

"They decided," Bomani said.

"Yes." Estlin blinked.

Sharp, bright light was striking lines through the tank. The frame of the greater vessel had rocked further back from the small tank. The air was cooler. The superstructure lifted slowly like a great beast. The tethers between it and the tank had released. The great tank climbed, creating more air space around the entire house. The walls of the smaller tank were wet and shining. It sank as the feet on its base melted into the soil.

"What's happening?" Bomani asked.

The two cuttlefish in the tank calmly watched them, extending a depth of thanks that Estlin could not share with Bomani until his refusal felt like a betrayal.

"They thank you," Estlin said. "For the gift."

"What gift?"

"The idea," Estlin said. "They understand it now."

He knew that *understand* was too small a word. The cuttlefish saw the idea with their acutely sensitive vision, and the idea was beautiful as sand was (infinite) beautiful. The idea was beautiful as a death bite predator was beautiful (terrifying).

The tank perforated, allowing the water to leak away, as it must, to let the terrible-beautiful-infinite idea die, drowning in air on the prairie soil.

"This cannot be," Bomani said.

"We knew there was a risk," Estlin said. "They knew the swarm did not want the idea to propagate."

"They cannot choose this."

"Their lives are short," Estlin said.

The cuttlefish were cold about necessary losses. Estlin's eyes were hot, but could not offer enough salt water to save them. Bomani reached out to gently touch the solid, delicate arms of each cuttlefish. A light snow was falling, the flakes melting before they reached the ground.

The tension in Spark's body released first, its extended arm uncoiling, releasing one of its beloved smooth stones.

⸺ «‹›» ⸺

Harry broke away from the scene, turning from the cuttlefish glistening on the wet ground to find the rest of the team clustered near the house. Troughton had returned, bringing Serese with him. Both of them watched the scene over their shoulders as they cast the bags they carried onto the porch. Harry joined them.

"Bernie, collect the video and photos of all completed drawings. Take them out now," Serese said. "Find out what is happening above us. I want a timeline."

Bernie looked up. "Soon. You know it's soon."

"Dr. Chandran, will you go with him?" Troughton asked.

"No," Adya replied. "I'll go when Estlin does."

"He may not," Troughton said.

"I know."

"You and Saeed have children."

"I am here for them," Adya said.

"Okay," Troughton said. "Estlin's next conversation with the Waes will be critical. Saeed or I will go out as soon as it's complete."

"I am going to find a shovel," Harry said. "Adya, we need a couple of towels—something to wrap them, please."

"There's a shovel in the shed." Saeed pointed to the left side of the house.

Harry nodded his thanks and continued. The small shed was open, and Harry found an old shovel propped in the corner. Leaving the shed, he knew that he needed something more. He unzipped one of the bags that was stacked nearby and filled his pocket with a handful of hazel nuts. When he returned to the front of the house, he found Adya waiting with the two towels he'd requested. Troughton stood with Serese by the steps.

Harry accepted the towels and slung them over his shoulder. "Thanks."

"Do we have time for this?" Troughton asked.

"We aren't sending them out for dissection," Harry said, "and I can't leave them to rot."

Damp cool wind swirled through the yard. A circular opening was expanding symmetrically above the house, and broken rainbows traced in from the upper rim of the ice structure.

"That's a lot of sky," Harry said. "We'll do what we need to. You can keep an eye on that and tell us what to do next."

Harry walked through the yard to where the splash of salt water had soaked the earth. He handed Estlin the shovel. "We'll follow you."

He gave Bomani the second towel and crouched down to wrap one of the cuttlefish. He lifted it and adjusted it in his arms until the twenty-pound burden was braced on his left forearm and into the crook of his elbow as though it were an infant.

"There's a place near the Saskatoon berry bushes," Estlin said. "Down by the well."

"Good," Harry said.

The ice structure above them rumbled like distant thunder.

Harry followed Bomani, who followed Estlin. Their small procession took a foot trail that curved down a hill covered with blue aster and the drying orange brush-like blossoms of prairie-fire. The water well was capped with a hand pump. A mechanical pump and pressurized storage tank were mounted on a small concrete slab.

Estlin stopped thirty yards away at a natural gap in a row of shrubs. He planted the tip of his shovel and began to dig. Bomani laid down his bundle and sat on the ground next to it. Estlin heaved up the soil, the blade of the shovel scraping and prying out fist-sized rocks. It became clear that he was digging a single trench. Once the trench was defined, Bomani stood, held out his hand for the shovel and continued digging.

There was a new sound above them. The ice structure, which had split wide open like an aperture roof on a vast stadium, was rebuilding itself in a complicated fold over fold over fold movement along the edge of the ring.

"Bernie's going out," Harry said. "He's got a better chance of figuring out what is going on out there than in here. Troughton's talking to the others about evacuation. Will you consider going after we're done here?"

"I dunno," Estlin said. "I don't find that there are many choices that I get to make."

Bomani planted the shovel in the heap of earth, obviously satisfied with the depth of the trench. He placed the first cuttlefish, still shrouded in the towel, and then took the bundle from Harry's arms.

Harry gathered the hazel nuts from his pocket and held them out to show Estlin. "I don't know if the squirrels will leave any to sprout, but I thought it was worth trying.

Estlin nodded and took up the shovel. He filled the trench to a suitable depth, handed the shovel to Bomani, and then took the nuts. He crouched to plant them in a spiral, and then stood back as Bomani covered them with the remaining soil. The largest rocks pried out during the dig were placed last to mark the spot.

Chapter 18

Paik was *being stupid* or at least that's what they'd been told, repeatedly, with a particular inflection that was now digging into their brain. They didn't exactly disagree with the point. Everyone else had bugged out of the research tent in the staging area. Paik had three empty carts ready and one cart loaded. Serese's note remained displayed as a shield, their token of power, their permission to be as foolish as they liked.

They had packaged a series of satellite images for the attention of an origami specialist who worked on radiation shielding for JAXA. They added the SAR X-band data. The quality of the satellite topographic radar images had deteriorated as the structure over the house split and folded, emitting noises like a calving glacier. The view of the house was now distorted by a series of curved ice sheets that acted like lenses.

As the camp shutdown had accelerated, Dr. Critoph had kindly brought tea and a scone. He hadn't questioned their decision at all, and it was comforting to know that he was one tent away, maintaining the last medical post in the staging area.

———— ⟨⟩ ————

Estlin led the way back to the house as the light faded. The evening transition was eerie because the structure had closed above them, and there was no way to distinguish nightfall from a gathering storm. Carrying the shovel over his shoulder, he felt bone weary. He thought about Harry's question, and what he'd do if everyone else evacuated. He couldn't think of a single place to go.

The lanterns were shining, and Serese sat on the porch swing, a resting readiness in every muscle. He knew there was work to do. He didn't know how he had missed it before, except that he had barely looked at her when she arrived.

"What is it?" he asked.

"I have a question for the Waes," she said. "Two objects are flying toward us from the Kuiper Belt near Neptune, where the Rosetta Bursts originated. We need to know more about them, anything the Waes will tell you."

"Do you want a *we-come-in-peace* pronouncement?" Estlin asked. "I doubt that would reassure anyone."

"I know," Serese said. "There was a strong reaction when the trajectory was confirmed, even though it was the foregone conclusion."

"You are worried." Estlin leaned the shovel against the porch rail. "About the objects or us? You know most of their answers cause problems." He waved a hand at the nearest example. "Bomani just drew a miniature fusion reactor."

"It was too beautiful for my skills to capture," Bomani said. "A reactor made out of diamond, where light is the heater and the hammer, creating a perfect cascade. The diamond itself is the machine, the fuel it consumes, and the window through which the energy flies."

"It is beautiful," Estlin agreed. "In a centre-of-the-sun gamma ray kind of way. Can I have the Wae's little Yidge-widget." He held out his hand and waited until Bomani surrendered the alien device. He lifted it to his lips and sang a name in two long tones. "Yidge?"

Yidge stepped into the air next to him, transitioning from invisibility to presence with a single stride. She looked different—slacks and practical shoes. He recognized her travel clothes from the day they met.

"Why are you shouting?" Yidge's question had a neutral, curious quality.

"I'm not shouting."

Yidge pointed a finger between her ear and forehead. "Yes, you are."

"I just buried friends," he answered. "I'm tired. I know the Waes like to stress us and see how we react, but we don't need mysterious lights in the sky. You can tell us what they are. Whatever it is, they can tell us. Trust me, everyone will still be stressed."

The pair of Waes leapt from the tree to the roof of the house. Turning in unison, they separated, walking down from the peak on opposite eaves, their attention fixed on Estlin.

"Are you changing your mind?" Yidge asked.

"I am moody," Estlin said. "What state do they think my mind is in?"

The Waes bristled as though this was a matter of concern.

"Two UFOs." Estlin addressed the Wae's. "What are they?"

"They told you," Yidge said.

"What?" Estlin asked. "For fuck's sake, when? You know there is some fragmentation. Some things do get lost in translation."

"You are swearing."

"I swear when I'm tired. I swear when people try to deflect their way around simple questions."

"One light carries the strange p□hutukawa." Yidge named a grand, invasive crimson-flowered tree. "The nsangunsangu, the entwined unbound one."

"One space tree on its way, okay."

"Transiting its canopy, its taps, and its home created the brightest burst," she said. "The first Rosetta Burst was the arrival of its annex of companions and needed things. The bursts emitted when the seeds of the pavers and observers arrived were small and easily suppressed…recovered."

"A space tree, and its house, and its friends, preceded by small advance teams," Estlin said. "Is the tree coming to examine the observations collected by the Waes? To make predictions about us?"

"No," Yidge said. "It would have, but it's not necessary now. It can proceed with its primary interest."

"Yidge, you're being vague," Estlin said. "The Waes have been pushing me around like a pawn. Please don't make me ask them."

"It has a particular obsession that it is here to study," she said. "The archivist found an ancient curiosity from the first visit here."

"First visit." Estlin wanted to go inside and lie down. He considered sitting on the steps, given the depth of the history lesson Yidge was threatening to launch.

"When the intelligence on the fourth planet made the loud error—the broken burst that rang out—the waetapu followed the sound and found the warm ash of the fire."

"Millions of years ago."

"Yes," Yidge said. "They assessed the effect of the fire throughout the solar system. The recollections are incomplete, but the archivist extracted a curiosity."

"The cuttlefish?"

"No," Yidge said. "But the Waes came to observe because the complexity of the cuttlefish was remembered. It is appropriate to estimate the effects—to consider ethical questions—before beginning research that requires interaction."

"We aren't the focus of the visit." Serese stepped into the conversation. "They started with an assessment of us in order to safely interact?"

"Not exactly," Yidge said. "Their aim was to learn if the effect of the visit would have any importance. For example, if we're headed to oblivion, a little extra push doesn't matter."

"It fucking does matter," Estlin said.

"They're still observing," Yidge said. "They cannot estimate our path yet, but the need for a detailed assessment was nullified by Sanford's understanding of the Rosetta Burst and our tendency to scratch every itch. I mean, if we're going to play with ideas that big and dangerous and unpredictable, there's no reason for them to sweat the small stuff."

"I told you their answers wouldn't help." Estlin turned to Serese. "I want to lie down. Do you need anything more? Do you want their widget?"

"No," Serese said. "Thank you."

Estlin climbed the stairs to the porch. When his hand touched the rail, it felt like the house was vibrating. The ice structure above clapped like thunder.

"What was that? Punctuation?" Estlin raised his voice, yelling at the Waes on his roof. "You are lousy house guests."

"Lyndie, wait." Harry had the look of someone who wanted to suggest a wiser, calmer approach.

"No," Estlin said, and he continued into the house.

——— «›» ———

Yidge vanished when Estlin closed the door behind him.

"He did warn us," Harry said, because someone needed to break the silence.

"It does generate mixed feelings." Troughton leaned against the stair rail, scratching his head.

"There's nothing mixed about it when you knock out our false bias," Saeed responded. "They say a tree is coming. We feel relief because we dominate trees. We invented the axe and the chainsaw, and feel the power of being able to instantly destroy a century of growth. We can kill defenseless giants that have stood for thousands of years. But whatever is flying at us, it is *not a tree*. It's a huge alien, likely the size of clonal tree colonies here. Those can survive for 50,000 years and this creature may be older. It sounds like it has a research obsession, and it has decided to skip the ethics review on its latest study because a partial dataset suggests that it doesn't matter if its research has catastrophic consequences for us."

"I agree," Adya said. "We imagine a blessed, life affirming tree, but we know nothing."

"It's insult and injury," Harry said. "Even as we are in the midst of self-destructing, the outside suggestion that we may self-destruct is rude, especially when it comes with a shrug that suggests that it doesn't matter if we do. To add an alien tree flying here to study something important, and it isn't us, is intolerable."

"No one is going to take this well," Troughton said.

"It won't be trusted or believed," Serese said. "The world is pivoting. The immense pressure on this point could collapse the global collaboration, but that is not our load to carry. We have to leave that to Ambassador Huo and others, because that struggle has an embedded time pressure. It demands the declaration of an accelerating cycle of victories—performative progress—that does not exist within the relationship we need to build here. Huo sees the fulcrum. He is dedicated to doing what he can to steady us through this transition, and he is not alone."

"The records created here will last," Serese said. "Those that view them will see when we are fully engaged, when we are tired, when we are distracted, and when we fall into stupidity. Within our moments, we can only do our best to be aware of ourselves and each other. We must invest in observation and reflection. We must rest when we need to rest." Serese pointed at Estlin's upstairs room within the house. "If you feel our collective effort starting to tip, reach out and steady the lever."

Chapter 19

"Paik, you need to pack everything now." Paik was alone in the tent, but the solo conversation was necessary, because they were not doing what needed to be done. They had invoked the power of the Governor General's note multiple times as the rumble of the nearby ice structure became continuous and unnerving. They'd sent out their last packets of data from the expansive tent with the other researchers and turned on every bank of lights when night fell. "You can unplug everything. Bernie will understand."

"Unplug. Yes." Bernie was at the door of the tent. He took a few steps, stopping at the carts Paik had assembled. "Time to go."

"What happened?" Paik asked.

"The crack is a half-step now." Bernie's hands were limp at his sides. "It's going to move. There was an electrical storm when the tank came through the mountains to settle over the house. When it goes, there could be sheets of lightning. We need to unplug and get out of the way."

Bernie wavered in place, which was alarming, considering that he was three steps from his chair. Paik pretended not to be alarmed, but they'd seen Bernie after he'd been blown up and this looked worse.

"What happened?"

"Can you shut it down?" Bernie pulled his chair closer and collapsed into it.

"Shutting down." Paik clamped down on the urge to push other questions. *Action first. Sheets of fucking lightning, and everyone else is smart enough to already be on a bus.*

They took the note from Serese, decided it was too useful to discard, and folded it into a pocket. There were three laptops, two towers, and a string of storage drives still spinning. They asked each system to wind down, took a long look at Bernie and decided it was the cumulative strain. He'd been riding the space-critter roller coaster for three times longer than any of the locals. If he needed to sit for a few minutes while they were being cranked up the next lift hill, so be it.

"Dr. Paik, you've done excellent work," Bernie said, his voice a tired monotone. "I don't think I said so, and I should have said so."

Paik never knew what to do with compliments.

"When I selected you, there was a *comment*," Bernie continued. "Someone said the situation was too critical for a *diversity hire*."

Paik kept their eyes on the screens, watching them blink to blackness one after another. This type of conversation usually went badly. They didn't want Bernie to disappoint them, and if he did, above everything, they didn't want Bernie to see the disappointment.

"I didn't know what they were talking about," Bernie said. "Research is a collective activity. The world doesn't need some well-connected narcissist in here, shouting his perspective into the biggest megaphone. We need everyone looking at this, and that means releasing clean information, complete information with context, but no garbage. I needed someone who could write excellent cover letters, so I only looked at cover letters. Yours had no presumptions. It didn't assume you were an exact fit for what you assumed the job to be. It didn't assume there was an interview to look forward to. It was relevant and concise. I didn't know you were different until the asshole made that comment, and I looked through the CVs and profiles of the people I'd selected trying to figure out what the fuck he was talking about. And when you arrived, I didn't acknowledge your difference because that asshole made me notice it and decide that it didn't matter. But I was wrong because who you are does matter, and you can expect assholes to be assholes. They start at unpleasant and escalate to unsafe, and he left you here alone when you should be with the team."

Paik spared a glance in Bernie's direction; he was watching them as though observing from a great distance. They crouched to pull eight plugs from one of the power bars and wondered if Bernie felt like he'd abandoned the team at the house.

"It was my choice," they said. "I had special permission from Serese Saie."

"This is still wrong," he said. "You're part of a team. That asshole should have stayed with you or found a volunteer."

Paik had deflections which they used whenever their difference was discussed in work environments, but none of them seemed necessary. They coiled cables, each second expanding.

"I'm sorry," Bernie said. "I'm awkward, it's not... with people I sometimes get things wrong." He scrambled to his feet. "I should be helping. I'll help."

Paik pulled the final plug and had a realization. "The generator. Do we have to move it, too?"

"We need help." Bernie turned and marched away, stopping at the open doorway of the tent, raising his hands and checking his watch. "I'll be back."

Paik continued packing and wondered whose job it was to drop the tent.

——— ⟨⟩ ———

"It was nice to see the stars," Troughton said.

Saeed cast a glance skyward. In the dark, the folding of the structure above them was all sound and subtle shifting shadows. He continued to change the drive on the camera in his hands. "I know it's my turn to take the walk, but—"

"I'll take the hard drives out," Troughton said.

"Okay." Saeed gave Troughton his full attention. "Why?"

"My instincts are screaming at me. If I don't go soon, I think I might startle and run, the way Estlin did when the bomb went off."

"Is this something we should all pay attention to?"

"I don't know," Troughton said. "How do you feel?"

"Steady."

"I've got a definite jitter. I can't tell if it's internal or external."

"Best guess?"

"Feels like a push," Troughton said.

"Any clues?"

"I don't usually remember dreams. But the last one was vivid. My partner's parents have a cottage with a deck facing Lake Huron. It was night, and I was closing the shutters because an ice storm was rolling across the water. The moon was huge, and the stars were so bright, it was like I was standing in the sky. The metal latches were freezing, and I can't say if I was preparing to shelter or leave. The wind picked up and black ice spread across the deck beneath my feet. I had to hold on. I knew that if I slipped, I would slide into the vortex, away from everyone I love. When I woke, my hands were aching."

"Should the rest of us worry about this warning?"

"I don't know," Troughton said. "It felt personal, and this situation is stressful. If it had felt bigger, I would have told you sooner. Now, I feel like I'm jumping off when my weight may be needed."

"The information needs to be carried out," Saeed said. "And while Serese is here, we need a strong advocate out there."

"Thank you." Troughton pulled on his headlamp. "Serese ordered them to shut the front gate behind us. I don't know if that will stick."

"The Waes control the gate," Saeed said. "It'll stick if they want it to."

Above them, two great plates met and fused together with a satisfied rumble.

"That's my cue." Troughton accepted the backpack from Saeed and swung it over his shoulder. "No long goodbyes."

"No goodbyes at all," Saeed said. "We'll see you later."

——— «» ———

"Pollock, it's time to reconnect with the rest of the team," Malone said. "Take Sanford and all the data. Every time you go through a gate, assume you'll never be back. Dewey, go find your Canadian friends. You've got free time and can help them load out. If you find an advantageous ride, take it. If you run out of opportunities, walk out and join Pollock."

Dewey accepted the order and was gone, leaving the older soldier who waited for Malone's nod.

"You aren't coming," Pollock said. "Do I want to ask?"

"No, you do not," Malone replied.

"Our politician will want to speak to Sanford," Pollock said.

"There's nothing to be done about it," Malone replied. "Sanford only speaks physics and his new topic is fusion reactors, so expect it to go badly."

"It's all going badly."

"Yes, it is," Malone said.

"Is your Hail Mary authorized or an improvisation?" Pollock asked.

"Bit of both," Malone responded. "Stop asking and go."

"Going, sir."

Malone grabbed a stack of plate-like wearable battery packs and connected an unsafe number of them in series. He used the wire cutters on his multi-plier and brute force to split open a chest pouch made to hold one battery. He dropped the stack on one flap and wrapped up the expanded pouch in olive drab tape.

The compact microwave that they packed in with their rations had not been used because its microwave emitter had been replaced with one tuned to the frequency that fried alien ovoids. It was useless for cooking, and they'd had no need to decontaminate small alien-tainted items. He tore the unit apart and did ugly, stupid, regrettable things to the transformer and emitter. The net result was a malformed high-energy microwave gun.

Cutting the power cord from the microwave, he threaded it down the right arm of his jacket and wired the battery pack to the gun, which he shoved in the jacket pocket. Strapping the battery pouch to his chest, he pulled on his jacket and zipped it up.

"Hail Mary," he said, and left the tent.

Chapter 20

The minibus shuddered as it turned to climb the next slope. Beyond the windows was a blur of green bush, and Bomani didn't know where he was or where he was going.

"Wake up."

"I'm awake, Bamama," he answered his mother. He can remember sleeping against her shoulder, and it feels like he is still dreaming.

He looked down and saw a turtle resting on the bright green folds of his mother's skirt. Fulu, the wise, stretched his neck, tilting one eye to gaze at Bomani.

Wake up.

Bomani heard the silent turtle speak clearly in Chitumbuka. "I've been with Estlin for too long."

"Wake up," Fulu said again.

"I am awake," Bomani insisted.

"No, you aren't." Kalulu, the trickster hare, argued from below the seats across the aisle.

Bomani did not want to listen to the clever hare. It would argue with anyone.

"Yendani makola."

The warm whisper into his shoulder, the wish that he *travel well*, was a goodbye from his mother. He turned to tell her he was not leaving and woke on the couch. He sat up, a pillow slipping from his arms. The room was dim, as though the bulb above him had lost half its glow. The shadow and light in the darker kitchen had a strange pattern. Bomani rose and the floorboards creaked and crunched as traces of ice fractured beneath his feet. The kitchen was full of hexagonal branching structures that spread a delicate lattice across every surface they touched.

It felt like midnight, like there was no point in calling out to the others. He turned and found the ice had covered the wall behind him with giant snowflakes. He watched as an ice sled formed on the couch, the kind that he had found on the beach in Samoa. He had lowered Estlin into one without knowing where it would go, and that decision forced him to take the same act of trust now. He picked up the pillow. The sled, being shaped to hold a human, was uncomfortably coffin-like. Taking his place, Bomani wondered if the calm he felt came from within or without, and then he stopped wondering.

《 》

Bursts of blue sheet lightning flashed within the clouds, illuminating the landscape and the space within the bus. As thunder clapped and rolled through in waves, Bernie turned to look at Paik, fixing on their calm dark brown eyes until his sadness subsided. Paik handed him a striped linen handkerchief. Bernie wiped his eyes and face, and then ruined it with snot. He stowed the ball of cloth in the netted pocket in the seatback and wiped his fingers on his pants. He'd held it together through the night and the dawn, when the coach bus joined the final convoy, but he could not endure being parked as the world changed outside his window.

The erratic weather had flipped two semi-trucks, trapping the bus in traffic, trapping Bernie with his thoughts. He'd twisted to press his forehead against the glass, hoping that Paik, sitting next to him, would assume he was fascinated by the weather. They had kindly not commented when he had to drag the back of his thumb across his eyes. It hurt—unexpectedly, deeply—that two of the cuttlefish had died to contain an idea—an idea that everyone he worked with would keep reaching for because they simply couldn't stop.

He wondered what Harry and Estlin were doing while the house hovered over the grassland and the encapsulation process continued, layering ice and other materials. He kept casting his imagination forward into a bright white wall. He had no idea where or when he would catch up to his friends.

The bus shuddered as the wind and rain shifted directions, splattering the tinted windows on the other side.

The storage compartments below were fully loaded, but Paik was the only other passenger.

Bolts of red lightning fired across the top of the cloud deck, filling the bus with a new colour.

"Red sprites!" Paik sprang to their feet to pull a backpack from the upper rack. "We should document this. I have some of the cameras."

Bernie was glad that Paik had chosen the seat next to him to help duplicate and notate the final recordings from the house. They dropped the backpack into the aisle and crouched to unload it onto the seat. "Do you think the Waes are releasing energy or gathering it?" Paik asked as their face was illuminated by the most beautiful flash of light.

They jumped into the seat behind Bernie, kneeling on it to press a small camera against the glass. Bernie twisted around and found himself watching Paik's deft fingers make a series of quick adjustments to the camera.

"Bernie, someone's waving at you."

Bernie looked out. Below his window, there was a man holding a black and white rabbit. He waved cheerily. Bernie recognized the Russian, Harry's Russian from Samoa, and raised one hand in acknowledgement. The next wave directed him to the front of the bus for a cheerful...reunion?

"You know him?" Paik asked.

"Sort of," Bernie answered. "He's Russian. The scary kind of Russian."

"He's holding a rabbit."

"His name changes. He can summon aircraft to remote locations. He air-dropped boxes of squirrels wired with tracking devices."

"That was legendary," Paik said. "Are you going to leave him out there in the rain?"

"No, I'll go," Bernie said. "He flew Harry here, so we kind of owe him."

As Bernie walked up the aisle, the Russian beyond the window matched his pace, so they arrived at the door at the same time.

"Could you open the door?" Bernie asked the driver.

The Russian and his rabbit were waving in the side mirror.

The driver took a long look.

"You know him?" she asked.

"We've met."

"Small world." She triggered the door, which slid aside admitting a gust of wet wind.

"Hello?" Bernie said.

"Dr. Bernie! It is good to see you."

"You have a rabbit?"

"Yes." The Russian planted one foot on the lowest step. "Can we come in? It's getting a bit electric out here."

"Are you armed?"

"Moderately."

Bernie considered the request. "It's not my bus."

"Of course." The Russian smiled, waving Bernie aside. "Bus driver! I have eight comrades who would be safer aboard your bus."

The driver looked to Bernie.

"I am Aleksi Zaytsev. I have eight friends here. I also have an array of local weather stations and one dedicated satellite."

"Welcome aboard."

Aleksi hopped up the steps. He pressed Bernie out of the aisle into the seat behind the driver and took a position at the top of the stairs, kneeling on the front seat above the door. His eight friends followed, wearing all-weather gear the colour of drying grass. They threw their bags and themselves into seats.

"Dr. Bernie, have you had lunch?"

"No."

"We have borscht," he said. "Very healthy. You will like. Little Nikita, feed everyone. Warm us up."

Bernie noted that little Nikita was an imposingly large man. "You have weather stations?"

"Bus driver," Aleksi said. "There is a decision for you to make. If we can move soon, we should move. But if we cannot move, we should tether your axels to the ground. We should cover the inside of all this glass with the canvas from the tents in your cargo hold. Can you decide in 10 minutes? Faster is better."

"I'll get an update." The driver dropped into her seat and picked up the radio.

"Good," Aleksi said. "Dr. Bernie, for you?"

Bernie accepted the offered bowl and spoon passed from Nikita to Aleksi to himself. There was a piece of heavy bread balanced on top of it. "What is happening?"

"The house is up, but you know this. The restructuring is complete and now it accelerates in a spiral. It creates the storm or creates a low-pressure pocket to fly through like the Wizard of Oz. Slow acceleration, but continuous. When it comes by again it may break the sound barrier. The aliens are clever. They fix many things. I don't know if there will be a boom, but we should prepare."

"What?" Bernie wondered where on earth the house was going, and why it would accelerate in place if it needed such velocity to get there.

"I am guessing," Aleksi said. "But it will pass moving eastward and turn westward. I think it may go into the mountains, turning and rising through the valleys, and then go eastward and up."

Aleksi pointed at the sky. "This is a good thing. If they are going up, whatever is flying at us may not come down. That is good. Big spaceships should stay in the sky. We just need to hold our hats."

The driver rose from her seat and addressed Aleksi. "The crew working on the flipped semis is waiting for the lightning to pass."

"The wrecks should be plowed aside."

"I told them. It will take them too long to agree." She pulled on a black jacket marked with reflective tape. "I have tow cables below. The semi behind us is fully loaded, and he stretches back far enough to tether to the last power pole. You're going to tie my axel to the hitch on his frame and borrow his sledgehammer. The truck in front of us has a light load and the driver is hesitating. I'm going forward to assess the situation and suggest he shelter with us. Forget his truck. There's enough room in front for you to drive a stake into the asphalt at an angle. The tent stowed below has a steel frame, and there are rebar signposts up and down this road. Whatever works." The driver swung her keys around her finger. "I'll open the holds now."

The door opened, admitting a blast of wind that got everyone's attention.

"Time to work!" Aleksi shouted at his team. He stepped into the aisle, offering the rabbit. "Dr. Bernie, will you hold my friend?"

—— ⟨⟩ ——

Malone shifted on the cot, careful not to disturb the IV line in his forearm. He raised his hand and pressed blistered fingertips against each other, an action that looked like it should hurt more than it did. "Ow?"

"You get no pity from me."

Pollock was by the foot of the bed, sipping a coffee.

The alien structure had yielded to the microwave emitter, the wall melting back, creating a narrow channel. Malone was sweeping the channel wider and deeper, when the emitter had failed and a burning cold slurry had cascaded into the channel, splashing across his hands. Malone stretched his stiff fingers, showing Pollock the damage.

"You have superficial frostbite," Pollock said. "And the electrical discharge singed your eyebrows off. It's a good look."

"Where are we?"

"Mary Lake. Our side of the border. Turns out Malmstrom Airbase has an RV Park here."

"What happened?"

"You don't remember our last conversation?" Pollock put down his coffee. He picked up a folding chair with one hand, flipped it around and sat on it. "I think the electrical arc may have scorched a bit deeper than your eyebrows. You should ask the doc about that."

"One of Dewey's sniper friends saw you attempt to walk into the alien ice wall. He saw it swallow your hands and spit you back, like a flashy, delayed ricochet. He recruited some help and hauled you out on a stretcher as the cuttlefish tank flowed by. He *apologized* to Dewey," Pollock said. "Said if he'd realized you were unhinged, he could have kept you from harming yourself."

"Hinges are overrated," Malone said. "I prefer sliding doors."

He wondered if his battery pack had died of natural causes or if alien magic had ripped the electricity from the wire before it reached the microwave blaster in his hands. When the device failed, for a split second, crush injury had competed with freezer burn, and then lightning had thrown him away from the wall.

"Want some water?" Pollock offered a bottle. "We have continuous seismic activity now. It is being compared to the signal for peat slippage… smooth landslides, the kind where a grove of scrub pine slides down a hill without breaking a branch."

Malone took a sip of water, assisted by Pollock. Once the water bottle was half empty, Pollock set it aside.

"When do we go back?"

"There is no place to go," Pollock said. "The house is gone. The beech tree is gone. There's a gaping hole in the ground. After the cuttlefish tank floated away, the space monkeys scooped the earth down to bedrock—or deeper—the hole filled with water from the aquifer while the house hovered over it."

"We knew this was coming," Malone said.

"I was surprised."

"When the ground cracked, we knew they were going to lift the house. Where is it now? Is it following the cuttlefish?"

"The house floated in place while the aliens wrapped it in icy armor, and the cuttlefish tank drifted off to the southwest like a low-lying cloud," Pollock said. "The tank is now folding itself through a valley on its way back to the ocean. The structure around the house went through an annealing process, forming and reforming. Now, the whole thing is accelerating in a spiral. We think it is going to climb the Sofa—the nearest, tallest mountain."

"What?"

"And the mountain itself is climbing," Pollock said. "It's gained a thousand feet of prominence in the last eight hours."

"Shit." Malone held up his hands, but there was nothing to be done with them.

"It's a magic mountain now. The new peak is fancy."

"Is anyone planning an intervention?"

"How the hell would I know?" Pollock said. "There is some kind of atmospheric slip coordinated with whatever railgun thing the house is sliding on. I don't think we should mess with it. You should see the fucking weather. Given the way tornados target RV parks, this is not a great place to be."

———— «◊» ————

Bernie paced the aisle, petting the rabbit, adjusting its position each time it wiggled.

"The Russians know my name," Paik said, the camera in their hands sweeping between the weather and the human activity outside. "I did not introduce myself."

"They must have watched us load and board."

"They're coming." Paik dropped lower in their seat.

The Russians piled aboard, one of them squeezing by Bernie to use the washroom at the back of the bus. The others stayed forward, bringing gear in, pausing to allow Aleksi to get through to Bernie.

"That was quick," Bernie said.

"It is good to be inside." Aleksi offered a smile that was almost disarming. "May I have my little friend?"

Bernie saw it as a butcher's smile and held the bunny close. "Why do you have a rabbit?"

"In times like these, everyone should have a rabbit." Aleksi sat on an armrest, blocking the aisle with his legs. "They are sensitive to Estlin's condition—like a living compass. In New Zealand, when the aliens vanished, the Chinese worked so hard to be sneaking, while all the rabbits were pointing. It was very funny. Even now, do you think my friend likes the view through the window?"

Bernie turned the rabbit. It resisted, squirming in his hands, until he handed it off to Aleksi who restored its preferred alignment.

"Soon Ilya will hang canvas over these windows, and Masha will bring you blankets. I believe we are safe, but I am a suspicious...a super-suspicious man."

"Superstitious?" Paik offered.

"Thank you, Dr. Paik," Aleksi said. "If we prepare, nothing will happen. But if we are dull and lazy, trouble will break our windows. Dr. Paik can you tape your camera to the glass? We should take the aisle to be safe. But all is fine. It is clear now the spiral is offsetting to the north as it expands, the bottom edge sweeping through where the house stood each time. My friends think they aim for a specific path into the mountains. I think they may be smart enough to avoid American airspace. Either way, this is good for us."

"They were generating power in the ground beneath the house," Bernie said. "If they come back along that line each time, it must be to maintain a connection to the power source."

"Wouldn't they take it with them?"

"Everything they do involves distributed technology." Bernie glanced out the window, considering the larger picture. "They will have several power sources with them, but they'll have ground-based power engaged in pushing them up."

"We are about to learn about a whole new way to get objects into space," Aleksi said. "The widening curve controls the centripetal force. It keeps that force in balance with the acceleration as the velocity increases." Aleksi adjusted his grip on the rabbit. "I think they have designed a launch that can lift earth without harming a worm. But it will have several phases. They must turn upwards with only a fraction of the speed they need. If they are too fast, the forces on the upward turn, even if it is kilometers long, would be too great."

The bus creaked.

"Just a gust," Aleksi said. "We found two ground installations along the loop. The satellites spotted a faint temperature difference, and we went to look. What we saw was subtle. We did not imagine the scale of this. The Canadians found something in the mountains. A day ago, they had a helicopter sweeping a valley with a tethered bird below it—a sensor bird the mining companies use to scan the earth for gamma rays and little twists in the magnetic field."

"I don't know what they will do when they stop pushing against the earth," he said. "Scoop and scram? It will be interesting to see. I think they are smart enough not to break all the windows in Calgary. If I were reckless, I would go outside to witness. I used to be reckless, but now my job has become too interesting to risk."

"I know what you mean." Bernie realized the Russians had accessed the cargo holds where his computers were stacked. "Did you follow us because I was the last one out of the house?"

"No, no," Aleksi assured him. "There was one more. The microbiologist."

Bernie nodded, trying to return the Russian's smile.

"He was not accessible." Aleksi tightened his grip on the squirming hare. "Be calm, little rabbit. You cannot hop into the sky." The rabbit escaped his grip and began to ricochet around the bus. "Nikita! When?"

"I don't know," Nikita responded. "I've lost the satellite."

"No more time." Aleksi abandoned his efforts to recapture the rabbit. "Everyone into the aisle and cover over with the blankets and canvas!"

Bernie dropped in place and reached out to take Paik's hand as they clambered from the seat. The blankets came down the aisle followed by the canvas, which was taken up by the Russian from the back of the bus who reached over their heads to pull it with him. Aleski was next to them, tucking the canvas down and illuminating their pocket with a small light.

"I must thank you again, Bernie, for your hospitality."

"Thank you," Bernie responded.

The boom was loud enough that Bernie felt it in his lungs. He tightened his grip on Paik's hand, counting through the after-rumble, which seemed to have no end. The compression wave arrived, heaving the bus up only as far as the suspension allowed before shoving it into the ground.

"All safe," Aleksi said to Bernie. "That was small compared to the force of our own launches. All very safe—"

Bernie's ears popped. The second wave struck from two directions at once. Everyone aboard shouted, and the bus moaned as it pulled against its tethers. When the tension released, Aleksi said nothing. Bernie counted seconds until he was certain there would not be a third shove. He relaxed his grip on Paik's hand but did not release it.

———— «» ————

The sky was green. The lightning had stopped but a continuous thunder-rumble was rolling in from all directions. Troughton put on his safety glasses and stayed close to the wall as he stepped away from the door. The dirt lot was full of G-wagons and the small dance floor inside was packed with infantry waiting out the storm. The convoy he'd evacuated with had followed dirt tracks to gravel roads, cutting back to a junction with the narrow Highway 6 where the Twin Butte Community Hall stood alone. The old wood structure had weathered the worst of it without any damage. The wind had dropped off as Estlin's house, and its protective ball of ice, had converted from spiraling on the ground to rising above them in an expanding helix. It had used a track through the mountains to the west to kick up into the sky. From the view, Troughton thought he might be standing in the center of the strange cyclone. The clouds above were swept into arcs, but not moving at aggressive velocities. He wondered what height and velocity the house would have before it turned onto an easterly track to arc across the country and out of the atmosphere.

"Troughton." Chief Warrant Officer Lacey had followed him out. Her eyes scanned the sky before she delivered the expected order. "Inside!"

Chapter 21

The hum was full of wandering harmonics and rhythmic ticks. Estlin felt fine threads weaving within it, the promise that it could tell him where clover was blooming. He woke within a lucid dream, within a facsimile of his room, and sent his dream-self staggering from the bed to the light switch by the door. He flicked the switch up, down and up. The action felt familiar to his fingers, but, being a dream, the ceiling light was not obliged to respond.

It felt like September had slipped away, lowering the cloak of colder, darker autumn. Beyond the walls of the house, he found a further time warp between the autumn twilight of the bedroom and the yard, where the squirrels were resting in an orderly array of leaf-lined dreys, all their instincts cued to stay in and secure, as though waiting out a harsh winter night. The insects on the tree were sheltered in each deep crevice-crevasse in the bark. From there, he fell into the fluttering flight of a lone moth circling on silent wings…until the Waes found him.

The push-pull they exerted on his attention was unmistakable because he'd never, ever cared about lichen. The copper beech had a second skin of thin, wrinkled lobes built by algae and fungi, and hordes of micro-critters were resting within each patch of grey bedding.

Estlin struggled against the false fascination that forced him into the interstitial layers. The stretch and shiver of fluid percolating through fungal filaments mapped into his lungs like a creeping cough. Trapped in whatever lesson the Waes were trying to deliver, he tried to ignore the pulsing fungi and focus on the simplistic joy of algae bathing in moonlight.

———— 《》 ————

Isolation? Sequestration? Quarantine? The motel blinds were kept closed by order of the Princess Patricia's. Troughton was certain they occupied every room in Pincher Creek. The town was less than an hour's drive north of Estlin's house—the hole where Estlin's house used to be.

He paced the small room, rolling the smooth stone in his pocket. He'd stolen the souvenir as he left the house. His flashlight found it shining in the center of the wet patch of earth where the cuttlefish tank had disintegrated, and then he was on the path with a solid piece of what he'd left behind in his pocket.

He was trying to be patient and professional. He didn't know why he'd been confined and isolated, aside from his status as *the last man out*. The card on the bedside declared a Wi-Fi password, likely useless, but he had no device to try it. There was no phone for requesting room service. Meals were dropped off at irregular intervals with minimal contact and no conversation.

The TV was off. He could only endure it for brief periods of time. It was disconcerting to watch a sensational situation be further sensationalized. The weather forecasters were fearful, the atmospheric scientists were alarmed, the volcanologists were excited, and the politicians were bending in the breeze. It was a bad idea to consume that level of anxiety while alone in a small space. The footage of him hauling a singed American serviceman on a stretcher was strangely popular. Reports that the soldier had been injured while extinguishing a battery fire were paired with conspiracy theories about *freezer burns* inflicted by malevolent aliens that could turn your blood to ice. It didn't help that both the soldier and the stretcher bearers had vanished from the public eye.

Troughton's eyes caught the black-eyed stare of the mountain goat print that shared the room with him. He wanted coffee. He could make coffee, but sleeping away the afternoon was a better idea. He flopped onto the bed, reaching out to place the stone on the bedside table. He didn't notice when the green pebble flattened into a coin-like disk, taking on the colours of the light cedar veneer. He did notice when a pair of ghost cuttlefish began to swim in circles above him.

Chapter 22

Estlin woke with his face planted on a pillow and his limbs spread like a starfish. Despite this position of maximum contact with the bed, he felt like he could float away—as though he hadn't fully returned from some mind-bending trip. He remembered climbing the stairs and kicking off his sandals. The blankets of the unmade bed were heaped beneath him, like the Waes had flipped the blackout switch as soon as he was close enough to fall on them. He rolled onto his side with great caution. Yidge was sitting on the edge of his bed.

"Damn."

"Are you thirsty?" she asked.

"Why?"

"You are thirsty," she said.

"Some spiked lemonade would be great." He pushed himself up, blaming Yidge for the extra spin this put on the room. "Did you....?" He pressed a hand against his face, his cheek felt swollen and wrong. He reminded himself that Yidge was made of light and could not have drugged him. "Did the Waes...?"

"They want me to talk to you," Yidge said.

Estlin found her youthful sincerity ominous.

"They are concerned you might change your mind."

"Change my mind?" One of his sandals was on top of his tall dresser. "What?"

"There wasn't time to discuss the decision of your true mind with your other mind," Yidge said.

That was confusing, and the sandal was distracting him. He stood and reached for it, felt himself fainting, tripped over his feet, and fell in an improbable way, bouncing between the floor and the dresser twice. He pressed his hand against the floorboards and his face against his hand. His eyes hurt like a headache that got stuck in the wrong spot. "I don't feel well."

Yidge was standing now, or appeared to be, her practical shoes in his field of view. Her image crouched next to him.

"Your fluids should redistribute soon," she said.

"What?"

"The Waes are concerned that your divided mind might disagree about what it agreed to do," she said. "It is extremely exceptional to be invited to meet the twisted giant."

"Yidge." Estlin sat up, pressing his back against the side of his bed. The view through the window was wrong. It was really wrong. "Did they steal my house?"

"You agreed to relocate."

"When?"

"You chose to climb the mountain two nights before your long rest."

Estlin cursed the prickly dreamwalkers, but there was a more important question. "Long rest?"

"The rest for the journey," she said. "The Waes protected your nervous system from the gravitational variations and acceleration, but your cells and lymphatic system still reacted to the transitions. You'll feel better when your fluids redistribute."

"Fuck. Where are we?"

"The moon," Yidge said.

"Fuck, fuck, fuck."

"It is a unique opportunity," Yidge said. "While seedling clusters sometimes travel, Crazy-tree is the only ancient nsangunsangu to amputate itself from the forest to travel from star to star."

"Fuck." Estlin pushed himself up. His first step went wrong and he caught himself against the dresser, which lurched against the wall. The sandal shifted and fell. It fell wrong because gravity was wrong. Everything was wrong. Estlin held on and looked out the window. The view hadn't changed. The tank wall was out there, glowing like a late morning fog on the verge of burning away.

"The moon," he said, and thought about puking.

"Yes," Yidge said. "You're on the moon."

"And I agreed."

"Yes."

"I'm going to appreciate this soon."

"The beech tree also agreed to the trip, despite the discomfort," Yidge said. "The impatient one did not allow time for the tree to transition into the quiet of its winter mind. There was no time for the shedding of leaves or budding back to wakefulness. Also, a longer trip would have been less compatible with your biology, so a compromise was required."

"You don't sound like you," Estlin said.

"I'm translating," she said. "I actually think it's an awesome way to travel. A few days of being shoved through space, and for you, it seems like a blink."

"No." Estlin slowly lowered himself to his knees, and then decided to lie on the wood floor. "This is more than a blink."

The room spun as he put his head down. There was a ringing in one ear. His view of the ceiling stabilized. Estlin imagined the beech tree standing taller, each leaf light on its stem. He imagined squirrels leaping in one sixth gravity and laughed so hard he had to roll onto his side, bouncing off the floor with each spasm of hysteria.

Yidge waited. The Waes peeked out from the closet shelf, and then returned to the shadows. The laughter subsided.

"Are you feeling better?" Yidge asked.

"No." Estlin's guts cramped creating an urgent need to get to his feet.

A chaotic scrambling of limbs got him to the door, where he stopped, gripping the frame, fearing the stairs. He grabbed the landing rail and pulled himself forward, sliding his feet along the floor despite the pressing need. He proceeded carefully onto the top step, lost his footing on the second step, missed the third step, and kicked the fourth step hard, falling with a stupid speed. He flew across the landing and managed to punch himself in the face, trapping his fist between bone and wall in a flailing attempt to catch himself.

He split his lip and bit his knuckle and was stunned enough to stop moving, which probably helped him to settle to the floor. He raised his hand to inspect it and catch the blood spilling from his lip. "Fuck."

"I don't think we caught that on camera, but it was hilarious." Harry was sitting on the floor in the kitchen. "You okay?"

"Great," Estlin said. "You?"

"The room spins when I move my head."

"We're on the fucking moon." Estlin used his shirt hem to catch the blood.

"Really?" Harry said. "That's good."

"How do you figure?"

"At least it's local, considering how freaking big space is." Harry paused. "Did you sign us up for this?"

"The Waes concept of informed consent is very different from ours."

"Well, that's not news," Harry said. "I'm going to get up again. Wish me luck."

"Luck."

"The others are outside," Harry said. "Saeed is springing around like an acrobat. I think he's digging a hole now."

"That sounds entertaining. Why do we need a hole?"

"Several of us woke with twisty guts."

"Me, too."

"Right," Harry said. "We will not discuss the low-G failure of Earth toilets in detail, but I suggest you hold out for the hole if you can."

"Noted."

Harry achieved a standing position via a series of slow moves.

"I have a suggestion," he said. "When you stop bleeding, I suggest you borrow one of my shirts. Don't go back upstairs."

"Good suggestion," Estlin said. "Thank you."

He wondered what the sink would do if he tried to wash his hands.

"What are you thinking?" Harry asked.

"I'm going to appreciate this soon." Estlin turned getting off the floor into a twelve-step process and left bloody handprints everywhere. "Who else got hijacked?"

"Adya, Serese and Bomani," Harry said. "Bomani got the couch. The rest of us got put to bed in random places."

"You didn't come to wake me," Estlin said.

"It's not the most dignified process," Harry said. "I suggested you'd be down in your own time."

"Good thought."

"I didn't expect the self-catapult from the top step."

"I'm glad it amused you." Estlin applied more pressure to his lip because it was necessary.

"Heard you laughing earlier. What was that?"

"Squirrels in space."

"That is funny."

"Everyone's outside?"

"It's the best place to hurl…given the toilet situation."

Estlin achieve the edge of the kitchen counter. It felt far more dignified and casual than trying to hold on to the wall.

"How are you doing?" Harry asked. "Do you need help getting outside?"

Estlin noted that Harry was still hugging the wall on the far side of the room.

"I'm good here."

"Good." Harry swallowed. "I'm going to…." He slid back down the wall.

"You'll feel better when your fluids redistribute," Estlin said.

"I'm trying to keep my fluids from redistributing," Harry responded.

"Sorry, it's just something Yidge kept saying."

"Did she explain anything?"

"Not really."

"Are we here so you can talk to a big alien tree?"

"I had a dream that wasn't a dream on the way here," Estlin said. "I think I'm here to help a giant alien tree talk to the lichen growing on the beech tree."

"They want you to talk to lichen?"

"It's a guess," Estlin said. "I could be wrong, but I had a stupidly long dream about lichen."

"I can't think of anything funny to say." Harry said. "Waewae kai pakiaka, but it's outside your skill range, isn't it?"

Estlin appreciated the honesty.

"Lichen are extremophiles," Harry said. "They can survive exposure to extreme temperatures, hard vacuum, cosmic rays...."

"Which could make them interesting," Estlin said. "Except that they're lichen."

"Still interesting." Harry shifted in place, sitting up straighter. "They could travel on tumbling space debris or on ship hulls. If you are obsessed with the currents on which ancient life flowed through space, you might use lichen to study the spread. Otherwise intelligent people have spent years of their lives sampling the genes of dead rats to understand their colonization history."

"Crap. We really are less interesting than a grey splotch on the trunk of a tree."

"Speak for yourself," Harry said. "I'm very interesting. Famous. Well-traveled... Kumara. We didn't pack enough kumara."

Estlin accepted sweet potatoes as essential stock for any moon landing. He wondered if he remembered the word from his time on Aotearoa or if the waewae tapu were messing with his wiring again. "How much did you pack?"

"None."

"Mō taku hē, mō taku hē" Estlin said, which was definitely the wiring because the Waes were watching him from the top of the stairs.

"You're sorry," Harry said. "Trip of a lifetime, and the Canadian apologizes for a catering issue."

"Sorry."

"Right. Help me up," Harry said. "Let's go for a moon-walk."

Epilogue

"This is more satisfying." Bernie adjusted the focus of the telescope. "I'm glad they landed on the near side of the moon."

"Yes," Paik agreed. "The direct view is better than live feed in a room full of overstressed people."

"At least we still have jobs," Bernie said.

"I haven't been paid," Paik said. "Have you been paid?"

"I don't know." Bernie hadn't seen a bank statement for a long time. It was an unfortunate moment to think of unpaid bills, so he adjusted the telescope eyepiece again and caught the sparkle of the dome near the Copernicus crater.

"It's an honour to serve?" he suggested.

"It makes me think of muppet adventures," Paik said.

"Pigs in space?" Bernie asked. "Or run rabbit run?"

"All of it," Paik said

"I saw a big brown moth resting on the siding of Estlin's house," Bernie said. "I hope it's up there."

He stepped aside to allow Paik another turn with the telescope.

"How long do you think it will take them to figure out how to signal us?" he asked, wondering what it would be like if the bank of lights flashed to life while they watched.

"They probably have more important things to do first," Paik said. "The UFOs haven't even parked yet. Give it time."

— «» —

Bomani sat on the porch stairs, his notebook and drawing pads stacked next to him. The break created an opportunity to review and organize his work, but then he hadn't had a true day off in weeks…and he was on the moon.

"Bomani, can I borrow you?" Serese asked.

She was glowing, having spent the last hour displaying impressive flexibility using a tree branch as a ballet barre.

Bomani bounced to his feet—he bounced higher than expected and took an extra step to catch himself. "Yes. Of course."

"I want to dance," she said. "It requires recalibration. Until I find my balance, I'll need an anchor."

"I am happy to help." Bomani also wanted to gain some competence. He'd achieved an effective stumbling walk, but it wasn't enough, given the joys of low gravity.

He considered the porch rail. "Should I hold on to something?"

"No," Serese said. "I'll make small, balanced moves, and my goal will be to not to pull you off the ground. You can always release my hand if things get silly."

Bomani shuffled his feet, moving forward, putting some bend in his knees before offering her his hand. He felt lighter than he had ever felt in his entire life, and then she began to move. Her hand communicated everything it needed, whether it needed to be held high or low, whether it wanted a tight grip or a loose one. It was fantastic even when they tripped and tumbled across the grass. He rose and offered his hand again.

As Bomani accepted the renewed trust of her hand placed in his, he knew he was doomed. He had fallen for Canadian royalty. It didn't matter how many had fallen before him— theatres full of people, he was sure—it was a wonderful, hopeful, helpless fate. It was the most unexpected place his travels had taken him, and he was standing on the moon.

"You are going to create something new," he said.

"Yes," she agreed.

"It will be fantastic," he said.

Bomani released himself from the role of static anchor and allowed himself to turn with Serese, as was essential to avoid another stumble. They settled into a stable, steady turn.

"We should ask the Waes to make one of their fishbowls for us, so we can see the Earth."

Serese smiled at him. "That's a good idea."

——— «◊» ———

From the canopy of the copper beech, Estlin considered his friends below. Bomani and Serese were now swirling slowly around each other. Harry and Adya were cooking sweet potatoes and fish in an earth oven. And Saeed offered him a slow wave from where he was sitting on the roof of the house.

Estlin had never climbed this high in the tree before, always stopping at the point where the thinning branches and distance from the ground made him uncomfortable. It was hard to judge the distance to the featureless dome above, especially with the light mist hanging in the air. He wondered if the balancers were preparing a rainfall to nourish the tree.

He descended to a natural seat created by a pair of branches and dug out the letter Serese had given him. The page was crumpled from living in his pocket. It was from Huo, and he had ignored it for a day. As he opened it, he found he was being particularly shiny, drawing all the squirrels to the top of the tree.

Dear Mr. Hume,

I am overwhelmingly grateful that serendipity brought you to Wellington. It was my duty to study your history. I found that you consider all of us—all people and all creatures—to be your neighbors, and that you have helped your neighbors so casually and frequently that it reflects your primary nature.

For the visitors who have arrived and the others who are coming, I imagine it is difficult to understand us. We are capable of great thought and creativity, but we are also capable of careless, contradictory actions. Please help our new neighbors. Help them as you have helped so many before. I believe they will be able to see our true potential in you.

With deepest respect,

霍伟

(Huo Wei)

Throughout the tree, the mist settled on the grey curling folds of the foliose lichen. The moisture seeped into the interstitial spaces from which a multitude of tardigrades emerged from their crevices. Their sensory bristles pricked up as they felt every change to their new-same world. They paddled through the fluid, carried by their eight strong limbs, grasping any debris encountered with hooked claws.

Each one reached out, taking hold of an invisible partner, to dance with the most distinctive variation in their environment, to dance in the light hold of lunar gravity.

If you enjoyed this read

Please leave a review on Amazon, Facebook, Good Reads or Instagram.

It takes less than five minutes and it really does make a difference.

If you're not sure how to leave a review on Amazon:

1. *Go to amazon.com.*

2. *Type in The Rosetta Mind by Claire McCague and when you see it, click on it.*

3. *Scroll down to Customer Reviews. Nearby you'll see a box labeled Write a Review. Click it.*

4. *Now, if you've never written a review before on Amazon, they might ask you to create a name for yourself.*

5. *Reviews can be as simple as, "Loved the book! Can't wait for the Next!" (Please don't give the story away.)*

And that's it!

Brian Hades, publisher

About the Author:

Claire McCague is a Canadian writer, scientist, musician, and science fiction fan. She works on sustainable energy systems, plays with words, and owns an excessive number of musical instruments. She's performed for community dances for decades. As a director and playwright, she's had productions in theatres, fields and forests from Victoria to New York.

Need something new to read?

If you liked The Rosetta Mind, you should also
consider these other EDGE-Lite titles...

The Rosetta Man
(Book One of the Rosetta Series)
by Claire McCague

Wanted: Translator for first contact. Immediate opening. Danger pay allowance

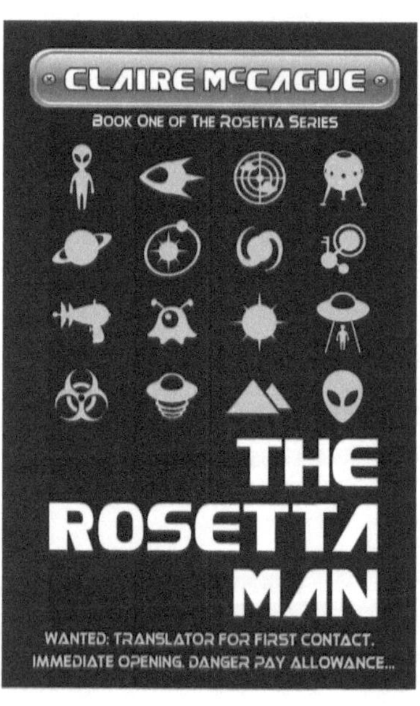

Estlin Hume lives in Twin Butte, Alberta surrounded by a horde of affectionate squirrels. His involuntary squirrel-attracting talent leaves him evicted, expelled, fired and near penniless until two aliens arrive and adopt him as their translator. Yanked around the world at the center of the first contact crisis, Estlin finds his new employers incomprehensible. As he faces the ultimate language barrier, unsympathetic military forces converging in the South Pacific keep threatening to shoot the messenger. The question on everyone's mind is why are the aliens here? But Estlin's starting to think we'll happily blow ourselves up in the process of finding that out.

"What makes The Rosetta Man stand-out? An unusually dense squirrel population for sci-fi. It's light-hearted, accessible sci-fi with exotic present day settings and a pair of aliens who are focused on observing the revealing chaos their visit creates." — Claire McCague

Pawns and Phantoms
(An Everland Mystery)
by Misha Handman

Todd Malcolm would be the first person to tell you that he's no Basil Stark. He's just a bouncer, part-time detective's assistant, and brawler who does his best to get by on the mean streets of 1950s Everland. But when Todd gets mixed up in an arson one night, he's thrown in over his head.

With his friends Glimmer and Vance Carson, Everland's 'other detective', Todd will have to contend with federal agents, angry tigers, murderous mermaids, and shadowy threats at every turn. Does Todd have what it takes to handle this case, or is he just a pawn in a dangerous plot?

About Misha Handman

Misha Handman Born on Vancouver Island, Canada, Misha Handman spent his early life immersed in the arts, with one parent a teacher and the other a manager of theatre and opera. Moving across the country to Ottawa, and then Toronto, he began writing at a young age – first writing comics and designing card games for his closest friends and then, buoyed by their approval, gradually expanding out to submissions to magazines and short story collections, and graduating from the University of Toronto with a classic English degree.

Wolf is a Four-letter Word
(Book 2 of the Eternal Spring, Invisible Forest series)

by Carrie Newberry

What do you do when the nightmare is real? That's the question facing Kellan Faolanni. Following the betrayal of her sister in the previous book, Kellan must set aside her own emotions and thwart an enemy who has the upper hand at every turn. Kellan, a member of the Sankhain, is a shapeshifter, half-wolf, half-human. Kellan's superiors task her to investigate a man killed by what appears to be a wolf pack. Meanwhile, Kellan's human friend, Darcy reveals that he's being stalked. Kellan learns that the killer and Darcy's stalker are one and the same: a faery named Aza. But Aza is a high-ranking member of the Shadow Court, and to kill him would start a war with the fey, a war that Kellan's superiors want to avoid at all costs. Kellan must find a way to eliminate the threat and save her friend. Her solution could cost her everything, including a new relationship with another Sankha, Tony, as well as her sanity.

About Carrie Newberry

Carrie Newberry studied creative writing at both the University of Wisconsin-Madison and UW-Eau Claire. But when she realized they would no longer let her take writing workshops for credit, she left academia and started work full time at a dog grooming shop. She lives in Madison with a dog who sings along with the radio, a cat who talks in her sleep, and an enormous collection of books. Also the author of Pick Your Teeth With My Bones, the first book in the Eternal Spring, Invisible Forest series, Carrie is hard at work writing Kellan's next adventure.

For more EDGE titles and information about upcoming speculative fiction please visit us at:

www.edgewebsite.com

Don't forget to sign-up for our Special Offers